First advanced proof copy

Don't Get Mad – Get Even

Getting Even

The Biggest Heist in History

To Zimena
Dick Sharples
X

by

Dick Sharples

Bloomington, IN   authorHOUSE®   Milton Keynes, UK

AuthorHouse™
1663 Liberty Drive, Suite 200
Bloomington, IN 47403
www.authorhouse.com
Phone: 1-800-839-8640

AuthorHouse™ UK Ltd.
500 Avebury Boulevard
Central Milton Keynes, MK9 2BE
www.authorhouse.co.uk
Phone: 08001974150

First published by AuthorHouse 4/10/2007

ISBN: 978-1-4343-0119-2 (sc)

Printed in the United States of America
Bloomington, Indiana

This book is printed on acid-free paper.

AUTHOR'S NOTE

GETTING EVEN is a work of fiction. While the British Museum, the Elgin (or Parthenon) Marbles and the Duveen Gallery certainly exist, the Museum's so-called Director of Operations, its Chief Resident Architect and its Temporary, Acting Head of Security – and all the other supposed Museum personnel who feature within these pages – are merely figments of the author's imagination.

ACKNOWLEDGMENTS.

My thanks to:

Peter Holliday & Associates, Structural and Civil Engineering Consultants, Pickfords Limited, DS Computer Graphics Limited and Tim Binding, the writer and novelist.

Dick Sharples

1

THE FIRST SHOT completely shattered the horse's head. Even before the last of the skull fragments had hit the floor, the woman had already lined up a second horse's head in the sights of her twin-barrel Purdey. The gun belched again. The second horse's head exploded into a thousand polyester-fibre pieces. The woman handed her gun to the soberly attired, gnome-like little man standing behind her, wearing a pair of earmuffs and a tortured expression. As the man gingerly took the gun, she said:

'That, Jefferson, is what I would like to do to your bloody British Museum and your bloody British Government.'

Her English was fluent, her accent Hellenic, the result of an expensive Greek education and an even more expensive Swiss finishing school. The little man saw her lips moving, hastily removed his earmuffs and said what English butlers have traditionally said since time immemorial:

'Will that be all, madame?'

'For the moment, yes.' She turned and moved towards the stairs that led out of the basement shooting gallery. As she reached the top of the stairway, over her shoulder, she said:

'You'd better order another half dozen,'

'Another half dozen. Yes, madame. Certainly, madame.'

And as his employer disappeared with a rustle of her designer silk gown, Jefferson's deferential expression was immediately replaced by a sullen scowl and a muttered:

'Rich bitch.'

Rich, Athena Papadopoulos certainly was – if only because she happened to be the multi-millionaire heiress of Greek shipping tycoon Andreas Papadopoulos who sadly, if somewhat predictably, had recently gone to join the Gods on Mount Olympus. After having imbibed his usual prodigious nightly intake of food, wines and spirits aboard his ocean-going yacht, it appeared that he had forgotten he had ordered his captain to put to sea and, possibly feeling the need for a little female company (a feeling, it seemed, he'd had at very regular intervals) he had attempted to step ashore. A few hours later, his dinner-jacketed remains had been discovered floating off the coast of Corfu and his beloved only daughter had joined the ranks of the world's poor little rich girls. Though rich in worldly goods, in one way, she was also undoubtedly poor, for Athena Papadopoulos, a volatile, twenty-eight year old classic Greek beauty, was not a happy woman.

Named Athena after the warrior goddess daughter of Zeus, she had been brought up by her fiercely patriotic father to be proud of her long Greek lineage, history and heritage. In particular, he had taught her to share his determination to right a grievous wrong (as he had invariably described it) concerning the Parthenon, the ancient temple that had been built and dedicated to his daughter's namesake nearly half a millennium before the birth of Christ, the ruins of which still dominated the skyline over the capital city of Athens. He had passionately believed that the ruins should be made whole again – or partly whole – by the return of the so-called Elgin marbles that had once formed part of the temple's façade, but which now resided in the British Museum. As every English schoolboy knows – or should know – the beautifully sculptured marble friezes, sculptures and figures, including the famous *Selene* horse's head, some small, some large, some massive, were taken, some say rescued, by agents of Lord Elgin, the then British Ambassador to the Ottoman Empire, which in the early eighteenth century, included Greece.

It appeared that many of the original marbles had, over the years, been broken up by the local populace to provide building materials for their domiciles, pig-stys and any other out-house that required a firm foundation. And what could be firmer than a hardcore of solid marble? Which is why, it seemed, that Elgin had decided to save as many of the remaining pieces as he could for the rest of the world – or at least, the rest of the world in the immediate vicinity of the British Museum – before it was too late. The Greeks – one Greek shipping magnate and his daughter in particular – had never been over-impressed by Elgin's reported rationalization for what they had long regarded as a straight-forward case of grand larceny and both father and daughter had vowed to do all they could to secure the return of the Parthenon marbles, as they preferred to call them, to their rightful home.

But despite approaching both the British Government and the British Museum, asking them to name their price for the return of the marbles, their pleas had always been met with a polite, but firm refusal – the reason why the mercurial Athena Papadopoulos had been driven to vent her anger on polyester-fibre replicas of the Parthenon *Selene* horse's head (which were readily available at the British Museum's souvenir shop) – in the basement shooting gallery of her imposing mansion in London's equally-imposing Belgrave Square.

While doing so gave her a satisfying, if only a temporary, relief from her feelings of utter frustration, it in no way affected her grim determination to secure the return of the marbles for the Greek nation. By any means possible. Politically, diplomatically, legally – or if needs be – totally illegally.

☞

The loud, gunshot-like crack of willow on leather echoed across the village green as the batsman sent the cricket ball soaring high into the air. The batsman didn't even bother to signal his fellow batsman at the other end of the pitch to try and steal a run. He knew what was coming. He just stood there, resignedly following the passage of the ball as it descended, with a depressing inevitability, into the hands of the waiting fielder.

The umpire signalled 'out,' the winning team gave a wild and derisive cheer and the batsman said 'oh shit.'

The match was over. As both teams drifted across the green towards the cricket pavilion changing room, the warm summer evening was already beginning to fade into twilight.

'Can you believe that?' said the batsman to the team captain, in tones of deep self-disgust: 'Two hundred and forty-three to our seventy-six, all out. Bloody grammar-school boys. And there wasn't one of them over the age of fifteen.' He shot a venomous glance towards the leaping, whooping, laughing schoolboys: 'Just look at them. Did you see their faces when they took the last wicket? Smug little sods. I hate kids like that, John. I really do.'

John Armitage merely shook his head and said, wearily:

'Oh come on, Ken. What you really hate is the fact that most of us are past it. Over the hill. Ready to be put out to grass.'

'Over the hill, me? I'm only thirty-two, for God's sake.'

Kenneth George Beynon was a cheerfully uninhibited, ruggedly good-looking young man. Of limited education, he had spent most of his adult life as a member of the British Army's elite Special Air Services, attaining the rank of Sergeant. According to most SAS men and to Beynon in particular, compared to them, the much-vaunted British Commandos were about as macho as a bunch of male ballet dancers and, as he had made a point of continuing to keep himself in good physical shape, the fact that he had been out-run, out-bowled and out-played by a bunch of rather puny and certainly spotty adolescents, had obviously hit a nerve.

'I said *most* of us were past it,' said Armitage, placatingly. He liked Beynon, despite their differences in age, background and way of life. For cricket, as always, was the great social leveller – the ultimate meritocracy where Playing The Game was the all that really mattered. The invisible glue that bound all those who took their cricket seriously, inexorably together.

Armitage was in his early forties. Deceptively mild-mannered, he was tall, well built and had once been described as 'quietly handsome,' although he'd had no idea what that meant. A businessman of the old school, over the years he had built up an international road-haulage company from a single truck to a fleet of vehicles that had once been one of the largest transport concerns in that part of rural Kent, before the financial demands of his now divorced wife and a series of bad business debts had taken their inevitable toll.

'Mind you,' conceded Beynon: 'I have to accept that I'm not quite as agile as I was and employment-wise, it seems I'm already due for the knacker's yard.'

'Tell me about it,' grunted Armitage, as they changed out of their cricket whites.

Beynon gave him a sharp look:

'Things still a bit dodgy?'

'Not so much dodgy as disastrous. The bank's now threatening to pull the plug on me and put in the receivers.'

"Jesus. I'm sorry John. I was just about to ask you if you needed another driver.'

'Are you serious?'

'Deadly. I was laid off this morning.'

The pair emerged from the pavilion in gloomy silence and made their way across to the other side of the green, to enter the pretty little public house that had been a vital part of village life, supposedly since the days of the somewhat less-than-devout Chaucer and his Canterbury Pilgrims. Legend had it that the free-spending, hard-drinking pilgrims once lost their way and had found, to their utter dismay, that they were destined to spend the night in an ale-free environment. The village elders had immediately decided that such a state of affairs should never be allowed to happen again and The Old Dun Cow had graced the village green ever since. The story was probably apocryphal, but generations of villagers had embraced it with enthusiasm. To the ever-credulous tourist, historical anecdotes – true or totally fictitious – were usually worth at least the price of a pint. The only modern anachronism in the main bar, with its low, oak-beamed ceiling and polished brass bed-warmers, was the large television set that was suspended from one of the ancient beams and which flickered balefully in the direction of the customers.

Beynon and Armitage automatically ducked their heads under an equally ancient beam just inside the doorway and joined a third member of the team who was already at his regular corner table, pint of beer in hand. The youthful opposing team had, presumably, been instructed by their parents to go straight home, to celebrate their victory with cups of nourishing cocoa. The moment Beynon and Armitage appeared in the doorway, the short, elderly, but wiry wicket-keeper signalled to the man behind the bar and said:

'One large scotch please Norman – and a pint of lager for young Ken, here. And make it snappy. They're one behind me.'

'Give us a chance, Mr. Messiter,' protested Mine Host, adding somewhat unnecessarily: 'I've only got one pair of hands.'

'Good Lord, Norman. So you have,' said Gavin Messiter: 'Never noticed that before. Must be quite a handicap.'

'Thanks for the Young Ken,' said Beynon, as he pulled up a chair: 'After today's fiasco, I feel more like a geriatric.'

'What's so bad about being a geriatric?' asked Messiter: 'I'm a geriatric. Well, almost. And I really fancy the idea of being a geriatric. That's why I opted for early retirement. No more having to catch the eight-fifteen up to London. No more having to design cheap and nasty office blocks or crappy little houses for crappy little property companies. In the words of the popular song – no more little boxes, all made of ticky-tacky, that all look the same. So roll on my retirement. I just can't wait.' His expression suddenly clouded. And half to himself: 'Not that it will be all that much fun without Joan.'

Said Armitage, softly: 'How long has it been now, Gavin?'

'One year, four months and twenty-three days. I do miss her.'

'I'm sure you do. She was a most remarkable woman.'

Joan Messiter had been a little more than that. Unable to have children of her own, throughout their marriage, she and her husband had fostered dozens of abandoned or orphaned children – some of whom who had been physically or mentally impaired from birth – and given them the love, understanding and the emotional security they needed, even though many of them had been written-off as 'unadoptable,' a term which invariably made both husband and wife extremely angry. And when commended for opening their home and their arms to such children, Gavin and Joan Messiter had been genuinely puzzled.

'Don't these people understand the love we get in return?' Joan Messiter had once said to Armitage: 'We're not bleeding-heart do-gooders, for God's sake. We just like children. And we need them, just as much as they need us.'

To Armitage, she was simply what he considered to be one of those very rare creatures called 'a good woman,' and he had long envied Gavin Messiter for actually finding and marrying one, especially as he'd had little success in finding such a paragon himself.

Gavin Messiter seemed to read his thoughts:

'And you, John? How do you find living on your own?'

'A lot less stressful than living with Laura.'

Apart from the subsequent financial settlement, Armitage had felt no sense of loss when his wife had finally walked out on him a few years earlier. A self-admitted workaholic – not by choice, but by necessity, if his business was to succeed – his long absences away from home had encouraged his very attractive and increasingly bored wife, who had elevated ennui to previously unknown heights, to embark upon a series of affairs that had culminated in divorce, enabling her to re-marry a man who was not only several years younger than herself but pleasingly virile – if not exactly over-burdened with brain cells.

While Armitage had had little contact with his wife since his divorce, it seemed that her relationship with her fresh-faced toy-boy had, so far, proved to be a success, if only because the financial settlement had enabled her to keep him in a state to which he'd been extremely happy to become accustomed. Fortunately, in one way at least, no children had been involved and the break had been relatively painless. Perhaps, Armitage had mused at the time, if he and his Laura had started a family, it might have saved their marriage.

And then he had recalled her flat refusal, on more than one occasion, to even consider the thought of motherhood. She was slim, pretty and wanted to stay that way – and not, as she had so vehemently and graphically put it – end up as a bulging brood mare, up to her ears in baby droppings and diapers.

Beynon had listened in silence, then said:

'As we seem to be discussing failed marriages, it's the kids I miss the most. But I at least know they're being well looked after. They really seem to have taken to Hester's new feller.'

And why shouldn't they? He told himself. The boys now had what they'd always longed for – a substitute father who was always there when he was needed, instead of someone they hardly ever saw for more than a few weeks or days at a time, when he came home on leave from Northern Ireland, Afghanistan or the Middle East – with the very real prospect of never coming home at all – except in a body bag. A father who'd play with them, who'd take them on family holidays, to the park, to football matches and who'd always be there on school sports days to cheer them on.

Like Armitage, he'd never been good husband material, from their wives' point of view, at least. No wonder Hester had finally decided she'd had enough and taken the boys back up North to her parents' place in Gosforth, a suburb of Newcastle-upon-Tyne, where she had been born and raised. And attractive as she undoubtedly was, it wasn't long before she'd met this apparently pleasant, middle-aged widower and had subsequently moved in with him. He still saw his sons, of course. Hester was not a bitter person and had never denied him access to his children, but over the last couple of years, the boys seemed to have become like a couple of distant little strangers who answered him in polite monosyllables, as if patiently waiting for him to go back where he'd come from and allow them to resume their now happy, secure way of life. And that hurt.

The three cricketers all lapsed into silence as they seemingly contemplated what might have been. It was Messiter who gave his two companions a sudden, metaphorical slap on the wrist and said:

'What a miserable bloody bunch we are. Why don't we all get pleasantly pixilated?'

'I'll drink to that,' said Armitage: 'At least, I would if I had something to drink.'

Norman caught Messiter's accusing look and shouted: 'All right! They're on their way!'

The tray of drinks miraculously appeared and as Norman served them, Messiter nodded towards the television and said:

'Turn the sound up a little, will you? I'd like to hear the news.' And by way of explanation to the others: 'See if the pound's gone up or down – that's the basis on which they'll be calculating my pension.'

As Norman turned up the sound, they were just in time to catch the image and the less-than-dulcet tones of Athena Papadopoulos at her latest Heathrow Airport press conference, before boarding her private jet prior to flying back to Athens. As on similar previous occasions, she was in full, tempestuous flow:

'But despite my offer of full compensation, which I know could involve a great deal of money, the British Museum and the British government refuse even to discuss the matter. But I warn them. This is only the beginning. The Greek people do not accept defeat easily and we will continue to fight for our rightful heritage until the marbles are restored to the Temple of Parthenon, where they belong.'

'Can you believe that?' said an incredulous Beynon: 'All that money for a few bits of broken marble? Must be up to her ears in the stuff.'

'It's not what they are,' said Armitage: 'It's what they represent. To her, at least.'

'For God's sake,' said Beynon: 'Who gives a monkey's?'

'She does,' said Armitage.

Said Beynon: 'I still think she must be one pip short of an olive.' He gave the screen another long look: 'Nice tits, though,' he conceded.

Said Armitage idly: 'Be interesting to know, though, wouldn't it?'

'Interesting to know what?' said Messiter.

'Just how much Athena whatever-her-name-is would be prepared to pay for the return of the marbles.'

'Legally or illegally?' said Beynon.

'Either. Or both.'

Said Messiter: 'It's all purely academic, of course, but I would have thought you could name your price.'

'You're probably right.' agreed Armitage, thoughtfully.

And that was how it all began.

ɩ ʂˊ

The post came early that Saturday morning. In the living room of his pleasant, half-timbered cottage, Armitage opened the single missive that wasn't a piece of junk mail. The letter was short and to the point, informing him that the bank was now not just threatening to pull the plug on him, but that head office had actually decided to do so, with immediate effect.

Dear God, thought Armitage. Was this all he had to look forward to? A bankrupt business, a house mortgaged to the hilt and an ex-wife who still demanded enough alimony to pay off the national debt?

His mobile rang while he was taking a shower.

'Can I ring you back, Gavin?' I'm in the – ' he paused and reached suddenly for a towel: 'A runner? Who's done a runner?' He turned off the shower: 'I'll be right over.'

Gavin Messiter's cottage was just a few doors along the village high street and by the time Armitage arrived, the coffee was already well and truly percolated. Messiter's face was a picture of utter despair. He pointed towards that morning's copy of *The Daily Telegraph* and said:

'It seems that our venerable company chairman has been milking the pension fund for years. Jesus W. Christ, John, this could well turn out to be a re-run of the Robert Maxwell saga. And in the last honours list, they even gave the bastard a knighthood.' With trembling hands, he poured two cups of coffee: 'I can hardly believe it. A month short of my retirement and after a lifetime of pension contributions, all I might end up with is a monthly handout from social security."

Said Armitage, from the heart: 'What a mess. What a bloody awful mess. I am sorry.'

'Yes, well,' said Messiter: 'You've got your own troubles. But I'll tell you this. Even though I've been your archetypal, law-abiding, upright British citizen since the day I was born, I'd do anything to get even with those gutless wonders who are running this country – the banks, the politicians, the judiciary and those faceless, fucking bureaucrats who've allowed this sort of thing to happen. God, how I hate them.'

He suddenly fumbled in the pocket of his dressing gown and brought out a small pill bottle, from which he shook a couple of capsules into the palm of his hand. Armitage looked at him enquiringly.

'Aspirin,' said Messiter quickly: 'I've got a migraine coming on.'

He went into the kitchen for a glass of water. When he returned, said Armitage, quite casually:

'Purely as a matter of interest, Gavin, just how far would you be prepared to go? Just to get even, I mean.'

'I've just told you. All the way. Why d'you ask?'

Armitage told him.

Messiter looked at him, mouth agape:

'You're joking, right?'

'Wrong. I've never been more serious in my life.'

'Then you're out of your mind!'

'Quite possibly. But in our situation, what have we got to lose?' He moved towards the telephone: 'D'you happen to know Ken Beynon's phone number?'

'Why d'you want to phone him?'

'To arrange a little trip to London. For just the three of us.'

Said Messiter a trifle irritably: 'Oh come on, John. Get real. I've heard some lunatic ideas in my time, but this one would make you the undisputed King of the nearest Funny Farm.'

'You're probably right. But indulge me. Just this once. Just to satisfy my curiosity. And at least, it'll be a day out.'

Messiter shook his head, helplessly: 'Suit yourself. His number's in the book.'

Armitage leafed through the telephone directory, dialled a number and within a couple of hours, all three men were on the train to London.

⌇

The Elgin (or Parthenon) marbles were on display in the purpose-built Duveen Gallery; a modern, well illuminated structure within the heart of the British Museum, which was situated, appropriately enough, in Museum Street, close to Tottenham Court Road.

Standing in the centre of the gallery, Armitage and Beynon gazed up at the marbles with something resembling awe. The sheer size of the largest sculptures and the intricate carvings and designs on even the smallest of the surviving fragments were, to them, quite unexpected, even breathtaking. Messiter simply gave the exhibits a cursory glance. He had been there before and as a professional architect, he was far more interested in the structural design of the gallery, rather than its artefacts.

Said Beynon, after a while: 'Well John? What d'you think?'

Armitage gave a wry smile: 'At a guess, the same as you. Ah well. It seemed like a good idea at the time.'

'It was a very interesting thought, though. Totally batty, mind, but very interesting. It would have solved everything. If, of course,' he added, with a grin: 'We didn't all end up picking oakum in the Pentonville pokey – with nothing to show for it but our double hernias.'

Said Armitage: 'Our what?'

'You saw the size of those pieces. Some of them must weigh at least a couple of tons. And even if we did manage to get inside this place, we'd need an entire weekend and a small army of men and equipment to get the bloody things out – let alone pack and load them.'

Said Armitage: 'You're quite right, of course. As soon as I saw them, I knew it wasn't really on. I just wanted to see for myself.'

'And now you have,' said Beynon: 'So let's go and find a drink.'

Messiter said nothing. As they walked out of the gallery, he seemed strangely preoccupied. They moved through the entrance hall towards the main doorway, passing the small, gnome-like little man who was trudging wearily towards the Museum's souvenir shop. They emerged into the sunlight and made for the nearest public house, which was conveniently situated on the opposite side of the street from the Museum's main entrance.

A few minutes later, from the relative comfort of a pavement table, each was sipping a drink, as they silently studied the nearby fire engine that was busily pumping away water that had flooded the gutters and part of the Museum's front forecourt, caused, presumably, by a burst water main. All seemed oblivious to the fact that *al fresco* eating or drinking in Central London was invariably garnished by a wide variety of toxic traffic fumes.

Inside the Museum's souvenir shop, the pretty girl assistant was welcoming her regular customer with a smile and a:

'Back again, Mr. Jefferson?'

'Back again, Miss.'

'How many this time?'

'Six – no, what the hell – make it a round dozen.'

Julie Baxter looked at him in utter astonishment: 'Another dozen Selene horse's heads? What on earth do you do with them all?'

'Don't ask, my dear. If I told you, you'd never believe me.'

A few yards away, outside the Museum Street pub, the trio were still gazing silently at the fire engine as they contemplated the failure of their fact-finding mission. It was Messiter who broke the silence. Somewhat to their surprise, he said:

'Look, um, I know I've been very dismissive about John's proposal, right from the start, but I've been thinking.' He nodded towards the Museum: 'As the three of us can't possibly get the marbles out of there on our own, what if we were able to get a little help?'

Beynon chuckled: 'You mean go in there mob-handed? Christ Gavin, you're as barmy as John, here. Must be catching.'

Said Armitage, with a smile: 'For a moment, I almost thought you were serious.'

'I am.'

Beynon and Armitage exchanged a look.

'All right,' said Armitage: 'We'll buy it. Or not, as the case may be. What have you got in mind?'

'Something so blindingly obvious that I can't understand why I didn't think of it before. What it boils down to is this.' He nodded towards the building: 'If we can't remove the marbles ourselves, why don't we simply persuade those in authority at the Museum to do it for us?'

Armitage and Beynon exchanged another look.

'Let's get this right, Gavin,' said Armitage carefully: 'Are you actually suggesting that we try and bribe half the senior staff of the British Museum to help us lift the marbles?'

Messiter chuckled: 'Of course not. It's all quite simple.' He indicated the nearby fire engine: 'It was that thing which gave me the first inkling of the idea and I really think it could work.'

Said Beynon, impatiently: 'Why don't we just finish our drinks and call it a day? In my considered opinion, having seen the bloody things, we've got as much chance of lifting those marbles as we have of nicking the Crown Jewels.'

'On the other hand, Ken,' said Messiter mildly: 'You're not an architect are you? Or a structural engineer. And I am. With certificates to prove it.'

'What's that got to do with it?'

'Everything. Or nothing. Now d'you want to hear what I've got to say or don't you?'

'And you really think it might work?' asked Armitage, as they boarded their train at Charing Cross main line station.

'Unless we give it a whirl, we'll never know, will we?' said Messiter: 'And can you think of a better way of getting even?'

Beynon was still not convinced: 'If we managed to pull it off, no. But like I said, even attempted theft carries a pretty long stretch with it.'

Said Messiter: 'It all depends on what you mean by theft. To my mind, the Greeks have got just as much right to the marbles as we have. So you could say we wouldn't exactly be stealing them, just…removing them, for their return to their rightful owners. Technically, of course, some might say we'd be committing a criminal act, but morally and ethically, I would have thought that was rather a moot point.'

Beynon sighed: 'God, it's like trying to get through to a brick wall.' He turned to John Armitage: 'Are you listening to all this, John? To hear Gavin talk you'd think he was a sharing, caring social worker, instead of a bloody-minded old-age pensioner, trying to screw the Establishment.'

Said Armitage: 'All right. Since you ask, the way I see it is this. Of course the odds are stacked against us – and on the face of it, the chances of us pulling it off are minimal. But on the credit side, we each have a very special sort of know-how. Gavin's an architect, you're ex-SAS – and I know the international transport business inside and out. To my mind, the only question is – do we at least go forward to the next stage, as Gavin proposes – or do we accept that the whole proposition is so ludicrous, so utterly insane, that we simply call it a day, here and now?'

'The first thing we'll need is a base,' said Gavin Messiter: 'An office would do, preferably overlooking the Museum.'

They returned to London a couple of days later, to sign a short term lease for a small suite of offices on the twenty-third floor of Centrepoint, the towering office block at the corner of Charing Cross Road and New Oxford Street, which looked directly down on to the front courtyard and main entrance of the British Museum. The trio stood in front of the office window and Armitage, a pair of binoculars in hand, carefully surveyed the courtyard, the Museum front entrance and the security men who were guarding the main gates. That same day, they separately entered the Museum itself, posing as typical tourists but making covert notes about the positions of each security camera, the numbers and positions of each security guard and, in particular, the doors labelled Private. Museum Staff Only.

The two men who were observed moving constantly from gallery to gallery, floor to floor, were later identified as the temporary acting Head of Security, an ex-Chief Inspector Charles Anderson, late of New Scotland Yard (traffic division) and Barry Lucas, his assistant. Physically at least, they were an ill-matched pair – Anderson well into middle-age and rather portly, who patrolled his manor (as he insisted upon calling it) with a slow, ponderous gait, his hands clasped firmly behind his back, like a minor member of the British Royal Family inspecting a parade of Chelsea Pensioners. Lucas was in his mid-twenties, an energetic, pleasant-faced young man who would seem to have been instructed to follow his superior like a Chinese housewife, always three steps behind him. Armitage noticed that both men seemed to spend an inordinate amount of time checking on security at the Museum souvenir shop and after positioning himself close to and within earshot of the shop counter, on the pretext of examining the picture postcards and the range of polyester-fibre reproductions of the Elgin marbles on display, he soon discovered why. After sending Lucas on a small errand, the temporary acting Head of Security had smiled ingratiatingly at the attractive young woman behind the counter and said:

'Good evening, Julie.'

The girl, seemingly named Julie Baker had forced a smile in return and said:

'Good evening, Mr. Anderson.'

Anderson had then glanced left and right, lowered his voice and with what he'd obviously hoped was a winning smile, had said:

'Charles, please. Out of working hours, at least. And as it's almost time to close for the day, I wonder if you'd care to join me for a little tête-à-tête at a local hostelry?'

Before the girl could answer, Barry Lucas had made a sudden and unwelcome reappearance, with the words: 'They're all ready for you, Chief.'

Clearly annoyed at Lucas's ill-timed interruption, his superior had smothered his irritation, nodded briefly towards the girl and said: 'Another time, perhaps.' He had then turned on his heel and walked stiffly out of the shop.

To Armitage's amusement, the girl, with a total disregard as to who might be listening, had then looked after the departing Anderson with an expression of utter loathing and said: 'Dirty old bugger. Makes my skin crawl. Keeps going on about having a tête-à-tête, whatever that is. What he's really after is a jig-a-jig. And him with a wife and three kids in East Croydon.'

To Armitage's continued amusement, the two-way conversation had then taken a rather different direction.

'Well, you can hardly blame him,' the young man had said, obviously from the heart: 'You are a very attractive girl.'

In truth, to Lucas, she was a little more than that. As a shy, unworldly ex-public schoolboy, born of middle-class parents in Surrey's so-called stockbroker belt, he'd never met a girl quite like her. Apart from her undoubted good looks, he admired the way she spoke her mind – albeit it with a very strong Estuary English accent – and who appeared to have little respect for any of the boring social niceties that had been all part of his own upbringing. The girl made a refreshing and quite intriguing change from the jolly, if somewhat hearty female members of his local Young Conservative Club.

Flattered, she had raised a coquettish eyebrow and said: 'If you think I'm all that attractive, why haven't you asked me out?'

'I've been trying to pick up the courage,'

'What's wrong with right now?'

'All right. Will you go out with me?'

And with the wilful perversity of an any attractive young woman who was well aware of her regular effect upon the males of the species, she had looked him up and down, sighed and, with a little shake of the head, had said:

'Do me a favour, sunshine. You're a nice enough feller, but I just don't fancy you. You're a bit too…you know…what's the word for it?'

Lucas's expectant smile had crumpled and he had hazarded a guess:

'Wet?'

'That'll do.'

'I'll work on it.'

'You do that. Now shove off. I've got to cash up.'

'Shove off. Right. Will do.'

And Barry Lucas had shoved off. Armitage had felt a twinge of pity for the disconsolate young man, who was obviously besotted with the girl. He was just glad that he wasn't that young, that vulnerable, any more.

When the last visitors had been escorted out of the Museum, the temporary acting Head of Security began his very first address to the team of uniformed security men and women, lined up before him:

'Right lads – and ladies, of course – my name's Anderson. Some of you may have heard of me. Ex-Chief Inspector Anderson of New Scotland Yard.' He gave a modest little smile: 'Otherwise affectionately known by the Met's other crime-busters by the nickname of Anders of the Yard. In the absence of Mr. Bracegirdle, who is currently attending an international security conference in New York, I have been brought in as temporary acting Head of Security and as such, I would just like to remind you of the need to be constantly on the alert against the ever-present threat to the security of this great national institution.' Some of his listeners secretly stifled a yawn. 'So let us all make sure that while he is away, Mr. Bracegirdle can rest easy in his bed, secure in the knowledge that the British Museum's priceless relics, antiquities, coins and medals are safe in my – in our – hands.' He nodded dismissively: 'Carry on.'

As they carried on, said one security man to another: 'Anders of the Yard? Jesus. What a prick. How did he get the job?'

His companion shrugged: 'Must know where the bodies are buried.'

After another couple of days of careful, covert surveillance and ironically, with the assistance of the British Museum's own information sheet, which helpfully included a diagram of the entire Museum complex, Armitage, Messiter and Beynon had successfully built up a picture of the security cameras and electronic detection devices in and around the Duveen Gallery and indeed, the entire Museum. Most of such devices appeared, not unreasonably, to be concentrated around the obvious targets for a break-in – the Portland Vase, the Sutton Hoo treasure, the medieval jewellery, the coins, small ancient relics and gold artefacts – anything that was relatively small, portable and easily disposable.

To Messiter's relief, the security equipment in the Duveen Gallery itself appeared to be minimal, presumably because the Museum's security advisors had come to the conclusion that there was little or no chance of anyone being able to steal such a huge array of exhibits as heavy and as unwieldy as the Elgin marbles.

Said Messiter: 'What we still need is the actual architectural plans of the gallery's structure. The location of the gallery's service tunnels and their entry points.'

'And where would we find them?' asked Armitage.

'All the plans would be in the office of the Museum's resident architect.' Messiter pointed to a section outlined on the official map: 'In the admin section. Just here.'

'And how do we get hold of them? They're not going to give them to us, surely?'

'Sadly, no.' He looked at Ken Beynon: 'This is where your SAS training comes in.'

Beynon looked from one to the other, then took a deep breath:

'Oh shit. This is getting heavy.'

'You're the only one who can do it,'said Messiter.

'But the decision is yours,' said Armitage: 'Say the word and we'll call the whole thing off right now.'

Messiter nodded: 'Like John says, the decision is yours, young Ken.'

There was a long pause. Then with a shrug of total resignation, Young Ken said:

'All right. I'll do it. But only on one condition.'

'Which is?' asked Armitage.'

'That if I'm nicked, you both come and see me on visiting days.'

༺ ༻

The following afternoon, Ken Beynon, dressed in a sweater, jeans and trainers, entered the gates of the British Museum. At the top of the steps at the front entrance, he turned, looked up briefly towards a window, high in the building that towered over the Museum's concourse, then disappeared through the main entrance.

Messiter lowered his binoculars, turned away from the window and said:

'He's gone in.'

Said Armitage: 'Now the only question is – how will he get out?

'Like I told him. Through the staff canteen. After six o'clock, it'll be closed for the night. So again, in that part of the building, the security should be minimal.'

'I wish I felt as confident as you.'

'Who's confident? All I've done is make an educated guess – and I could be wrong.'

When he was sure that Armitage wasn't looking, Messiter took a small pill bottle from his jacket pocket and surreptitiously shook a couple of pills into a trembling hand.

༺ ༻

When Beynon entered the men's toilets, the two men standing in front of the urinals, united in blissful relief, didn't give him a second glance. He entered one of the cubicles and locked the door behind him. He sat down on the closed toilet seat and waited patiently until he heard the door close, first once, then twice, as the men departed. As he had ascertained on a previous visit, above the toilet cubicles was a mains water pipe that ran from one side of the room to the other and, after unlocking the cubicle door, he climbed on to the toilet seat, grasped the overhead pipe and effortlessly heaved himself up towards the cistern inspection hatch in the ceiling. A moment later, he was through the hatch, which he closed carefully behind him. There was more than enough room for him to stretch out and begin his wait for the sound of the first warning bell, that signalled to the visitors that the Museum was about to close.

The bell rang exactly on time and after ushering the very last visitor – or who they assumed to be the very last visitor – out of the main entrance, the security men closed and locked the massive doors firmly into place.

ເ⊼

In the main entrance hall, the self-styled Anders of the Yard, his assistant in his usual position, a few feet behind him, gave his team their final briefing of the day.

'Right everyone. You all know your places. Check every possible exit, egress, nook and cranny – and remember, always expect the unexpected. You never know who or what might be lurking in the shadows. But before you disperse – any questions?'

Muttered the same disgruntled security man, sotto, to his companion: 'Just one. When is Mr. Bracegirdle coming back?'

Anderson looked at them expectantly: 'Well? Anyone? Come on – don't be afraid to speak out.' They just looked back at him, stonily and he had little option but to answer himself: 'No questions at all? Right. Great. Fine. Fantastic. Carry on then.'

As they all made their way to their predetermined destinations, the eager Lucas stepped forward and said: 'What would you like me to do, Chief?'

Anderson thought for a moment and, still mindful of the fact that if it hadn't been for his assistant's ill-timed reappearance when (or so he believed) he had been on the point of persuading the nubile Julie Baker to take the first step along the road to an out-of-office-hours intimate relationship, he said, maliciously:

'You can check out the public conveniences.'

'Again?' said Lucas. Then with weary resignation: 'If you say so, Chief.'

As Anderson stalked off towards his office, Lucas moved disconsolately towards the nearest toilet, passing Julie Baker as he did so. While she was not exactly over-burdened with sensitivity, she could not help but notice his doleful expression and to her surprise, felt a twinge of guilt for the way in which she'd first encouraged him to ask her for a date, only to slap him down, a few moments later. Why had she done that, she wondered? He wasn't a bad little feller. Quite nice, really. In a naff sort of way. And in an effort to make amends, she gave him a ravishing smile and a bright:

'Hallo sunshine. Where are you off to, then?'

He did not return her smile. He simply glowered and said:

'Where I usually end up, at this time of the day. In the shithouse, where else?'

Her smile vanished and not a little aggrieved, she called after him:

'Charming. Really charming, that was.'

But he had already entered the door of the men's toilets.

☙

Beynon was on the point of dozing off in the darkness when he heard the door to the toilets being flung open and the angry footsteps of a disgruntled Lucas, who kicked open the door of each cubicle, one after the other, to check the interiors. When he came to the last cubicle, Beynon heard him groan and mutter 'oh, that's gross,' followed by the sound of a flushed toilet, presumably because its last occupant had unhelpfully and even more unhygenically neglected to do so. Lucas then walked out of the toilets, slamming the door behind him, but it was another hour or so before Beynon cautiously opened the inspection hatch a few inches and peered out. The toilet was in darkness, the Museum silent.

Beynon eased himself down through the hatch and, hanging from the overhead water pipe with one hand, he closed the trap door with the other. After dropping silently to the floor, he pulled out a small pocket flashlight and checked the hand-drawn map of the administrative block, given to him by Messiter. The architect had done his homework well. The door to the admin complex was situated in a corner of the nearby gallery that housed an ancient tomb in the shape of a scaled down Greek temple, named in the Museum's guidebook as the Nereid Monument. Built around 300 BC for a king of Lycia, it rested on a large, richly decorated podium and again, presumably because of the sheer size and weight of the exhibit, the security devices were mostly concentrated elsewhere and within minutes, Beynon had by-passed the single security camera that was scanning the gallery and had reached his destination – a door marked *Private. Museum Personnel Only.*

He tried the door handle. It was locked. From one of his pockets, he produced a slim, strangely shaped piece of metal, previously the property of Her Majesty's Armed Forces, but which he'd found to be such a useful little tool, that upon his honourable discharge from the SAS, he had decided to forget to hand it back. He inserted the probe into the keyhole. After a couple of experimental turns and a jiggle of the instrument, the lock clicked open and he was able to negotiate his way down the deserted, dimly-lit corridors of the admin block towards one office in particular – that of the Museum's resident architect.

The misted glass-panelled door, with its black lettering bearing the legend *J.C. Caldwell, Chief Architect*, was also locked and was also just as swiftly *un*locked. Beynon went straight to the row of filing cabinets against the wall. Messiter had advised him that in most, if not all architectural departments, large or small and particularly for departments with a regular staff turnover, a detailed list of each filing cabinet's contents was deemed vital – and that such a list was invariably kept on the desk or in one of the drawers of the chief architect's secretary.

Beynon moved to the smaller of the two desks and opened the unlocked top drawer. He could hardly believe his luck. There, as Messiter had suggested, was a black exercise book in stiff cardboard covers, clearly labelled *Files – A-Z*. Within minutes, he had located the original architectural and structural plans of the Duveen Gallery, opened them out on to the desk and, standing on the secretary's chair – and with the aid of a desk-lamp and a small, but expensive digital camera, he took a series of photographs.

So far, it had been a textbook operation and it was with a sense of mounting relief that Beynon carefully replaced the plans, the chair and the list of files and moved silently towards the office door. If Messiter's directions for the final stages of the operation proved to be as accurate as the others, they would lead him straight to the deserted staff canteen, where, with a little luck and a quietly opened window, he would be able to make his escape through the staff car park. It was then that he heard the sound of a larger door at the end of the corridor being abruptly opened, followed by the voice of one security guard as he said to the other:

'Harry? You check the left side and I'll check the right.'

Then came the footsteps and the rattle of each office door handle as they moved along the corridor towards the office of the chief architect. At the same moment, Beynon suddenly remembered he had forgotten to switch off the desk lamp.

2

JOHN ARMITAGE TOOK a sip of his now lukewarm coffee, glanced at his watch and said: 'Where the hell is he? According to your calculations, he should have been out by now.'

Messiter checked his own watch and moved to the window: 'So I miscalculated – but that doesn't mean he's been caught.'

'Then what else can it mean? He's nearly an hour overdue, for Christ's sake.'

'Then where are all the police cars, for Christ's sake?' Messiter pointed down towards the Museum front forecourt, illuminated by the many lamp posts along the length of Museum Street: 'If he'd been arrested, the place would be swarming with police, by now.'

Armitage considered, then nodded: 'You're quite right, of course. I wasn't thinking. It's the waiting. The not knowing what's happening. Makes me very edgy'

'Not just you, John.' Messiter groped in his pocket for his bottle of pills: 'God, if I'd known just how agonizing this was going to be, I'm not at all sure I would have asked Ken to do it.'

He swallowed two pills and took a sip of his lukewarm coffee.

Said Armitage, quietly: 'More aspirins, Gavin?'

'What else? Stress always gives me a migraine. You know that.'

'I also know that they're not aspirins. They're TNT, right? For your angina.'

Messiter looked at him, angrily: 'How did you know that?'

'The last time you took them, you left the bottle on the desk. I read the label. Why didn't you tell us you had a heart condition?'

'Because it wasn't important. It *isn't* important. Dammit, just because I've got a touch of angina doesn't mean I'm not up to the job. You need me, John. And I need to see this thing through. And having come this far, I've no intention of backing out now.'

'We need you all right. But I know how stressed-out you are. How stressed-out we both are and if there's the slightest chance of you having a full-blown heart attack all because of this, I'd rather we called it a day, here and now.'

'I've told you. I'm fine. Now let's close the subject, all right?'

'God, you're a stubborn old sod, Gavin.'

'You'd better believe it.'

Messiter went back to the window to continue his surveillance of the Museum's front concourse. Armitage took another sip of his coffee and eyed his companion's rigid back with some concern.

 train

Beynon had a choice. To either switch off the desk lamp or relock the chief architect's office door from the inside. There was no time to do both. It was not a difficult decision. As he was already at the door, he inserted the probe into the keyhole and the lock clicked into place, moments before the shadow of a security man appeared in the door's misted glass window. The door handle rattled and, as Beynon had anticipated, a voice said:

'Hallo?' A tap on the door: 'Anyone in there?' Another rattle of the handle: 'What d'you reckon, Harry?'

Another voice: 'I reckon the dozy bugger's left his light on.'

'Got the keys? Best switch it off, right?'

From his prone position on the floor, immediately behind the door, Beynon began to pray. To his relief, his prayers appeared to be answered.

'Why bother?' said the one called Harry: 'Could take ages to find the right key. And at least he remembered to lock the bloody door.' He apparently glanced at his watch: 'What's more, we'll be off duty in another couple of minutes. So come on, they're still open.'

Beynon waited until their voices had died away and carefully, quietly, clicked open the door. It was relatively easy to find his way through the corridors to the staff canteen which, as Messiter had said, was in total darkness. He moved quickly to the nearest window, then to the next, then on to the next and paused, in dismay. Each window was protected by a hinged metal mesh, screwed securely into place. In desperation, he went behind the serving counter and into the kitchens, in the hope of finding his way out via an exit door or goods entrance – to be met by a goods entrance that was protected by a heavy metal shutter door and a row of metal barred windows, which made even the thought of escape quite out of the question.

Said Beynon, to the deserted kitchens: 'So much for your minimal security, Gavin.'

He was trapped inside the Museum and he knew it. There was only one thing to do. Beynon retraced his steps down the corridor and, on reaching the entrance door to the administrative complex, again unlocked and re-locked it, before making his way back to the men's toilets, intent on spending the night in his original hiding place. When the Museum re-opened in the morning, the moment it was safe to do so, he would emerge from the service hatch and assume, once again, the role of a typical visitor.

Unfortunately for him, however, two other people were heading for the same men's toilets, albeit from a different direction. The two plump, cheerful, middle-aged cleaning ladies, trundling their trolley full of cleaning gear across the main entrance hall, had been employed by the Museum for more years than either of the women cared to remember and as a result had, almost without knowing it, picked up a great deal of knowledge about the Museum's exhibits, which was reflected in their conversation.

Said one: 'You're not going to believe this, Dot, but Annie Parkinson – her in charge of dusting the Egyptian antiquities – took one look at the bust of Theodosius in the mezzanine and told me it was ancient Anatolian!'

'She didn't!' said the one called Dot.

'She did!' insisted her fellow worker: 'And I mean, anyone can see it's early Byzantine – sticks out a mile, don't it?'

'Sticks out a mile,' agreed Dot: 'Silly cow.'

They reached the entrance to the men's toilets, pulled out their mops from the trolley and disappeared inside. The sight of the trolley a couple of minutes later halted Beynon in his tracks. He warily edged the door open a fraction and saw that not only were the room lights on, it was also occupied by two members of the Museum's staff. Once again, with mounting dismay, he was forced to retrace his steps, looking desperately around him for somewhere, anywhere, to conceal himself for the night, before he was inevitably apprehended by a patrolling security man, or picked up by one of the cameras.

As he reached, once again, the gallery housing the Nereid Monument, he heard the sound of approaching footsteps and with no time to unlock and escape back through the nearby door to the admin block, he knew it was only a matter of seconds before he would be seen by the security men. Bitterly resenting the fact that the entire operation had been well and truly foiled, albeit unknowingly, by two middle-aged cleaning ladies, he prepared to give himself up. But only for a moment. He glanced wildly around him and suddenly realised that he was still in with a chance. A small chance, but a chance nevertheless. If he could only make it in time.

&

During the night they had taken it in turns to survey the front entrance for any sign of a police vehicle. Messiter was dozing on one of the camp beds while a bleary-eyed Armitage, standing at the window, said:

'Still no sign of him. And the Museum's been open for almost half an hour.'

Said Messiter wearily: 'Of course there's no sign of him. You were right and I was wrong. He must have been caught.'

'Even though there's been no sign of a police vehicle?'

'Perhaps they used the side entrance.'

'I can see the side entrance from here, too.'

'Look. Face up to it. It's all over, John. Somewhere along the line, I must have cocked up and as a result, put young Ken up to his ears in deep shit.'

'Yes, well, it's still very early in the day and I'm still not convinced that he isn't inside the Museum – maybe waiting for the place to fill up with a few more visitors as his cover. Because if he's not been arrested and is not still inside – where the hell is he?'

'Right here,' said Beynon as he came through the door.

'God!' said Armitage: 'You had us worried.'

'I had me worried, too.'

'What happened to you, for God's sake?'

'Later. I'm completely bushed.' He pulled the little camera out of his pocket and held it out to Messiter: 'As the man said – why don't you and John go into the darkroom and see what develops?'

❧

It was in the early hours of the morning that Beynon had emerged from the inner recesses of the Nereid Monument, into which he'd just managed to scramble as the security men had turned the corner. Though cramped inside, the ancient tomb had served its purpose and, after allowing more than enough time for the two cleaning ladies to complete their various tasks, he had then made his way back to the men's toilets and spent the rest of the night inside the cistern inspection hatch, before venturing out into the front entrance hall, to mingle with the Museum's early morning visitors. As he made his way out of the main doors, he had come face-to-face with the temporary acting Head of Security and his assistant and to Beynon's dismay, both Anderson and Lucas had given him a swift, but curious glance. Beynon had immediately realised why. Unshaven and with uncombed hair, he must have looked unusually scruffy for a visitor to the hallowed corridors of the British Museum and he could only hope that neither would have any reason to remember his face at some time in the future.

Anderson, however, had other things on his mind. Another visit to the souvenir shop to exchange (albeit unwelcome) pleasantries with the hopefully soon-to-be recipient of his affections. And this time, the presence of his assistant would not be required. Anderson looked at his watch and said:

'10 a.m. and all's well, Lucas. Another uneventful night in the annals of the good old British Museum, right?'

'Seems like it, Chief.'

'And let's keep it that way. Constant vigilance. That's the answer.'

'Constant vigilance, yes. Right. Got it.'

'And don't you ever forget it.'

'I won't. Never. Not once.'

'That's why I want you to go and remind every other member of my team that the Chief says that they must never forget it, too.'

'Forget what, Chief?'

'Constant vigilance, for Chrissake.'

By now, Lucas was beginning to find the conversation lurching into the surreal and he was glad to escape. Even so, he cast a quick glance towards the souvenir shop, knowing full well that the dirty old bugger with a wife and three kids in East Croydon (as Julie Baker had pointedly described him) merely wanted him out of the way so he could come on strong with his would-be girlfriend.

'Tell them what you said, Chief. Right,' he repeated, reluctantly: 'Got it. Will do.'

Another glance full of longing towards the souvenir shop and Lucas walked away towards the staff canteen. Even though he had been trusted to be the carrier of such a vitally important (if totally pointless) message, he might as well deliver it over a cup of coffee and a sticky bun.

ᴄ☞

'Well?' said Beynon: 'What d'you think?'

Messiter filled the computer screen with the images from the digital camera and said:

'They'll do, Ken. Well done.'

'You still think we're in with a chance, then?'

'Having seen these, more so than ever. Yes, I'd definitely say it was on. Technically, at least.'

'In that case,' said Armitage: 'I reckon it's time I had a word with our sponsor.'

Three days later, a taxi drew up at the door of an imposing mansion in Belgrave Square and a sober-suited John Armitage emerged from the passenger door, to walk briskly up the few steps to the equally imposing front doorway and ring the polished brass bell-push. The door swung slowly open to reveal an impassive Jefferson, doing his utmost to cultivate the English butler's polite but aloof demeanour. Although being somewhat vertically challenged, he drew himself up to his not-very-full height, raised his eyebrows in the approved manner and said, loftily:

'Yes?'

'Mr. John Armitage to see Miss Papadopoulos.'

A cold: 'Do you have an appointment?' Jefferson knew full well that Armitage had an appointment, but for Jefferson, calculated obtuseness was all part of a butler's calling. Besides, he enjoyed being awkward.

'Yes,' said Armitage: 'I do have an appointment. As I'm sure you're well aware. Now may I come in?'

Jefferson's expression tightened and without another word, he stood to one side. Armitage smothered a grin, surprised to discover that in the circumstances, he was still relaxed enough to find the butler's posturings rather amusing. With his carefully rehearsed, measured tread, Jefferson led Armitage straight to a door at the rear of the long hallway, then down the staircase to the basement shooting gallery, where Athena Papadopoulos, dressed in another, similarly exotic and similarly costly designer dress from her extensive wardrobe, was in the process of demolishing another row of *Selene* horses' heads with her matched pair of hand-made, Purdey double-barrelled shot guns. Although she had seen Armitage the moment he had entered the gallery, she completely ignored him until the last of the horses' heads had been blown to polyester-fibre smithereens. Then handing the guns to the waiting Jefferson, she turned, looked Armitage up and down and said:

'Well, Mr. Armitage?'

'Well what, Miss Papadopoulos?'

'Aren't you in the least curious to know why I should be shooting at plastic replicas of one of the most famous of the Parthenon marbles?'

Armitage smiled: 'The ways of the rich and famous have always been a mystery to me, but since you asked, I suppose it could be a form of therapy.'

'It's a great deal more than that. It's an expression of my utter frustration, my total anger at your British Museum's refusal to return the marbles to their rightful home.'

'So you said on television. But there is a strong body of opinion which believes that by removing the marbles from the debris of the ruined temple, Lord Elgin actually saved them from their total destruction.'

'Nonsense. It was an act of sheer vandalism.'

'Do you really think they would have remained there, buried in the debris, if Elgin hadn't reclaimed them? Or would they have been broken up like so many other pieces were – to provide the foundation for a peasant's pigsty?'

'That's totally irrelevant.'

'Not to the British Museum, it isn't. And as possession, as they say, is nine-tenths of the law…'

Athena gave him a long, speculative look, which was returned with polite equanimity.

'Whose side are you on, Mr. Armitage?'

'Mine. And my two business partners.'

She picked up a business card from a nearby table.

'Why did you send me your business card?' She read the inscription out loud: '*Armitage Transport International.* John J. Armitage, Managing Director.' She turned the card over and read: 'Marbles a speciality. What does that mean, Mr. John J. Armitage?'

'It means why I'm here and why you agreed to see me – if only out of curiosity.'

'Please get to the point.'

'Certainly.' He nodded pointedly towards the butler: 'For your ears only, I'm afraid.'

She turned to the attentive Jefferson: 'Please leave us, Jefferson.'

He nodded, made a dignified bow and walked up the stairs and out of the gallery, leaving the door slightly ajar. Armitage raised his eyebrows and Athena Papadopoulos turned towards the stairway with a loud, impatient:

'And close the door behind you.'

There was a moment's pause, then, to Armitage's inner amusement, the door clicked firmly shut, indicating that the butler had obviously intended to remain in the immediate vicinity, presumably with his ear glued to the door jam. Athena Papadopoulos turned back towards him, with an abrupt:

'Now, Mr. Armitage.'

'Quite simply, I'm here to ask you if you'd care to negotiate a fee for the unofficial return of the Elgin marbles – I do beg your pardon, the Parthenon marbles, back to Greece.'

Athena Papadopoulos gave a long sigh, turned towards the nearby bell-push and pressed it. A few moments later, the gallery door was re-opened and the butler was framed in the doorway:

'You rang, madame?'

She indicated the man in front of her and said, imperiously: 'Jefferson? Throw him out.'

Jefferson looked down at the tall and well-built Armitage and visibly blanched:

'*Me?* Throw *him* out? You've got to be – '

'Just do as you're told.'

She was halfway up the stairs before pausing and turning for a contemptuous:

'As you said, Mr. Armitage, I agreed to see you mostly out of curiosity. But I might have known. You're just another, rather pathetic confidence trickster – and a very inept one, at that.'

Said Armitage quietly: 'Payment on delivery.'

Another pause, another long stare. Then: 'Jefferson?'

Jefferson edged nervously down the stairs: 'Now look, madame – '

'Tell Chef that Mr. Armitage will be staying for dinner.'

A slightly bemused Armitage calculated that the opulent dining table must have been all of twenty feet long. The carpets and furnishings in the dining room itself were equally luxurious. Ostentation obviously ruled. Sitting at each end of the long table, they sipped their soup in silence. After Jefferson had served the second course and departed, Athena Papadopoulos broke the silence with a casual:

'I had you checked out, of course.'

'I would have been surprised if you hadn't.'

'And while you are undoubtedly who and what you say you are – the managing director of a small, privately-owned transportation business, with an excellent reputation throughout the profession, it appears that for various reasons, your business is on the point of falling apart. In exactly the same way as your marriage fell apart, approximately two years ago.'

Armitage nodded: 'Yes. I'd say that was a fair assessment of my present situation.'

'Then why should I listen to some quite preposterous proposition concerning the removal of the marbles from the British Museum – especially from a man like yourself? A self-confessed failure – both privately and professionally.'

'Because you have nothing to lose and everything to gain. The marbles in particular.'

'Very well. Tell me exactly how you intend to do it.'

Armitage smiled and shook his head: 'You know I can't do that.'

'And why not?'

'I would have thought that was obvious. The fewer people who know about this the better. For all our sakes – including your own.'

'I still wish to know. In fact, I insist upon it.'

'With all due respect Miss Papadopoulos, you're in no position to insist upon anything. All we need from you is your agreement to pay a fair price – in cash, of course – for the safe return of the marbles.'

His hostess looked at him in total disbelief. Was the man actually refusing to tell her what she desired to know? No one had ever dared to refuse Athena Papadopoulos anything, even when she was a little girl. It was obvious that the Englishman was genuinely unaware that whatever Athena wanted – Athena always got. She carefully put down her solid silver cutlery, rose to her feet and said, grandly:

'Mr. Armitage. I don't think you quite understand the situation – which is, unless you tell me what I wish to know, here and now, your audience with me is at an end. Is that quite clear?'

'As a bell, Miss Papadopoulos.'

She pointed a quivering finger towards the door, like an actor in a Victorian melodrama and said: 'Then tell me what I wish to know, or go.'

All that was missing, thought Armitage, were the words 'and never darken my door again.'

'The choice is yours, Mr. Armitage.'

'It always was, Miss Papadopoulos.'

He replaced his fork and knife with equal deliberation, rose from his chair, turned towards the door and, with mock sadness, said:

'What a pity it isn't snowing outside.'

As he took the first step towards the door, it suddenly opened as Jefferson reappeared to serve the wine. Armitage proffered the butler an arm and said, quite straight-faced:

'Jefferson? Throw me out.'

Jefferson looked apprehensively towards his employer, but his employer was staring in obvious bewilderment at the totally unfazed Armitage, not quite believing what she was hearing. Could it be that he had actually called her bluff? For that is what it was. As the man had said, no matter how ridiculous his proposition might have sounded, she had nothing to lose and everything to gain. For the first time in her life, she realised that she had no choice but to swallow her pride – plus a substantial helping of humble pie. She looked in fury at the man at the other end of the table, who merely returned her look with an expression of bland indifference. Then finally biting on the bullet, she gave an angry, child-like pout and abruptly sat down again, gesturing to Armitage to do the same. Then through firmly gritted teeth, she said:

'Jefferson? You may serve the wine.'

A little while later, over coffee and cognac in the beautifully carved, oak-panelled library, Athena Papadopoulos nodded towards the large oil painting of an elderly, unsmiling man, hanging over the ornate fireplace and said:

'My father, Andreas Papadopoulos. A quite remarkable man. And a patriot. For his sake, in his memory, I would be prepared to pay anything for the safe return of the marbles to Greece. Legally, illegally, peacefully or by force.'

'Illegally, possibly,' said Armitage: 'By force – certainly not. Violence has no place in our operation. To pull it off, it's going to be difficult enough as it is. Which is why if we succeed, our fee will be one millions pounds. Each.'

'Three million pounds?'

'In cash. Plus expenses, of course.'

'What sort of expenses?'

'The purchase of the necessary equipment, transportation and storage costs and any other items that may be needed for us to be able to complete the operation and for which you'll be given a detailed, itemised account." A knowing smile. So that was it: 'With payment in advance, of course.'

'Certainly not.'

The smile vanished. What in the name of Zeus could the man up to? It just didn't make sense. Where was the catch? There had to be a catch, *somewhere*. The situation was becoming more interesting by the minute. Fascinating, even. She looked at him searchingly, as if seeking a tell-tale flaw in his relaxed, calmly confident composure, but found nothing. She shrugged. What he hell? As he had said, what had she got to lose?

'Very well,' she said finally: 'I agree to your terms. You see? Even though I do not believe for one moment that you and your partners will succeed in fulfilling your part of the bargain, I am prepared to snatch at straws.' She raised her glass: 'To the success of Operation Parthenon, Mr. Armitage.' And with more than a hint of menace: 'And God help you if this is nothing more than an elaborate hoax.'

Armitage smiled and raised his glass:

'Nice doing business with you, Miss Papadopoulos.'

☙

'One million pounds each?' repeated Beynon: 'Plus expenses? You've got to be joking.'

Armitage smiled: 'That's what I thought *she'd* say. But she didn't even blink.'

'But even if we did get that far, how do we know she'll pay up?'

'For one thing,' offered Messiter: 'Three million is petty cash to her. For another, she knows it'll be payment on delivery. No marbles – no money.'

They were sitting at their original table outside the public house in Museum Street, directly facing the front forecourt of the British Museum.

'So it's all systems go,' said Beynon.

'Seems like it.'

Beynon glanced casually towards the passing pedestrians then hastily turned his head away, with a muttered: 'Oh shit.'

'What is it?' said Messiter.

'I forgot to tell you. They clocked me the other day. The security feller and his assistant. The assistant's coming this way. He's the one with the pretty blonde girl.'

Said Armstrong: 'It's the girl who works in the Museum souvenir shop.'

Beynon kept his head turned away: 'The last thing I need is for him to get another good look at me.'

But Lucas was too intent in engaging Julie Baker in earnest conversation to even glance in their direction. As they walked through the main gates of the Museum, Lucas was making yet another attempt to persuade the girl to go out with him and, to his surprise, this time she actually seemed to be giving the idea serious consideration.

Said Lucas eagerly: 'But if you don't fancy the theatre, we could go to a disco. Y'know, somewhere really hep. Swinging. Far out.'

The girl giggled: 'Hep? Swinging? Far out? I haven't heard anyone talk like that since my dad wore flared trousers and a gold medallion.' She shook her head in mock despair: 'You shouldn't be allowed out on your own, Barry Lucas. You really shouldn't. What am I going to do with you, eh? What am I going to do with you?'

'Dunno, really.' said Lucas with a sigh: 'What would you suggest?'

Julie Baker smiled, gave his arm a little squeeze and said: 'I'll give it some thought.' Immediately, she wondered why she'd said it. Give it some thought? Why on earth should she? He was just a little boy. And a complete and utter dip-stick. Always was, always would be. So why had she suddenly become so concerned about him? As they mounted the steps to the Museum's entrance, she again shook her head, this time in total bewilderment at herself.

From the other side of Museum Street, said Messiter: 'It's all right, Ken, they've gone in.' He drained his glass and rose to his feet: 'Come on, you two. We've got some shopping to do.'

The newly purchased wrench, rope ladder, additional flashlights and high-speed, miniature cordless drills were lined up on the desk of the Centrepoint office. As they stood at the computer, Messiter used a pencil as a pointer at the series of Beynon's illicitly obtained digital photographs of the Duveen Gallery's detailed structural plans.

'Like I reckoned, as it's obviously essential for all the exhibits to be maintained at a constant temperature, all the year round, the Duveen Gallery has its own independent air conditioning and central heating system. It's housed here, in this boiler room, just behind what is called the East Pediment and this is the access door.' His pencil traced a path around the walls of the Gallery: 'Off the boiler room are a series of narrow passageways, running around the gallery between its inner and outer walls – with just enough room for an engineer to crawl through for maintenance. And that's where we have to go.'

'All three of us?' asked Beynon.

'All three of us,' confirmed Messiter: 'It's far too big a job for one man – or even two. It's going to be a race against time as it is.'

'Just one question, Gavin,' said Armitage quietly: 'Are you sure you'll be up to it, health-wise?'

Said Beynon: 'Why shouldn't he be?'

'Because he's got a heart condition.' To Messiter, he said: 'Sorry Gavin, but he has a right to know.'

'It's only a minor heart condition, Ken,' insisted Messiter: 'Just a touch of angina and I'm damned if I'm going to let it stop me pulling my weight. And like I said, you just can't do this without me.'

'If you're sure,' said Beynon dubiously.

'I'm sure. Now for God's sake, let's get on with it.'

Even Messiter had not anticipated that something as basic as a service hatch in the British Museum's men's toilets would be destined to play such a key part in the entire operation, but as Armitage, then Messiter emerged from the hatch and made a shaky descent down the lightweight, nylon rope ladder, the hatch and the space above it was more than proving its worth. After pulling the ladder up and out of sight, the athletic Beynon slipped easily into view and, after closing the trapdoor behind him, dropped silently to the floor of the cubicle.

He looked at the heavily breathing Messiter with some concern: 'You all right, Gavin?'

'Don't fuss. I'm fine. Just fine. A little out of condition, that's all.'

'Okay. But stay close to me.'

Their passage through the darkened Museum was uneventful. Beynon had been there before. Following his mimed directions, they successfully eluded the few security devices between the toilets and the gallery housing the Nereid Monument. The Duveen Gallery was immediately next to it and, after Beynon had paused in the open doorway to check out its interior, he nodded to the others and led the way past the rows of marbles towards the East Pediment.

Surprisingly, or perhaps unsurprisingly, the door to the boiler room was not locked and as they entered it, closing the door behind them, they were met with an array of control panels, stopcocks, air-conditioning units and a large boiler. The gentle pumping sound came from the adjoining equipment, over which Messiter cast a professional eye, before a quick nod and a whispered:

'First, we need to shut down the pumping system' He pointed to the large hexagonal screw bolt: 'I'll need the wrench.'

The wrench was produced from Beynon's shoulder bag and after a few turns, the pumping sound ceased.

'Drills and torches, Ken?'

The drills and torches were also swiftly produced and Messiter pointed to the cupboard-like door, to one side of the boiler.

'Through here.'

As they crawled along the narrow, tunnel-like duct, the sides of which carried both lagged and unlagged pipes and electricity cables, Messiter checked his computer prints-out of the structural plans, paused and pointed his finger at an exact spot on the piping. Armitage immediately began to drill through the lagging and the pipe beneath, as Messiter and Beynon crawled on to repeat the process along the entire length of the tunnels, one after the other.

It was a long and arduous process. When they finally retraced their steps to the boiler room, even Beynon showed signs of weariness. A panting Messiter reached for his pills and mutely gestured to Armitage to turn the pumping system back on again. That done, their tools safely packed away in Beynon's shoulder bag, they cautiously made their way out of the door and back into the Duveen Gallery.

Behind them, the first beads of water were already beginning to ooze from the piping, along the entire length of the service passageway.

Beynon swung himself up into the cistern service hatch and lowered the rope ladder down to the waiting Armitage and Messiter.

'You first, Gavin. And get a move on. We've got just over five minutes before the cleaning ladies get here.'

The still breathless Messiter grasped the rope ladder, took a tentative first step and shook his head:

'I'm sorry. I can't make it.'

'For Chrissake, Gavin,' said Beynon: 'You've got to make it – or we'll all be sitting ducks.'

Messiter shook his head again and sank down on the toilet seat, utterly exhausted: 'I'm sorry. I really am.' To Armitage, he said: 'You go on up, John. There's no point in us all getting caught.'

'For God's sake, Gavin!' snapped Beynon: 'You can't just chuck in the towel! Not after getting this far.' To Armitage he said: 'John – you come up here and we'll haul him up between us.'

Armitage nodded and started to scramble up the ladder.

'It's no good, John,' whispered the ashen-faced Messiter: 'I haven't even got the strength to stand up. I'd just fall over.'

Armitage paused halfway up the ladder, looked up at Beynon and held out his hand: 'Give me the wrench, Ken. Quickly, now.'

The two cleaning ladies, pushing their trolley before them, made their way across the main concourse towards the men's toilets, their conversation again reflecting their place of employment:

'So I said to her – Annie Parkinson I mean – Annie, I said, now you've been transferred from the Egyptian rooms to the Duveen Gallery, what do you think about the contribution Mycenaean culture made to ancient Athens? Was it a good thing or not?' She chuckled: 'Of course, Dot, she didn't have a clue as to what I was going on about. But would she admit it?'

'No she would not,' hazarded the one named Dot.

'No she would not,' confirmed the other: 'And d'you know what she said?' She gave another chuckle: 'You're not going to believe this, Dot. She said well, she said, they did teach them how to carve them Elgin marbles, didn't they? Them what's in my gallery.'

'She didn't!' said the one named Dot.

'She did! And I mean, the marbles were carved about four thousand years later, circa four hundred and thirty eight BC – right Dot?'

'Right,' said Dot: 'I thought everyone knew that.'

'Everyone but Annie Parkinson.'

'Silly cow,' said Dot.

'Silly cow,' agreed her companion.

They reached the men's toilets and leaving their trolley behind them, they pushed open the swing door and entered the toilets, re-emerging almost immediately with identical expressions of wonder:

'God almighty,' said the one named Dot: 'What are we going to do about that?'

'Call security,' said the other: 'And quickly. They'll know what to do.

3

ATHENA PAPADOPOULOS SWEPT through the front door of her Belgrave Square mansion and said:

'Have there been any telephone calls for me, Jefferson? From a Mr. Armitage in particular?'

'No madame,' said the butler, closing the door behind her.

'Are you sure?'

'Quite sure, madame.'

'Damn the man.'

Jefferson gave a secret little smile. His employer was obviously very pissed off with the man who'd come to dinner, a few weeks previously. He liked it when she was pissed off, especially when, for a change, she was pissed off with someone else, instead of him. But in truth, his employer was more disappointed than annoyed. Armitage had promised to keep in touch with her to inform her as soon as he'd reached each stage of the operation, on a need to know basis, but without going into detail. And his long silence would seem to indicate that either the whole thing was an elaborate, if pointless, hoax – as she'd originally suspected, or that he and his associates had decided the plan was too risky, too difficult to carry out and had called it a day.

Either way, it would mean that she'd seen the last of John J. Armitage who, despite his quite infuriating and very English insouciance, had proved to be a very interesting dinner companion and a great deal more entertaining than anyone at the Anglo-Greek charity function she had attended that same evening.

She shrugged off her Russian silver fox stole, which her butler just managed to catch before it dropped to the polished floor and said:

'Cognac, Jefferson. In the library. Now.'

'Cognac, madame. Yes, of course, madame. Right away, madame.'

And as she disappeared through the doorway, his deferential demeanour was replaced, as usual, by an aggrieved expression and a one fingered salute.

The security man looked reluctantly through the door of the men's toilets, at the water cascading from one of the washbasins and on to the already flooded tiled floor.

'Jesus. What a mess.' He tiptoed gingerly through the water to the basin and attempted to turn off the tap, but without success: 'It's locked solid. The thread must have gone.' He bent down and peered under the basin: 'Where's the hell's the stop-cock? Ah.'

This time he was more successful and managed to turn off the stop-cock before moving back towards the doorway. But as he crossed the now slippery floor, his feet went from under him and he abruptly sat down in two inches of cold water:

'Damn, blast and bugger it,' muttered the security man, as he crawled to his feet: 'I'm soaking.'

The two cleaning ladies standing in the doorway did their best to muffle their snorts of laughter.

Said the one named Dot: 'Oh dear, Mr. Hargreaves. You're all wet.'

Said the other: 'You'd better get out of those trousers before you catch your death.' She reached out towards him: 'Here. Let me help you.'

'Gerroff,' said the security man, backing away: 'I'm a married man.'

'But what do we do about the toilets?'

'There's nothing you can do until that tap's fixed. I'll leave a note for maintenance. In the meantime, stick up an Out Of Order sign.'

'Whatever you say, Mr. Hargreaves,' said the one named Dot, taking a sign from the trolley and hanging it on the door. As the security man squelched miserably away across the entrance hall, they masked their grins and pushed their trolley in the opposite direction.

Inside one of the cubicles, Beynon and Armitage were standing on the rim of the toilet bowl as they supported a heavily breathing Gavin Messiter.

Said Armitage, gently, reassuringly:

'You can relax now, Gavin. They've gone.'

Said Beynon: 'And by the time the Museum opens, most of the water will have drained away.'

Messiter nodded weakly, gratefully and closed his eyes in relief.

☞

It was several days before a keen-eyed security man happened to notice the appearance of several damp patches on the walls of the Duveen Gallery. These were followed by a series of tiny vertical and horizontal cracks around several of the exhibits. The small, plump and somewhat agitated little Scotsman who went by the self-chosen title of Director of Operations, gazed up at them with growing dismay and turned to the man beside him, who was also studying the walls, but with a professional eye.

'Is it serious, Caldwell?'

The museum's resident architect absently fingered his neat bow tie and ran a hand through his expensively coiffeured, iron-grey hair.

'Serious enough, Director. As far as I can tell, it looks like a case of subsidence. At a guess, it's all down to that burst water main a few weeks back.'

The Director shook his head: 'Surely not. I know it flooded the East basement, but the water company assured me that there'd be no lasting damage.'

'Yes, well, they would, wouldn't they?' drawled the architect. 'I reckon the water then seeped into the upper walls and started to weaken the brickwork. But we won't know for sure until we've hacked off the plaster facings and the brickwork is fully expose.'

The Director looked at him in some alarm.

'But won't that create a bit of a mess?'

The architect nodded, cheerfully:

'Not just a *bit* of a mess – an almighty mess. But unless you wish to run the risk of the inner walls collapsing and bringing the marbles down with them, you'll have to remove the exhibits and close down the gallery. And the sooner the better.'

The Director glared at him. Godammit, the man seemed to be actually enjoying the situation and Hamish Munro's usually soft, carefully cultivated Edinburgh Morningside accent spontaneously degenerated into a rough, Glaswegian patois that betrayed his real origins:

'Close down the Duveen? Are ye off your heid? I dinnae believe it!' His angry voice echoed around the gallery, startling the handful of visitors around them: 'At the height of the tourist season? I canna do that, Jimmy!'

'I'm afraid you've no choice, Director. And the name's Julian, by the way. Now if you'll excuse me, I have to go and talk to the builders.'

'But where are we going to store the blasted things? The cellars are crammed from floor to ceiling as it is.'

The architect feigned sympathy: 'I'm afraid that's your problem, Director. I'm just a simple architect.'

He turned his back on the director and moved swiftly towards the doorway, masking a smile of grim satisfaction as he did so. It was nice to have a break in his invariably boring, daily routine and be actively involved in doing something important, for a change. It was even nicer to show the pompous, jumped up so-called Director of Operations that he, J.C. Caldwell, the British Museum's resident architect, was now in charge, whether he liked it or not And the Director did not like it. He took one, last, agitated look at the damp patches along the walls, then angrily followed his colleague out of the gallery, passing a man seemingly deeply immersed in a book devoted to the marbles. As the Director went out of sight, Armitage closed his book and smiled.

☞

'The most likely storage place,' said Messiter: 'Would be the old underground vaults in Essex – just outside Colchester.'

To Armitage's and Beynon's relief, he seemed to have completely recovered from his near collapse a few days previously.

'I told you,' he'd said, on their return to London: 'All I needed was to put my feet up for two or three days. And now let's get back to the job in hand.'

He, Armitage and Beynon were sitting around their Centrepoint office desk, studying a road map of South East England.

Continued Messiter: 'According to *Gray's History of the British Museum*, they were built at the start of the second World War, specifically to house the Museum's most valuable artefacts during the German blitzkrieg on London – including the Elgin marbles – and the vaults are still very much in use today.'

'Even so,' said Armitage: 'We can't be sure that's where the marbles will end up *this* time, surely?'

'Obviously not. We'll need to check it out.'

Said Beynon: 'And just how do we do that?'

Messiter smiled and reached for the telephone: 'That's the easy part.'

☞

At the end of the long, winding, Essex country lane, the sign outside what was once a wartime army camp, complete with wooden guardhouse and a high security fence, announced itself as the now privatised *Sentinel Security Vaults*. When the telephone rang within the guardhouse, the duty security man reluctantly put aside his tabloid newspaper and the undoubted appeal of the pneumatic young lady who was coyly gracing that day's page three and picked up the receiver. He listened intently, then said:

'Just one moment, sir.' Putting his hand over the mouthpiece, he turned and called towards the half-open inner-office door: 'Mr Johnson sir? A gentleman from the British Museum wishes to know if we've been informed about a very special delivery.'

Said the manager's disembodied voice through the open doorway: 'If he's referring to the one I think he is, the instructions came through this morning. It's due a week on Saturday. Via Avery Transport.'

The security man removed his hand from the receiver and said: 'The delivery due a week on Saturday, sir? Via Avery Transport? Yes, everything's in order. And don't worry, sir. They'll be safe with us. Not at all, sir. Goodbye, sir.'

He replaced the telephone, just as the manager appeared in the inner- office doorway, shaking his head in disbelief. He was obviously not a lover of ancient artefacts.

'Dear God. They do get into a flap, don't they? We're talking about storing a few tons of broken marble, for Chrissake – not the bloody Mona-Lisa and her dam' silly smile.'

In the Centrepoint office, Messiter replaced the receiver and said: 'See what I mean? They're due to be picked up a week on Saturday, by a company called Avery Transport.'

'I know them,' said Armitage: 'Well, I know *of* them. Very old established. Based in Fulham.'

Said Messiter: 'Yes, well, that was the easy part. The next bit's a little more tricky – and this is where you come in, young Ken.'

'Oh shit,' said Beynon, not for the first time: 'Not again.'

'This one should be fairly straightforward – all you'll have to do is nip in and out and pick up a couple of forms. At best, all they'll have is a single night watchman.'

'Who's they?'

The offices of *Avery Transport's* London depot were situated in an old Victorian building that had once been a warehouse, within a sprawling, flood-lit yard in a quiet West London back street. Lined up in the yard were rows of trucks – from furniture vans to large container pantechnicons – each bearing the distinctive Avery Transport logo. Just inside the main gate was a small wooden hut and, as Messiter had anticipated, its only human occupant was an elderly night watchman, a flask of tea beside him, a copy of *The Racing Times* in his lap and a couple of German shepherd guard dogs at his feet.

Neither the night watchman nor the dogs had sensed the silent arrival of the ex-SAS man who had quickly scaled the high perimeter wall at the other side of the yard and who had lock-picked his way into the office building via a side door in less than a minute. But it was some time before Beynon, with the aid of a small flashlight held between his teeth, had finished checking through the first floor office filing cabinets, none of which seemed to contain what he was looking for. For a moment, he just stood there, in an agony of frustration and indecision, before his glance fell upon the two over-flowing filing baskets on the top of the large central desk – one labelled *In* and the other, somewhat predictably, labelled *Out*. He gave a grunt of satisfaction as a quick riff through the *IN* basket provided him with what he had been instructed to look for. In the best traditions of contemporary bureaucracy, the signed order forms from the British Museum were in triplicate and after checking that the photocopier in the corner of the office was switched on, he began to run off several copies.

Whether it was because they were alerted by the small flashes of light coming from the photocopier through the uncurtained office window on the other side of the yard, or because of the night watchman's canine companions' natural sixth sense, Beynon was not to know. But the twin low growls from the German shepherd and his sibling brought the night watchman reluctantly to his feet and prompted him to peer out of his window and into the yard. To the dogs, he said:

'What is it?'

But by then, Beynon was making his way back down the stairs of the building towards the side doorway.

'Daft buggers,' said the night watchman: 'There's no one out there.' The dogs, however, were obviously less than convinced and continued to growl like a couple of basso profundo opera singers. The night watchman sighed: 'Smell the office cat do you? Why don't you leave the poor little sod alone? She's never done you any harm.' But the growls continued, followed by a frantic scratching at the door. The night watchman gave up: 'Have it your way.' He opened the door and let the dogs out, closing it behind them.

A moment later, Beynon opened the office building side door a few inches and peered out – to come face to face with two slavering, malevolent German shepherds, sitting side by side outside the door, their considerable fangs bared in eager anticipation. His immediate reaction was to try to slam the door shut again, but he was too late. The guard dogs hurled themselves at the closing door and despite Beynon's efforts, one managed to get a paw and a muzzle into the narrow opening, while the other barked, howled and scrabbled at the door in fury. The last thing Beynon wished to do was cause pain to an animal that was simply doing what it had been trained to do, but with his shoulder to the door, he slowly increased the pressure on the snarling dog's muzzle until the snarls turned to a whine and the dog tried desperately to withdraw both his paw and muzzle from the narrow opening. Beynon immediately pulled back the door a fraction and, the moment the dog had backed away, he slammed it shut again, this time succeeding in closing it properly, before either dog could make a second attempt to get to him. At that moment, the door of the night watchman's hut was thrown open and a voice bellowed:

'What's all the bloody noise about? Come here, you daft buggers!'

The dogs paused momentarily at the sound of their master's voice and began to whine:

'I said come here!'

The dogs refused to move. This was unusual. His word was normally their command and his curiosity finally aroused, the night watchman moved warily across the yard to the barking dogs and, as they continued to scrabble at the closed door, he grasped the door handle and turned it. From his prone position on the roof of the building, which he'd reached via an upper-storey skylight, Beynon looked down on the night watchman and his two guard dogs and silently congratulated himself on having the foresight to re-lock the side door before racing back up the stairs and on to the roof. The night watchman gave the whining dogs an angry look and, as if lecturing a couple of stubborn little schoolboys:

'What *is* the matter with you two? Started seeing things, have you? One more sound out of either of you tonight and it'll be the Battersea Dogs Home for the pair of you. Is that quite clear?'

The dogs sniffed the air and with the scent of their quarry having long since evaporated, combined with their keeper's tone of voice, their tails drooped apologetically and they attempted to lick his hand. Mollified, he gave them a brief pat and walked back across the yard towards his hut, muttering as he went, for the third time that evening, his semi-affectionate 'daft buggers.' After the door had closed behind the night watchman, Beynon, his previous exit route still blocked by the two dogs, which were now padding aimlessly around the yard, unwound the thin nylon rope from around his waist, looped it neatly over the long-dormant chimney stack and abseiled silently down the rear of the building. Once on the ground, in a matter of seconds, he had flicked the rope to dislodge it from the chimneystack, scaled the nearby perimeter wall and had dropped, with feline ease, into the deserted back street.

Well within the hour, he was sipping a cup of black coffee in the Centrepoint office, as Messiter and Armitage studied the photo-copied documents. Said Beynon, wearily:

'I tell you, I'm getting too old for this sort of thing. Another couple of inches and those bloody dogs would have made a meal out of my wedding tackle.'

'Don't worry, Ken,' said Armitage reassuringly: 'No more breaking and entering, we promise you.'

'Thank God for that. I've come to the conclusion that I'm just not cut out to be a burglar.'

Messiter held one of the photo-copies up to the light and said casually:

'Then how d'you feel about forgery?'

The following day, they inspected each other's attempts to forge the signature that appeared on the photo-copied order forms that had been nefariously obtained the previous night. The florid, somewhat ostentatious signature was that of Hamish C. Munro, the British Museum's Director of Operations, whose written authority was obviously required before any valuable artefact could be removed from the building. It was Beynon's near-perfect duplication of the Director's signature and the ease and panache with which he executed it, that both surprised and impressed his partners.

Said Messiter, wonderingly: 'Where did you learn to do that, young Ken?'

Beynon smiled, modestly: 'When I really *was* Young Ken. I used to write sick notes, signed by my mother, so I could skive off from school and play footie in the park. Did the same for some of the other kids, too. For fifty-pee a time. Happy days.'

'Talk about a mis-spent youth,' said Armitage, with a grin.

'Came in handy, though, didn't it?'

Using the computer, it was comparatively easy to print exact replicas of the order forms before handing them to Beynon for signature. This done, the three critically studied the original photo-copies and the new forged documents, side by side.

'Seem okay to me,' said Armitage finally.

'I think that's about as good as we'll get,' agreed Messiter.

Said Beynon: 'Let's go for it then.'

Armitage picked up the telephone and dialled a number. His conversation with the manager of *Avery Transport* was brief and to the point:

'Hamish Munro, Director of Operations, the British Museum. The consignment for *Sentinel Security*. We're running late, I'm afraid. The packing's taking much longer than we thought – so we'll need at least another couple of days before they'll be ready for collection. I suggest the following Monday. That's the twenty-fifth, instead of the twenty-third. You'll need written confirmation, of course. I suggest you simply scrap the original instructions and I'll have the replacement documents biked over to you within the next couple of days. I trust that will not present any problems.'

When *Avery Transport's* manager finally managed to get a word in edgeways, it appeared that the new arrangements presented no problems whatsoever. Armitage replaced the receiver and nodded at the others.

'Now what?' said Beynon.'

'We also inform *Sentinel Security* that the British Museum consignment will be delivered a couple of days late, then you two can go home, sit back and wait,' said Armitage: 'I have to go and see a woman about a tanker.'

⟨≈⟩

'I'd almost given you up, Mr. Armitage,' said Athena Papadopoulos, as they relaxed in the comfort of her opulent library. Turning to her seemingly ever-present butler, who was in the act of pouring two overly generous cognacs, she said: 'You can leave the decanter, Jefferson.'

Jefferson gave his deferential bow and, as always, repeated his instructions:

'Leave the decanter. Yes, madame. Of course, madame. Will that be all, madame?'

Armitage could not help but wonder if her servant was ever given any time off. No wonder his expression seemed to be permanently frozen into that of a fair imitation of an Easter Island stone idol and, as if sensing

Armitage's unspoken query, she continued: 'Yes, that will be all, Jefferson. You may now retire.'

For a moment, Armitage thought he detected a slight change of expression in the butler's doleful visage – a certain wistfulness at even the thought of retiring, not just to bed, but permanently. But if he disliked his job – and his employer – so profoundly, why on earth did he continue to remain in her employment? Armitage immediately answered himself. Money, what else? Employers like Athena Papadopoulos were invariably more than willing to pay well above the going rate to ensure that their servants would be on call whenever required. And with a woman as professionally demanding as Athena Papadopoulos, Jefferson couldn't have much of a life. He almost felt a twinge of pity for the little man. But only for a moment. After all, if the money was all *that* important to him…he stopped in mid-thought. You hypocritical, holier-than-thou bastard, Armitage. Of course money was important to the man. Money was important to everyone – himself, Gavin Messiter and Ken Beynon, in particular. Why else would they have embarked upon a totally lunatic operation which, if it failed, would almost certainly make all three of them long-term guests at one of Her Majesty's penal establishments?

'I said I'd almost given you up, Mr. Armitage.'

'Um? Yes, well, as *I* said, any subsequent contact between us would be on a need to know basis. And what I need to know is – could the Papadopoulos tanker, which, according to *Shipping News*, is due to arrive at the South Essex Oil Terminal around midnight on Saturday, the twenty-third of this month, be made available to me?'

'For what purpose?'

'To take on board the Parthenon marbles for their return to Greece. I'd planned to use a Portuguese merchantman. The Captain's an old business associate of mine, but he won't be getting into port until the following day.'

Athena Papadopoulos said nothing. She just looked at him speculatively over the rim of her brandy glass. Then after a while:

'You're saying you're already in possession of the marbles?'

'Not exactly. Had I been so, it would probably have been all over the newspapers by now.'

'Indeed.'

'But if everything goes to plan, by this time on Saturday the twenty-third –'

Athena Papadopoulos laughed out loud.

Armitage raised his eyebrows: 'You find that amusing, Miss Papadopoulos?'

'Oh come now, Mr. Armitage. D'you really expect me to believe that?'

Armitage sighed: 'Not to put too fine a point on it, Miss Papadopoulos and my apologies in advance for any intemperate language, but I really don't give a tuppenny fuck if you believe it or not. All I want from you is an answer to a very simple question. Will your tanker be made available to my associates and me or not? Time is of the essence and if the answer's no, I shall have to look elsewhere.'

She shook her head in wonder, sipped her cognac and looked at him in open admiration: 'I really have to hand it to you. You're nothing if not consistent. Just how long d'you intend to keep this up?'

'Keep what up?'

'This…silly little game of yours. This charade. You know that sooner or later, it all has to come to an end.'

Armitage drained his drink in one quick gulp and rose to his feet. He'd had enough. The events over the last few weeks had been fraught enough for all of them without him having to justify himself to a spoilt, arrogant, albeit beautiful young woman who was asking for a swift kick up her elegant backside.

'Ah, well. It was just a thought. One of your tankers seemed to be the logical answer, that's all.'

'Where are you going?'

'Back to work. As I said, time is off the essence, but as you obviously have some difficulty in taking me seriously…'

She suddenly realised that she didn't want him to go. He was proving to be far too entertaining, far too amusing, to be allowed to walk out on her before she was ready to dismiss him.

'Sit down, Mr. Armitage.'

'Look, it's been a hard last few weeks and it's going to get even harder. Thanks for the cognac, but as I said, I've work to do.'

'Did I say you *couldn't* have the tanker?'

'You didn't need to say it.'

'Sit down.' He hesitated. She smiled winningly: 'Please?'

'The magic word. But first, do I get the Goddam tanker or not?'

'Let's talk about it."

He sat down. She reached for the decanter and refilled both glasses.

It was exactly eleven o'clock the same evening when Gavin Messiter, in the process of preparing to go to bed, felt a sudden, massive pain, first up his right arm, then across his chest, before collapsing into unconsciousness in the hallway of his cottage, where he would continue to lie until his discovery by his regular cleaning lady, the following morning.

At the time of Messiter's heart attack, Armitage was thoughtfully regarding a relaxed, slightly mellow Athena Papadopoulos who, propped up by a plethora of cushions, was now stretched out on the long leather couch and who, somewhat to his surprise, appeared to find his company quite enjoyable. She nodded towards the decanter:

'Your glass is empty. Have the other half, as you English say.'

'I've already had it. Several times over.'

'So have another. Live a little, Mr. Armitage. Don't be so bloody English. Let your hairs down.'

Armitage masked a smile. The very fine cognac was obviously beginning to affect her normally effortless English, which had suddenly become a little less than perfect. She waved a hand airily in the direction of her late father's portrait:

'My father could drink a whole bottle of cognac at one sitting and still remain as sober as one of your judges.'

Said Armitage, dryly: 'I won't ask you what he died of.'

'Of life. And living it. To the full. And in some ways, you and he are very much alike.'

Christ, thought Armitage. I hope not.

'There was a touch of larceny about him, too,' she continued: 'He was equally rude, outspoken, very impatient with those who disagreed with him and, like you, he didn't give a – what did you call it? – a four-penny fuck what people thought of him.'

'It was a tuppenny fuck, actually.' Why, mused Armitage, did the woman seem to have this strange compulsion to pay over the odds for everything? Force of habit, presumably. Or more money than sense, as Beynon had once put it. He prepared to leave: 'Yes, well, thanks for the brandy and the use of your tanker –'

'The strange thing is,' she went on remorselessly: 'Even though I'm sure you're a complete charlatan – the only reason why I've agreed to your ridiculous request for the use of my tanker – I do find you rather interesting. And I can't say that about many men of my acquaintance.'

'You must have led a very sheltered life.'

She looked at him in surprise: 'Of course I've led a very sheltered life. My father had me watched morning, noon and night. And any man who even looked at me more than once was quietly warned off. He was convinced that the men I met were not really interested in me as a person, as a woman, but as a meal ticket – and a *cordon bleu* meal ticket at that.'

'I can see his point.'

Athena Papadopoulos swung her shapely legs off the couch, sat angrily upright and said:

'What d'you mean, you can see his point? How dare you say I'm not attractive! I've had men grovelling at my feet, telling me how much they loved me, how much they wanted me, pleading with me to have their babies! I am a very elegant, very desirable, very cultured woman!'

And modest to a fault, thought Armitage, wearily.

He rose to his feet: 'Look. As it happens, I do find you extremely attractive. But the fact is – '

But Athena Papadopoulos now had the bit firmly between her gleaming, perfectly matched teeth. She rose unsteadily to her feet and demanded:

'Am I not beautiful?' She raised the hem of her dress above her knees: 'Are my legs not beautiful, too?' She cupped her breasts to emphasise her impressive cleavage: 'And what about my bosoms? Pretty hot stuff, no?'

Armitage sighed: 'I do believe you're pissed, Miss Papadopoulos.'

'I am not pissed! And what an ugly word. I thought you English were supposed to be a nation of poets. No, I am just bloody angry with you!'

'And I'm just bloody tired. Now if you'll excuse me, I have a long way to go.'

'We can soon fix that.'

She moved over to the fireplace and pressed a bell push on the wall. It was all of three minutes before a somewhat rumpled and out of breath Jefferson, his hair all awry and struggling to pull his butler's jacket over his pyjama top, entered the library in some haste and wheezed, somewhat predictably:

'You rang, madame?'

'Mr Armitage will be staying the night.'

Thought Armitage: so much for the poor bastard's early night. But it did make sense. As some one who'd spent his life in the transport business, he'd always made it a rule never to drink and drive. And with the last train long gone and the cost of a mini cab into deepest Kent quite prohibitive, the thought of having to spend yet another night in the Centrepoint office was of little appeal.

'Thank you,' he said: 'That would be most acceptable.'

The *en suite* guest bedroom was as gratuitously ostentatious as the rest of the mansion, with a bed the size of his Kent cottage living room. Armitage slipped out of his clothes and climbed gratefully between the silken sheets. He was sliding effortlessly into the arms of Morpheus when the bedroom door slowly opened to reveal Athena Papadopoulos standing in the open doorway, framed in the light from the hall. Armitage blinked at the light and sat up in bed.

'What is it?'

As he reached for the bedside lamp, she closed the door quietly behind her and moved to the side of his bed. Barefoot and draped in a sheer, diaphanous nightdress that left little to the imagination, as she had obviously intended, she just stood there, looking at him, with the nervous demeanour of an anxious, vulnerable little girl desperately in need of reassurance. Then, in a very small voice, she said:

'Tell me, John J. Armitage, do you really find me attractive? It's very important to me. I must know.'

'For God's sake,' said Armitage: 'What d'you want from me – a signed affidavit? Yes. I really, truly, find you extremely attractive. Now please. Let me get some sleep.'

'Prove it.'

'Prove what?'

'That you think I'm attractive. Make love to me.'

He sighed: 'Are you sure you know what you're saying? While I have to admit that's the best offer I've had all week, the way I'm feeling at the moment –'

She placed a gentle finger on his lips and said: 'I need you, John Armitage. I don't care what you really are and what you're really up to. All I do know is, I find you very…attractive, too. More so than any man I've ever met. I don't know why. In some ways you are also a – how d'you say it? – a pain in the bottoms?'

Armitage chuckled, despite himself: 'That's near enough.'

'And no, I am not pissed, as you so elegantly put it. The thing is, when you have been as alone and as lonely for as long as I have…'

Said Armitage: 'Spare me the poor little rich girl crap. You're here because you're a normal, healthy young woman who, to put it equally inelegantly, thinks it about time some one gave her a good seeing to.'

Athena Papadopoulos shook her head in wonder: 'You really know how to make a woman feel wanted, don't you?'

Armitage gave a gesture of resignation. Since his divorce, his carnal relationships with women had been few and far between. Particularly relationships with women as desirable as Athena Papadopoulos and, he reasoned, if only for the sake of good company-client relations, perhaps it would be advisable for him to simply lie back and think of England – and the Elgin marbles in particular. He pulled aside the bedcovers and said abruptly:

'Why don't you shut up and get into bed?'

First a glare, then a long, throaty chuckle: 'You smooth-talking, English bastard. Move over.'

She shrugged off her nightdress and slipped into bed. As she wound her arms around his neck and pressed her body against his, Armitage could not help but wryly reflect that even if the whole marbles operation ended in disaster, he at least would have come out of it with *something* to show for his trouble.

᙮

'Where the hell have you been?' demanded Beynon: 'I've been trying to get you all morning.'

'Sorry,' said Armitage, as he climbed out of his car: 'I had the mobile switched off.'

He had arrived back at the village to find a grim-faced Beynon sitting on his front wall of his cottage, obviously waiting for him.

'Not that you could have done anything,' said Beynon, as Armitage fumbled with his front door keys.

'About what?'

'About Gavin. Massive heart attack. He's been whipped into hospital.'

Armitage paused in the doorway: 'Oh God. How serious?'

'Serious enough. They're going to have to operate. Multiple by-pass.'

Armitage felt a sudden pang of guilt. From the moment he'd discovered that Messiter had a cardiac problem, he should have tried harder to convince him not to continue to be involved in such a stressful and physically demanding operation. Beynon obviously felt the same way:

'Should we have called the whole thing off, John? Would it have made any difference?'

Armitage shrugged, helplessly: 'I don't know. Possibly. I did try. Not all that hard, I admit – and you know how pig-stubborn the man can be. What are his chances of pulling through?'

'That's what I asked the surgeon and all he'd say was – how long is a piece of string? Now I ask you, what sort of prognosis is that, for Christ's sake?'

'But he's still in with a chance.'

'Seems so. Yes.'

Armitage came to a decision: 'Then I think we should try and finish the job. On Gavin's behalf. Otherwise, all he's gone through, everything he's done – will all be for nothing. Agreed?'

Beynon thought for a moment, then nodded: 'Agreed.'

Armitage went into the kitchen and switched on the coffee percolator.

From the living room, Beynon called: 'How did you get on with little Miss Moneybags? Get what you wanted?'

'Oh yes,' said Armitage: 'She was most co-operative.' And half to himself: 'Generous to a fault, in fact.' He returned to the living room, pulled a sheaf of papers from a side cupboard and said: 'The first thing we have to do is map out, step by step, exactly what, with a bit of luck, should happen on Saturday, the twenty-third.'

'We hope.'

'We hope. Yes.'

4

THE MORNING OF SATURDAY, the Twenty-Third dawned bright, warm and sunny, with little cotton-candy clouds drifting lazily across the azure blue skies, high above the British Museum and presumably, most of London. Inside the building, Barry Lucas was feeling a little less than sunny as he faced a tight-lipped Julie Baker across the counter of the souvenir shop.

'But you promised, Barry. And my mum's expecting you. She's even made a fruit trifle.'

To his – and certainly to her own surprise, Julie Baker had suddenly asked her mother if she could bring a young man to tea, perhaps hoping that both her mother and her down-to-earth, builder and decorator father would take one look at him and tell her, in no uncertain terms, that their worlds were so far apart, there was no future, no point, in continuing their relationship. If relationship was the word. While she had undoubtedly developed a strange soft spot for Barry Lucas – God only knew why – she did need a second opinion. And tonight was the night.

'I didn't ask to supervise the loading,' protested Lucas: 'That was Anderson's idea. Today was supposed to be my day off, but you know what he's like. You'd think he did it on purpose.'

'Probably did,' admitted the girl: 'On account of him finding out that I'd agreed to go out with you tonight.'

'How did he do that?'

'I told him. Yesterday. When he started coming on strong again.'

Lucas sighed: 'That explains everything. Anyway, I should only be a little late and as soon as the marbles are on their way, I'll drive straight over.'

Julie Baker pouted and grumbled: 'I don't know why I bother with you? Why do I bother with you? I don't know why *I* bother with you.'

'Neither do I,' said Lucas truthfully. Then with a wistful little smile: 'Unless you're beginning to fall for my boyish charms.'

'Oh, knock it off, will you? It's just that I had nothing else on tonight. Now go and load your rotten marbles. Go on. Hop it.'

Lucas hopped it. She looked after him and again shook her head in total perplexity. How on earth had she allowed herself to become even mildly involved with such a daft, pathetic – if quite sweet – little pratt like him?

༄

Exactly on time, the massive pantechnicon, once part of *Armitage International's* haulage fleet, but now emblazoned with a large *Avery Transport* logo, reversed carefully through the side entrance of the British Museum. As he had anticipated, Armitage's bank had yet to complete the lengthy legal procedures required to force his company into bankruptcy and send in the official receivers which, over the previous couple of days, had enabled him and Beynon to transform the truck into an Avery Transport facsimile, in the privacy of *Armitage International's* huge, hangar-like depot on a quiet Essex Industrial Estate. They were even more resolute in their task, encouraged by the fact that Gavin Messiter had successfully survived the four-hour emergency operation and, although still in intensive care, his condition was said to be relatively stable.

With a uniformed Beynon at the wheel and a similarly dressed Armitage in the co-driver's seat, the vehicle backed inch by inch towards the loading bay. Squinting through the rear mirror, Beynon suddenly reacted, then muttered:

'Oh Christ. Look who's guiding us in.'

The temporary acting Head of Security had evidently decided to act as parking supremo as he strutted, clipboard under arm, along the elevated loading bay, his free hand signalling like a demented windmill:

'Steady as you go. Left hand down a bit…I said *left* hand down… that's it. Careful. Easy now. Easy! I said EASY for God's sake!'

The truck's rear doors finally came to rest at the edge of the bay, which was already piled high with hermetically-sealed wooden crates of varying sizes.

Muttered Armitage: 'You stay in the cab, Ken – and keep your head down.'

As Beynon nodded and switched off the engine, Armitage clambered out of the truck, climbed up on to the ramp, nodded politely towards the temporary acting Head of Security and began to open the pantechnicon's rear doors. At the same time, Barry Lucas appeared from within the interior of the Museum and approached his superior:

'Right, Chief. What d'you want me to do?'

Anderson handed him the clipboard:

'Check the crate numbers against the manifest as they're being loaded. And make sure the numbers tally. I'll inform the Director of Operations that the marbles are safely on their way. And remember –'

'Constant vigilance. Yes. Right. Rely on me, Chief.'

Believing that he had taken his young rival out of the equation, Anderson moved swiftly back into the Museum, probably, thought Lucas bitterly, to make yet another bid for the delectable Julie Baker's after-hours affections. Armitage nodded towards the open pantechnicon:

'Ready to start loading?'

'Sure,' said Lucas. He waved an arm towards the two Museum personnel waiting patiently by their forklift trucks. Armitage pulled out the bunch of papers from his uniform pocket and held them out.

'The paperwork. In triplicate, of course. Mind if my co-driver and me grab a cup of tea while you're loading?'

Lucas glanced at his watch: 'You're in luck. The staff canteen's still open.'

'Ah,' said Armitage: 'Nice thought. But when we have to come into town on a job, we usually go to that little caff round the corner.' He winked and nodded towards the cab: 'Young Nigel fancies one of the waitresses.'

Lucas smiled: 'Gotcha. See you later, then.'

Armitage went around to the blind side of the truck and called up towards the cab:

'Nigel? Tea-time.'

Beynon clambered swiftly to the ground and they both moved towards the side exit. As they went, an aggrieved Beynon muttered:

'Nigel? Why Nigel, for Chrissake? Do I look like a Nigel?'

☞

When Beynon and Armitage made their way back to the Museum, the pantechnicon had been fully loaded. Two security men stood guard on each side of the open doors and the twin fork-lift trucks were already disappearing back into the Museum's storage section, the large metal roller-shutter doors descending noisily behind them. As Beynon slipped unobserved into the driving seat, Armitage climbed on to the loading bay and as he went to close and lock the double doors, he looked questioningly towards Lucas.

'All done?'

'All done.' Lucas handed him a copy of the manifest: 'Your copy. Which route will you take?'

'Route?'

'To the *Sentinel Security* Vaults.'

'Ah.' Armitage pretended to consider: 'At this time of day, we'll probably join the M25 at Potter's Bar, then on to the A12.'

Lucas nodded: 'Good thinking. Have a good trip.'

'Thanks. Cheers.'

He jumped down from the loading bay, went along the side of the truck and climbed into the cab. The engine burst into life and, followed by the two security men, the pantechnicon moved slowly forward and out through the side gates, which were immediately locked behind them. Lucas looked at his watch and smiled. The whole operation had taken far less time than he'd anticipated. He was going to make his date on time, after all. So up yours, temporary acting Arsehole of the Yard. There was a spring in his step as he went back into the Museum.

Armitage and Beynon said little to each other as the truck proceeded at a steady, legal pace along the busy Motorway. It was when they were approaching the turn-off to the A12 that Beynon finally expelled the air from his lungs and said:

'I can't believe we've done this. It was so easy.'

'Yes, well,' said Armitage: 'I happen to be a great believer in Sod's Law – that if anything *can* go wrong, it will. And we've got a long way to go yet.'

'Oh come on, John,' said Beynon: 'Lighten up. It'll be another couple of days before the real Avery Transport truck turns up to collect them – and by tonight, they'll be safely on board the tanker. So what can go wrong now?'

☞

Barry Lucas was escorting a smiling Julie Baker towards the Museum staff car park when he tapped the clipboard under his arm and said:

'I've just got to drop these papers off into security. Won't be a minute.'

As he slid them from the clipboard, he glanced at the top copy and blenched. A quick look at the duplicates was followed by a:

'Oh my God! You idiot, Lucas! You absolute twat! Anderson's going to go right through the roof!'

'What is it?' asked the girl in alarm: 'What have you done?'

'It's what I haven't done. Sorry, but I've got to go. I'll explain later. Sorry. I really am.'

With the clipboard under his arm, he raced towards the car park, leaving an angry and confused Julie Baker wondering, once again, just what she had let herself in for.

As he crouched over the wheel of his battered Ford Fiesta and roared out of the car park, an agitated Lucas was beginning to wonder what on earth he was doing in the security business in the first place.

He already knew the answer. Although a university graduate, he had failed a series of interviews for the position of management trainee with a wide variety of well-established companies, including *Marks and Spencer, Sainsbury's Supermarkets, F.W. Woolworth, The Cooperative Wholesale Society* and, the most humiliating rejection of all, The *Happy Haddock* fish bar chain.

In desperation, his father, who had understandably come to the reluctant conclusion that his son was probably not destined to be a Captain of Industry, had called in a favour from a fellow member of his golf club who knew a man who ran an agency for security personnel and his son had finally secured the position of trainee assistant to the British Museum's temporary acting Head of Security, another of the agency's clients. The agency's client list included many ex-policemen and Anderson had been very grateful for the opportunity to work for the British Museum, even in a temporary acting capacity. Who knew where such a prestigious appointment might lead?

In truth, since his retirement from the Metropolitan Police, the ex-Chief Inspector, late of New Scotland Yard (traffic division), had not exactly been inundated with offers of gainful employment, which was why, on being prevailed upon by the agency to employ Lucas as his assistant, he had been more than happy to do so. Or so he'd said. Lucas, however, suspected that he'd been chosen only because Anderson had probably considered him to be none-too-bright, eager to please and someone who wouldn't answer back, no matter how much he was imposed upon. Even so, Lucas had been determined to make a go of it.

But now, after having been given the chance to prove himself, he'd blown it. He obviously wasn't up to the job, he told himself. Or any other job, come to that. And the question was – where would he go from here? For a start, his second class, Mickey Mouse degree in Media Studies and Street Theatre, which included such commercially viable subjects as the art of chainsaw juggling, had turned out to be about as useful a qualification for obtaining regular employment as would a Certificate in Undertaking in *Shangri La*. And not for the first time in his somewhat less than scintillating professional career, the depressing image of his local Jobs Centre loomed large.

As soon as he hit the M25, he gunned the engine to its maximum. The car had been passed to him by his mother who, after failing her driving test for the umpteenth time, had decided, much to the relief of his father, who'd developed a nervous tic while trying to teach her the rudimentary rules of the road, that perhaps she wasn't cut out to join the ranks of the horizontally mobile.

'Come on!' he shouted aloud at the wheezing little car: 'We've got to catch up with them! If we don't I'm fucked! Fucked, fucked, fucked!'

As if in sympathy – or perhaps because they were now driving downhill – the Fiesta's speedometer edged slowly upwards.

☞

It was already dusk when Lucas caught sight of the pantechnicon, with its distinctive Avery Transport logo, half a mile or so ahead of him. As the truck roared steadily onwards, Beynon glanced at his companion and said:

'We're just about to join the A12. How far before our turn-off?'

Said Armitage: 'A good few miles yet.' A strong light flickered in his side mirror: 'Who the hell's that?'

Beynon looked into his mirror, worriedly: 'God knows.' He took a second look: 'At least it's not a police car.'

Lucas's car, its headlights flashing on and off, finally managed to overhaul the truck and as he drove alongside it, he gestured frantically for Beynon to pull over.

'Oh shit,' said Beynon: 'It's the lad from the Museum. What the hell can he want?'

Said Armitage, tersely: 'We'll soon find out. Stop at the next lay-by.'

As the truck came to a halt, the Fiesta close behind it, said Beynon: 'You go, John. He's had one good look at me already.'

Armitage nodded, clambered quickly down from the cab and approached the advancing Lucas, who was waving a bunch of papers.

'What's the problem?'

'Thank God I managed to catch up with you. You forgot to sign for the shipment. And I forgot to ask you to do it. Sorry.'

'No problem.' Armitage tapped his uniform pockets: 'Got a pen?'

'I think so. Ah, yes. Here.'

Through the rear mirror, Beynon watched Armitage signing the papers against the side of the truck, before he and Lucas briefly shook hands and they both returned to their respective vehicles.

'What the hell was all that about?' demanded Beynon, as Armitage climbed back into the cab. Armitage told him.

Said Beynon: 'Is that all? God. For a moment, I thought I'd need a change of underwear. Dozy little sod.' He turned on the engine: 'Come on, let's get out of here.'

Armitage glance in the mirror: 'Hold on. He's coming back.'

Lucas appeared below Beynon's side window and gestured to him to open it.

Muttered Beynon: 'Jesus, what now?' Resignedly, he wound down the window, doing his best to mask his face with his peaked hat.

'Sorry to bother you again,' said Lucas apologetically: 'But your friend's got my pen.'

Beynon turned to his co-driver: 'For Christ's sake! Have you got his pen, John?'

'Sorry,' said Armitage, passing over the pen, which Beynon then passed down to Lucas.

'He's always doing that,' said Beynon. But before he could wind up the window, Lucas gave him a sudden, puzzled look and said:

'Don't I know you? I'm sure we've met somewhere before.'

Said Beynon quickly: 'How about this afternoon? The British Museum? When you were loading the truck?

'Ah. Yes. Of course. That's it. Must be.' He gave a friendly wave of his hand: 'Cheerio, then.'

Beynon nodded briefly and sent the truck moving forward.

'Well saved,' said Armitage dryly.

'I'm not so sure. Not once he's had time to think about it.'

Lucas watched the rear lights of the truck until they disappeared into the darkness. Then with a puzzled shake of his head, he climbed back into his Fiesta.

☞

The pantechnicon moved slowly through the open door of the *Armitage Transport International* depot, with its *For Sale or Rent* sign hanging forlornly above the entrance. From within the massive garage, which still housed the remnants of the company's once extensive fleet of trucks, vans and lorries, Armitage operated the switch that sent the heavy steel door sliding back into place. Beynon turned off the engine, climbed quickly out of the cab and grabbed a mobile ladder, which he then wheeled to the side of the truck. As Armitage dialled a number on his mobile telephone, Beynon climbed the ladder and started to peel away the large, adhesive plastic sheets, which bore the Avery Transport logos, to reveal the original *Armitage Transport International* lettering beneath.

Said Armitage into the telephone: 'Miss Papadopoulos? Athena? John Armitage. Just checking to make sure your captain's been properly briefed.'

'You're telling me you've got them?'

'Oh yes. We've got them. Each and every one of them.' He smiled: 'Oh ye of little faith.'

The voice on the phone grew loud and shrill: 'You've got them? You're actually saying you've got them?!'

'We've got them,' repeated Armitage patiently: 'And all I need to know is –'

'You wouldn't lie to me, would you, John J. Armitage? Not after what's happened between us? Please say you're not lying to me.'

'I'm not lying to you. I've never lied to you.'

There was a long silence. Then with what sounded suspiciously like a sniff, she said: 'I believe you, John Armitage. I really believe you. I can't imagine how you've managed to do it and I apologise for ever having doubted you, but the fact is –'

'The fact is,' interrupted Armitage: 'That we're running a bit late and I have to know the situation with the tanker.'

'My latest information is that it's on schedule and should be docking at pier seven at approximately eleven p.m. this evening. The captain's been told to pick up a large consignment of tanker spares – engines, piping, pumping equipment – exactly as you requested on the manifest.'

'Thanks. That's all I need to know. See you in Athens.'

He switched off the telephone and joined Beynon at the top of the mobile ladder. In the bedroom of her Belgravia mansion, unaware that the two-way conversation had suddenly become rather one-sided, Athena Papadopoulos spoke softly into her beside phone:

'And I really thought that once you'd had your way with me, you would cast me aside like an old shoe and I'd never see you again. You make me feel ashamed of myself. But I'll make it up to you, darling John Armitage. I promise you…John? Are you there?' The drachma – or rather, the euro – finally dropped: 'John! Talk to me, you bastard! Talk to me!'

She slammed down the phone in a fury and flung herself back against the pillows. Damn the man. How *dare* he treat her like that? How *dare* he seduce her, ravish her, then act as if it was just another one-night-stand? Even if, she had to concede, what a remarkable one-night-stand it had turned out to be. She had never thought that an Englishman – albeit a tall, handsome and intelligent Englishman – could prove to be such a strong, yet gentle lover. She gave a little smile as she re-lived the uninhibited enjoyment of their night together. She'd never met a man quite like John J. Armitage and though he was still, in some ways, an undoubted pain in the bottoms, she had already decided that this was only the beginning of their relationship – whether or not he *did* succeed in delivering the Parthenon marbles back to where they belonged.

☜

The *Armitage Transport International* pantechnicon reached the South Essex Oil Terminal at exactly five minutes to eleven. Armitage leaned out of the cab and handed the gateman a fist-full of papers:

'Has the Papadopoulos tanker docked yet?'

'The one due in at pier number seven?' The gateman shook his head: 'No sign of him yet, mate. Could be on account of the fog. Everything slows down a bit, then.'

'What fog?'

'In the channel.' He nodded towards his gatehouse, which was warm and inviting in the cold night air: 'Heard it on my radio. Seems it came down all of a sudden. A good, old-fashioned pea-souper.'

Damn, thought Armitage. That was all they needed. The gatekeeper first checked, then handed back the documents.

Said Armitage: 'Ah well, in that case, all we can do is go to pier seven, have a fag and wait for it to turn up.'

'Suit yourself. It's first right then second left.'

The gateman raised the steel entrance barrier and Beynon sent the truck surging forward. Armitage decided to look upon the bright side. Apart from the small hiccup involving the Museum's pleasant, if somewhat feckless assistant Head of Security, the entire operation had, up until then, been working entirely to plan. So what did it matter if the tanker arrived even a couple of hours late?

☜

The captain of the Papadopoulos Line oil tanker was not a happy man. He had always disliked, even feared, navigating the narrow English Channel, one of the busiest shipping lanes in the Northern Hemisphere. And in bad weather, with poor visibility, it was also one of the most dangerous, even with the best navigational aids. His fears were well-founded.

It was almost midnight when, without warning, through the swirling mist, came the towering bows of a Panamanian-registered container ship, its radar navigation system disabled because of a flagrant disregard for the need to regularly service its on-board electronics. Seconds later, with a grinding screech of metal on metal, the container ship ploughed straight into the side of the Papadopoulos tanker. The Panamanian vessel had been sailing three miles off course and had been travelling in the wrong lane.

Armitage waited until four a.m. the following morning before coming to the reluctant conclusion that something had gone seriously wrong. He dialled a number on his mobile phone and, much to his surprise, it was answered immediately by an agitated Athena Papadopoulos, who had seemingly been sitting by her telephone most of the night, waiting for him to call.

'Why haven't you rung me before?' she demanded: 'I had a call from my captain just after midnight to tell me that he's in big trouble.'

'What sort of trouble?'

She told him. Beynon woke up from his doze: 'What is it? What's happening?'

Into the phone, Armitage said: 'Hold on a minute, Athena.' And to Beynon: 'Sod's law rides again. The tanker won't be coming in tonight. It's been in collision with another ship and is having to make for Cherbourg for repairs.'

'Oh shit,' said Beynon: 'And it was all going so well. Now what do we do?'

'There's only one thing we can do. Get the marbles back under cover and try to arrange alternative transport.'

'Before Monday? When the balloon goes up? How the hell are we going to do that?'

'I know it's a tall order, but – '

A loud squawk from his mobile reminded him that he was still in communication with his client: 'Sorry. My partner and I are trying to work out what we do next.'

'I'll tell you what you do next,' said Athena Papadopoulos crisply: 'You take the marbles to Cowes in the Isle of Wight and meet me there.'

'Why Cowes?'

'Because that's where my boat will be coming in. On Monday morning.'

'*Your* boat? Oh yes.'

Through the television newsreels, Armitage had been made well aware of what Athena Papadopoulos casually referred to as her 'boat,' the obligatory toy of every wealthy Greek shipping heiress, though he would have hardly called the *MV Athena* a boat. It was, at the very least, a well-appointed ocean-going yacht, complete with a ten-man crew and every conceivable luxury. He was also well aware that his patron was known to regularly attend the annual Cowes sailing regatta, if only for the social activities, when the distaff side of international society, in designer summer dresses and pretty hats, met to exchange the latest gossip and imbibe countless litres of *Pimm's Number 1,* while their partners vainly attempted to recapture their lost youth, by what was generally known as 'messing about in boats.' Even so, reflected Armitage, both Athena Papadopoulos and her floating gin palace would undoubtedly serve their purpose.

🙢

'It's still going to be very tight,' muttered Beynon, as Armitage took his turn at the wheel. As the pantechnicon thundered towards the South Coast and the Isle of Wight Ferry terminal, the first rays of the rising sun were turning night into day. Beynon checked his watch, anxiously: 'If the Avery Transport truck's on time, all hell will break loose at around ten o'clock tomorrow morning.'

'It's going to be even tighter than you think,' said Armitage: 'We've got another job to do first.'

'Another job? What are talking about?'

Armitage told him. In great detail.

Beynon shook his head bemusedly: 'You're crazy. We'll never do it. There's not enough time.'

'We'll just have to find the time – even if the Museum does blow the whistle before we've finished. Trust me Ken. I know what I'm doing. That's why I've been on the phone for the last hour and a half and got at least half a dozen people out of bed.'

Armitage had been in the transportation business for a long time and his professional contacts embraced half the globe. The time had come to call in a few favours – with no questions asked. And as someone who had been both liked and respected by his peers throughout the transport industry, the response had been immediate and positive.

Beynon sighed: 'All right. I take your point. Where do we go first?'

'The Royal Naval dockyards in Portsmouth. There's an old, disused warehouse in the East basin. Everything will be ready and waiting. And after that, it's on to the local ferry terminal for the Isle of Wight.'

Beynon thought for a moment, then gave a sudden, spontaneous grunt of amusement. Armitage looked at him questioningly. Beynon grinned:

'I was just thinking. I'd love to be a fly on the wall.'

'Where?'

'At the British Museum. At ten o'clock tomorrow morning. Just to see their faces when the genuine Avery Transport truck turns up and they finalise realise that someone's nicked their precious bits of marble.'

ᴛ s

'Forgeries,' said an agitated Hamish C. Munro. He peered at his supposed signature on the manifest: 'And damned good ones too.'

The Director of Operations, his resident architect and the temporary, acting, Head of Security each silently examined the documents in turn, then, with a sad shake of his head, Anderson turned to his hapless assistant and said:

'Dear, oh dear, oh dear. I'm afraid you've really done it this time, lad.'

Snapped the Director: 'Oh no, Anderson. It's no use trying to pass the buck. This is all down to you. You were supposed to be in charge.'

'Yes, of course I was, Director,' said Anderson hurriedly: 'All I'm saying is, anyone could have made the same mistake. You said yourself the forgeries would have fooled anyone.'

Said the architect to the forlorn Lucas: 'What did the men look like, Mr. Lucas?'

'Both white. One around forty. Quite tall. The other around thirty. Medium build.'

'Come on, lad,' said Anderson: 'You can do better than that. We want to know if there was anything special about them. Distinguishing marks. Tattoos. Colour of hair.' He automatically touched his receding hairline: 'If any.'

Said Lucas: 'Hard to tell. They were both in uniform. But I'm pretty sure I'd seen one of them before. The younger one. Here, in the Museum. You saw him too, Chief. A couple of weeks back. When he passed us in the entrance hall, remember? – and you said "what's a scruffy, unshaven sod like him doing in the British Museum?"'

Said the Director: 'You were that close to him, Anderson?'

'Seems I must have been.' The temporary acting Head of Security glared at his assistant: 'Not that I can recall the incident,' he lied.

He remembered the man right enough. As a young conscript, he had completed his National Service as a member of the British Military Police and spit and polish had become a way of life, which meant that even the sight of anyone who failed to measure up to what he considered to be an acceptable level of dress, appearance and personal hygiene resulted in a knee-jerk reaction and a gratuitous expletive. Oh yes, he remembered the bastard all right. He might have known he was up to no good. To Hamish Munro, he said:

'I'd better get on to my friends at the Yard. Right, sir?'

'Wrong. Well, not yet.'

'But a felony has been committed.'

'We must take into account the political implications. If the Greek Government discovered they've been stolen, they might claim that the marbles were not safe in our hands.'

'And they'd have a point,' said J.C. Caldwell, looking straight at the uncomfortable temporary acting Head of Security, who'd obviously had hopes of eventually ending up without either of the temporary, acting, prefixes.

'Even worse,' said the Director: 'If the police laid on a big operation for their recovery, the thieves may panic and dump them.'

Said Caldwell: 'Then you think they're still in the country.'

'They have to be. They're far too heavy to be flown out and they know that from now on, every port will be watched around the clock. No, my guess is, they've been hidden somewhere. In some remote warehouse. And all we can do is wait for the inevitable extortion demand for their return.'

'Good thinking, Director,' said his Head of Security, ingratiatingly, in a desperate attempt to repair the damage to his professional reputation: 'What would you like me to do?'

'As little as possible,' snapped the Director: 'Just get young Lucas here to have a quiet word with every harbour master from Tilbury to Tyneside.'

'Yes. Right. Will do.' He turned to his assistant: 'You heard what the Director said. So get on to it, lad, double quick.'

Lucas nodded and walked out of the office. Anderson turned to the Director and his architect and made one last attempt to repair the damage:

'Don't worry, gentlemen. I've cracked harder cases than this and you can rest assured that we'll soon have those marbles back where they belong. Yes indeed. You just leave it to me.'

He drew himself up to his full height, turned on his heel in the approved military manner and strode out of the office.

'Good God,' said the architect: 'For a moment, I thought he was going to salute. What an awful little man. Who hired him?'

'How about a cup of coffee?' said the Director quickly, moving swiftly towards his personal percolator. Caldwell smiled to himself. He might have known. To the man's back, he said:

'Oh, by the way, Director, the good news is that an inspection of the Duveen Gallery has revealed that the damp patches were not caused by the burst water main, but by leaks in the Gallery's heating system. It seems that the water pipes were very neatly sabotaged by some person or persons unknown who knew exactly what they were doing.'

The Director turned back towards the architect and looked at him in blank disbelief: 'That's the good news?'

'Well at least we won't have to pull the walls down. Once the pipes have been sealed, the gallery could be re-opened for business within just a few days.'

The Director took a deep breath: 'How the fuck,' he asked slowly, ominously, but not unreasonably: 'Can we re-open the Duveen marbles Gallery for business again, ye arty-farty, fancy-nancy, public-school idiot, when we've got nae fucking marbles to exhibit?'

The architect returned his angry gaze unperturbed. He enjoyed winding the Director up:

'I agree that could present a bit of a problem, Director.' A bland smile 'But I'm sure you'll think of something.' He nodded brightly towards the percolator: 'Oh good. I do believe the coffee's just about ready.'

☞

The *MV Athena* had dropped anchor in the early hours of Monday morning and by Monday mid-day, Athena Papadopoulos was already hosting her first on-board cocktail party. Some of guests were dressed nautically, as befitted members of the Royal Yacht Club, even though many of them had not actually taken to the water in so much as a *Mirror Class* sailing dinghy, or even in a little plastic *Pedallo*, for some considerable time. Others were dressed more formally, in the uniforms of assistant harbour master, a deputy chief commissioner of police and a senior member of Her Majesty's Customs and Excise. To add to the ambience, the hostess had employed a string quartet of pretty lady musicians to play everything from Mozart to Lennon and McCartney, for the entertainment of her guests. When her tiny mobile telephone trilled inside her *Gucci* handbag, Athena Papadopoulos moved quickly through her guests towards the bow of the ship, where she could talk without being overheard.

The voice of John Armitage came over loud and clear:

'We've just driven off the ferry and we're on the road to Cowes.'

'Everything's ready for you. The crew are standing by to unload.'

'Hold on,' said the voice: 'What's all that noise? And the music?'

'Um? Oh, I'm having a party.'

'A party? How the hell can we unload in the middle of a party?'

'Trust me, John J. Armitage. I know what I'm doing.'

'Now look. This isn't going to work. Let's call it a day, all right?'

'Having got this far? No way. See you in half an hour.'

Before he could reply, she clicked off the phone and dropped it back into her handbag. Then moving back to her guests, she deftly lifted a glass of champagne from the tray of the passing Jefferson and turned to the man on her right:

'I'm so glad you could come, Commissioner. I wanted to have a word with you about crime prevention during Cowes Week. I hear the regatta attracts many of the wrong sorts of people. Petty criminals. Pickpockets. Even international smugglers.'

Athena Papadopoulos was beginning to enjoy living dangerously.

☞

The pantechnicon approached the dock gates and came slowly to a halt. Armitage leaned out of the cab and held out the wad of papers towards the uniformed customs officer:

'Special assignment. *MV Athena.*'

The man waved the papers aside: 'You're expected. Away you go.'

Said Armitage: 'Don't you want to check the manifest?'

The customs officer shook his head: 'More than my job's worth, squire. The Papadopoulos woman's holding a party aboard and my boss is one of her guests. And if he thought I was being difficult…'

'My God,' muttered Beynon, sotto: 'The nerve of the woman.'

He sent the truck surging forward and a few minutes later, he and Armitage were sitting silently in the cab as they watched the crew of the *MV Athena* expertly transferring the heavy crates from the jetty and into the capacious storage hold, aft of the main deck. The crew had obviously had a lot of experience in loading heavy crates for their shopaholic employer and the senior customs officer watched with interest, as crate followed crate. When one of the crates, with the words *THE BRITISH MUSEUM* stencilled clearly across it, was being winched from the dock, Athena Papadopoulos noticed the customs officer's interest and stepped quickly in front of him, effectively blocking his view. With an airy wave of her hand, she said:

'Just a few little bits and pieces for my new villa on Thiros, Mr. Battersby.'

The incriminating crate was lowered out of sight. The senior customs officer gave a wry little smile: 'How ever would Harrod's survive without you, Miss Papadopoulos?'

Armitage looked up towards the deck of the ship to see Athena Papadopoulos leaning on the rail, looking down at him, with a little smile on her face. At least, thought Armitage, she'd had enough sense not to go the whole hog and blow a kiss to one of the truck's co-drivers. Even though the dedicated hedonists of Cowes' café society were renowned for their open-mindedness, it would still have raised quite a few eyebrows, followed by the inevitable slyly-whispered speculations concerning

Athena Papadopoulos possible involvement with a bit of rough trade. It was another half hour before the loading was finally completed. Armitage gave the sweating crewmembers a thumbs-up sign and Beynon sent the pantechnicon roaring into life.

It took a further five hours of non-stop driving before the truck finally arrived back at the Armitage International depot. Both men were completely exhausted, but Armitage still insisted on using one of his light vans to get them back to their little Kent village. After grabbing a few hours sleep, he dialled his employer's mobile. She answered immediately and was obviously quite euphoric with excitement:

'It was pretty damn fantastic, no? And no one suspected a thing.' Her voice softened: 'I miss you, John J. Armitage. And if you want your three million quids plus expenses, you'd better be waiting for me. In Piraeus. On my private jetty. With a big bunch of flowers.'

Armitage had little time for pleasantries: 'Look, the sooner you set sail the better. Before someone makes a connection. Have a good trip.'

He clicked off the phone and went back to bed, leaving her looking angrily at the mute handset and muttering a string of colourful Greek epithets that would have even evinced the admiration of the Gods of Mount Olympus who, according to legend, had also been inordinately fond of a well-crafted obscenity.

                               ⬧

'My mother thought you were very nice and polite,' said Julie Baker, as she began to open up the British Museum souvenir shop: 'My dad liked you too. Especially after you told him you supported Tottenham Hotspurs. How did you know that was his team, too?'

'You happened to mention it last week,' admitted Lucas: 'I've never been to a professional football match in all my life.'

She giggled: 'You cheeky little devil. It seems there is more to you, Barry Lucas, than meets the eye.'

'Go on say it. You're not as daft as you look.'

'Oh, I don't think you are daft. Not any more. And the thing is, my parents really like you. Dad even said he thought you were quite good-looking.'

'He did?' said Lucas, pleased despite himself.

'Yes. Honestly. Can't see it myself, mind,' she added gratuitously. His smile faded: 'But there's no accounting for tastes, is there?'

A sigh: 'I suppose not.'

'But what really matters is that you made quite an impression on them.'

'It won't last,' said Lucas morosely: 'Wait until they find out that their daughter's going out with a dead-beat. A born loser. A no-hoper, who's just about to join he ranks of the unemployed.'

'Oh come on, Barry. I'm sure it won't come to that.'

'It might, if we don't get those marbles back. What I don't understand is why some one should go to all that trouble to steal them. Why didn't they go for something smaller, just as valuable and easier to get rid of? I mean, what's so special about a pile of broken marble?'

Julie Baker considered: 'Well, some people seem to like them. That Greek woman for one.' She patted the polyester-fibre replica of the *Selene* horse's head: 'Her butler must have bought a couple of dozen of these things over the last twelve months.'

'Greek woman? What Greek woman?'

'You know. That Athena Papa-whatsit. The shipping heiress. Her who's always in the newspapers and on television. God knows what she does with them.'

While, over the past few weeks, due to the unremitting demands on his time by his superior, Lucas had had few opportunities to either peruse a newspaper or watch television, he did recall the name. He thought long and hard: 'Jesus,' he said softly: 'I wonder.' And on an impulse, he grabbed Julie Baker by the shoulders, planted a grateful kiss on her lips and walked quickly out of the shop. The girl looked after him blankly, touched her lips in surprise and took a deep breath:

83

'Well now,' she said softly, thoughtfully: 'There really is more to you than meets the eye, little Barry Lucas.'

[.s]

'I'm not saying there *is* a connection, Chief,' said Lucas, as he and Anderson walked across the entrance hall: 'But I've checked with the harbour master and the *MV Athena* arrived in Cowes a couple of days ago. And on Monday, in the middle of a cocktail party, she took on board a big delivery.'

'Of what?'

'She said it was furniture. For the new villa she's had built on Thiros – that's a little island in the Aegean. She owns it. But it could have been anything in those crates. And as she's always going on about the marbles being sent back to Greece…'

Anderson paused, thought for a few moments, then shook his head, dubiously: 'I don't think so, lad.'

'But it's worth checking out, surely?'

'And create a diplomatic incident? No, she's too well known, too well connected. Wouldn't be surprised if she was an intimate of the Duke of Edinburgh's. He does a bit of boating at Cowes, too. I suppose he got a taste for it when he was in the Andrew.'

'The Andrew?'

'The Royal Navy, lad, as we old sea-dogs like to call it.'

As a youth, Anderson had once been a member of the local Sea Cadet Corps, until he had discovered, during a day-trip to Calais, that the rise and fall of the Channel Ferry and his stomach were totally incompatible and the moment he was back on terra firma, he had eschewed the Sea Cadets for the rather less nautical Boys' Brigade. Even so, whenever given the opportunity to do so, he would invariably bring up his own, though less than illustrious maritime experiences, somehow managing to give the impression that compared to him, every British seafaring hero – from Sir Francis Drake to the fictional Captain Horatio Hornblower, were merely twice-around-the-lighthouse, pleasure-boat sailors – which had once prompted a police colleague to make the observation that Charles P. Anderson not only liked to build castles in the air, but that he actually moved in.

'The point I'm trying to make,' continued the self-styled old sea dog: 'Is that to accuse a woman with her connections of stealing the Elgin marbles, well, it's just not on, is it?' A patronisingly pat on the shoulder: 'It was an interesting thought, though. Keep it up, son. We'll make a security man out of you yet.'

Anderson turned and walked quickly back the way he had come, leaving a crestfallen Lucas wondering what else he had to do to convince his superior that the events of the last couple of days had to be more than just a series of coincidences. What was the matter with the man? Couldn't he see that they were really on to something?

Back in his office, Anderson made a couple of swift telephone calls, then moved a few doors along the corridor to the office of the Director of Operations.

'What is it, Anderson?' said Hamish Munro irritably. The man kept popping up like a damned jack-in-the-box.

Anderson told him. And Hamish Munro listened.

'I'd always had my suspicions about that woman, Director,' continued Anderson. And quite shamelessly: 'Oh yes. Call it a hunch – a gut instinct, if you like, born of my many years at the Yard. And when I checked with the harbour master…'

Munro nodded, thoughtfully: 'It certainly adds up. And it's the best lead we've had so far. The only lead. Well done, Anderson.'

Anderson gave a modest little smile: 'Thank you sir. Just one small snag. It appears that the *MV Athena* sailed from Cowes in the early hours of this morning and by now, she'll be well out of British territorial waters.'

The Director looked at him, aghast: 'Then we've lost them! We've lost the Elgin marbles!'

Anderson smiled, smugly. He'd been waiting for this moment: 'Not necessarily sir.' He gave a knowing tap to his nose and repeated: 'Not necessarily.'

'What d'you mean, man?'

'The boat will still have to pass through the Straits of Gibraltar – through British territorial waters – and if you had a quiet word with the Admiralty…'

†

'What a shit,' said Lucas bitterly, as he walked Julie Baker to her bus stop: 'What a bastard. Not only does he get a free trip to Gibraltar, but he gets all the kudos, too.'

The girl took his arm and squeezed it: 'Never mind. I'll make it up to you.'

'How?'

She batted her eyelashes and with the totally spurious demeanour of a *femme fatale*, she said huskily: 'Oh, I'll think of something.'

He scowled: 'Don't fart about, Julie. I'm in no mood to play your daft little games.'

She pouted: 'I was only trying to cheer you up.'

'The only thing that would cheer me up is to see our temporary acting Head of Sodding Security fall flat on his ugly face.'

But by then, Anderson's plane was already landing at Gibraltar airport and, far out to sea in the Bay of Biscay, the *MV Athena* was making its way steadily towards the Straits of Gibraltar.

†

The sea was calm, the night was warm and Athena Papadopoulos, was relaxing on the afterdeck, a glass of champagne in hand, thoughtfully contemplating the enormity of what her clever, wonderful, very own John J. Armitage and his two friends had achieved over the last few days. They had done it. They had actually done what they said they'd do and she could hardly believe that within a few days, the Parthenon marbles would be back where they rightfully belonged, in Athens, in the capital city of her beloved Greece and the Temple of Athena. Once through the Straits of Gibraltar, they'd be on the last lap and when her ship finally sailed into the

Port of Piraeus, there he'd be, waiting to welcome her, with a loving smile and a huge bunch of flowers. She paused for a moment.

All right, she conceded. So he probably wouldn't be holding a huge bunch of flowers. It just wasn't him, somehow. Come to that, she wasn't at all sure about the loving smile, either. Being English, he wasn't the demonstrative type. Not that she really minded. He had so many other lovable qualities. She mentally ran down the list. Or tried to. After five minutes of furious thought, she finally admitted defeat. Why not face up to it? The man was a bastard. A clever, handsome, charming bastard – but a bastard, never the less. And she could hardly wait to see him again. To hold him again. Just to *be* with him again.

She drained her glass and called for the ever-attentive Jefferson who, despite the glass-like surface of the sea, was currently leaning over the guardrail, staring with nauseous intent towards the waters below. She rose to her feet, announced she was going to bed and as he turned groggily towards her, she said, not unsympathetically:

'Oh dear. You never were a good sailor, were you, Jefferson?' Then in an ill-conceived, if well-meant attempt to offer a little solace: 'Still, that's nothing to be ashamed of. Your famous, one-eyed Admiral Lord Nelson was known to throw up at very regular intervals. Couldn't keep anything down, poor man. Even the sight of just one of your English pork sausages would be enough to make him reach for his bucket.' She opened the door of her stateroom.

'Good night, Jefferson.'

She closed the door behind her, leaving Jefferson with a sudden, unasked-for image of a plate of greasy pork sausages, swimming in a pool of rapidly congealing fat. He groaned, turned back to the rail and involuntarily followed in the footsteps of the famous, one-eyed Admiral Lord Nelson. And, like him, at very regular intervals.

☞

It was in the early hours of the following morning, when the ship finally entered British territorial waters, that Athena Papadopoulos was abruptly awoken by the sound of a strident voice coming through her cabin's open porthole. Said the voice, through a hand-held loud hailer:

'MV Athena? This is the British Royal Navy and we wish to board you. Heave-to.'

The steady drumming of the engines faltered and fell silent. Athena Papadopoulos leapt out of bed and reached for her *peignoir*. She ran to the porthole and looked down. Below her was a British Royal Navy pinnace containing a young, but determined-looking naval sub-lieutenant, four armed naval ratings and a somewhat queasy Anderson, who was clutching the sides of the boat, as it rose and fell with the gentle swell of the waves. Beyond them, the lights of Gibraltar twinkled invitingly in the distance.

Horrified, Athena Papadopoulos looked wildly around her. Dear God, no. It couldn't end like this. Not after getting so far. She sat down on the edge of her bed and put her head in her hands, drained of all emotion. Reality finally intruded. Of course it ended right there. She rose wearily to her feet. It was all over. And she might as well face up to it.

5

ACCOMPANIED BY THE SUB-LIEUTENANT and two of the armed naval ratings and watched by a silent Athena Papadopoulos, Anderson descended into the hold, his flashlight sweeping the stacked crates, stores and boxes. Within moments, the beam of his torch had picked out one particular crate, on which was clearly stencilled the words *THE BRITISH MUSEUM*. He gave short grunt of triumph and dramatically pointed a quivering finger towards it:

'That one. Open it up.'

One of the able seamen stepped forward, crowbar in hand and began to prise it open. It took only a few minutes. Once open, Anderson pushed aside the seaman and ripped away the packing. This time, he could scarcely control his elation at what was finally revealed. Anderson turned to the sub-lieutenant, indicated the *Selene* horse's head that was gazing stonily out of its container and said:

'I think I've found what I was looking for, lieutenant. Please instruct the captain to take his vessel into Gibraltar.'

His self-satisfaction was almost palpable. He looked up towards open hatch cover, where an expressionless Athena Papadopoulos was staring down at him. The woman was obviously close to tears. Yes, well, she shouldn't have chosen to tangle with Anders of the Yard. He'd done it. He'd actually recovered the Elgin marbles for the British nation. After a lifetime of thinly-veiled derision from his fellow police officers, whom he knew thought of him as, at best, a bit of a joke and at worst, a complete and utter prat, he'd finally, actually made it. There had to be an OBE in it. At the very least.

An excited Anderson was in a dockside telephone kiosk as the last packing case was finally unloaded from the moored MV Athena.

'Seems my hunch was right, Director. We've just unloaded them and as soon as I've checked their contents against the manifest...' He gave a modest, self-deprecatory chuckle: 'Oh, I just got lucky, that's all.' His smirk broadened: 'You're very kind, Director. Thank you.'

He hung up the telephone and walked back along the jetty towards the *MV Athena*, with a distinct spring in his step. Move over, Mr. Stanley Bracegirdle. On his return from the International Security Conference in New York, the erstwhile Head of Security might well discover that employment-wise, he was not quite as secure as he'd thought and that the British Museum now had a *new* Head of Security. Yes, life was undoubtedly sweet and once he and the marbles were safely back in the UK, life would become even sweeter.

The naval ratings began to jemmy open the rest of the crates, watched by a mute, grim-faced Athena Papadopoulos, from the deck of the *Athena*. She was well aware that her arrest was imminent, to be followed by a trial in a British Court of Law and, almost certainly, a substantial prison sentence. She shuddered at the thought. The prospect of being locked away in a prison cell, in the company of genuine female criminals and every other form of low-life, most of whom would undoubtedly have a personal hygiene problem, was quite horrifying.

Having once accidentally switched on her television and found herself watching an English television drama that had graphically portrayed life and living in a dark and depressing English women's prison, she now had little doubt as to what she might expect during her incarceration in such an establishment. Being rich and famous, she would immediately become the target of her more malevolent fellow inmates – the openly envious, the financially predatory and, worst of all, as she was still young and attractive – those of a Sapphic persuasion. And how would she be able to do her porridge, as the English called it, under those circumstances? It didn't even bear thinking about.

She looked towards the row of crates with deepening despair as Anderson stepped forward and ripped off the final packing from the second crate to be opened – to reveal the stack of rectangular paving stones within.

Paving stones? Totally bewildered and with increasingly agitation, Anderson ripped away the inner packing from crate after crate as, one by one, the contents of each crate were revealed to be nothing more than stacks of identical paving slabs, none of which bore the slightest resemblance to any of the missing Elgin marbles. Anderson looked wildly up towards the equally astonished Athena Papadopoulos. They couldn't *all* contain just fucking paving stones, surely? If they did, he was fucked too.

He paused as he suddenly remembered the crate that had been opened aboard the *MV Athena*. He ran back to the half-open crate and pulled the *Selene* horse's head from its packing. For its size, it seemed amazingly lightweight. Which is when he realised he was actually holding one of the British Museum souvenir shop's polyester-fibre replicas. Who'd ever planted it among the paving slabs had, he thought bitterly, a really shitty sense of humour. Still clutching the replica, he again looked up at the openly incredulous Athena Papadopoulos who, after shaking her head in total disbelief, gave him a slow, triumphant smile.

Dear, wonderful, clever John J. Armitage. She might have known that he would have something extra up his sleeve. Then her smile, her relief and her euphoria evaporated as quickly as they had come. Why hadn't he told her? Why had he allowed her to believe that she had been caught red-handed in possession of purloined property, with all that implied? She'd nearly had a heart attack. How could he have done that to her? Switched the cargo and used her and her ship merely as a decoy, a diversion, without even bothering to tell her? What a callous, insensitive, utterly selfish bastard he was. She grimly promised herself that when next they met, she would have great pleasure in making him undergo an equally painful experience, via a swift drop kick to his private parts, which she was well qualified to administer.

As a teenager, already blossoming into ripe young womanhood, her late father had insisted that she took a course in the art of self-defence, in order to defend her virtue (as he'd so quaintly put it) should ever the occasion arise. The lessons had turned out to be far more enjoyable than she'd anticipated as, during the course of her private, one-to-one tuition, she had developed an intense, puppy-love crush on her muscular young instructor and had actively encouraged him to instruct her in another form of unarmed combat, one that she understood would not only be equally physically demanding, but far more pleasurable.

Her instructor, not wishing to disappoint his naive, breathlessly ardent, nubile young student, had agreed to her request with some enthusiasm and by the time her father had found out about their amorous *pas-de-deux,* the instructor had wisely taken to the hills. But by then, Athena Papadopoulos was well versed in the martial and associated arts and more than capable of dealing a swift, immobilising blow to any predatory male who had less than honourable intentions – particularly to that very sensitive area between a man's lower limbs, which she understood the English euphemistically called 'the family jewels.'

She paused, struck by a sudden, second thought. But in the case of John J. Armitage, wouldn't that be tantamount to cutting off her nose to spite her own face – in a manner of speaking? Pragmatism finally ruled and her anger gradually subsided. It was a time for rationalization. Well, after all, no one was perfect, even her clever, handsome John J. Armitage. Perhaps he had a very good reason for not telling her that he had switched the cargos and surely, any reasonable woman, such as herself, would at least give the man the opportunity to *explain* his actions or, in this case, the lack of them? Her feelings of relief and euphoria at her escape from certain incarceration quickly returned and in a now pleasantly relaxed state of mind, she leaned over the rail to address the sub-lieutenant, displaying an impressive cleavage, a winning smile and a sweetly spoken:

'Lieutenant? Would you and your men be good enough to assist my crew in re-packing and loading my paving stones, so we can on our way by this evening?'

The young sub-lieutenant tore his eyes away from her generous décolleté, took a deep breath and said: 'Um? Oh. Yes. Right. Of course, Miss Papadopoulos.'

A dazed, despairing Anderson, conscious of the grins on the faces of both the sub-lieutenant and his men, threw the replica back into its crate and vented his anger and frustration on Athena Papadopoulos and her openly derisive crewmembers, now lining the rails:

'You're enjoying this, aren't you, Miss Papadopoulos? Revelling in it! Well I'll tell you this, madam. You haven't seen the last of me. Oh dear me no. I know you're up to something. I can feel it in my water. And it's only a matter of time before I nail you – *and* the bloody Elgin marbles.'

Infuriating, she just smiled at him and, with a totally bogus expression of injured innocence, said:

'Dear oh dear, Mr…whatever-your-name-is. Things in your country have come to a pretty fine pass if a foreign visitor can't even purchase a few paving slabs for the patio of her new villa, without being accused of attempting to steal the Parthenon marbles – the *Parthenon* marbles, please note – not the *Elgin* marbles.'

'All right! Have it your way. But just tell me this. If you haven't got the sodding things – then where the hell are they?'

'That,' said Athena Papadopoulos, thoughtfully: 'Is just what I'd like to know.'

ᛤ

Lloyd's Register of Shipping, now simply known as *Lloyd's Register*, the British publication that listed the names, owners and condition of almost every ship that sailed the seven seas and which were available for charter, was first printed in 1764, as an aid to the import and export merchants, the marine insurance underwriters and all others connected to the international shipping industry – both then and now. How the Lloyd's shipping surveyors had rated the *SS Rosetta*, an ancient, wheezing, tramp steamer, supposedly out of Opporto, but registered in Guatemala, Armitage shuddered to think.

The old merchantman was one of the very few ships afloat that still free-lanced around the high seas, sailing from country to country, port to port, picking up commissions to transport a wide range of cargos, from fruit to fertilizer, coal to chemicals, with no questions asked. With its patchy-red, rusting hull and superstructure, it had long been a leading candidate for the maritime knacker's yard. But it had also been the only ship available to Armitage at such short notice – the ship he had originally, if somewhat reluctantly, planned should transport himself, Beynon and the marbles back to Greece. Other options had been limited and most importantly, Armitage knew that unlike other senior mariners of his acquaintance, the captain of the *SS Rosetta* had more than a touch of larceny about him and would accept the commission without demanding to know full details of the cargo he was being paid to carry.

Armitage and Beynon stood on the bridge alongside the *Rosetta's* Portuguese-born captain, who also happened to be its sole owner, navigator and first mate, feeling the deck beneath their feet vibrating steadily in time to the throb of the vessel's ancient, clanking engines, as the aged vessel edged arthritically towards the Straits of Gibraltar, like a floating, steam-driven, Zimmer frame. It was its infuriatingly slow, snail-like progress that made Armitage wonder if it would have been wiser to have kept the marbles under wraps for a few more days, in the anonymity of the disused warehouse in Portsmouth Dockyard's East basin, where the exchange of the cargos had actually taken place. They could then have awaited the arrival of another Papadopoulos Line tanker at the South Essex Oil Terminal. But that could have taken weeks and if they were to avoid being apprehended, time was of the essence. So all in all, he felt sure that he had made the right decision. Even so…

Armitage turned towards the man at the wheel.

'Can't you make this old rust-bucket go a little faster, Jaime?'

Captain Jaime Carlos António José da Souza looked him with an expression of hurt surprise and, in tones of deep reproach, said:

'Rust bucket, Senhor Armitage? My Rosetta? She is a very fine ship. She may be a little old, but like an old servant who has done whatever you have asked her to do over many, many years, she must now be treated with a little tender loving care. Treat her gently and she will never let you down.'

'Please don't bullshit me, amigo,' said Armitage wearily: 'We've known each other far too long for that. Can you crank this bloody old thing up a few notches, or can't you?'

The Captain considered his request, thoughtfully stroking his drooping Zapata mustache while scratching the left armpit of his grubby, food-stained, off-the-peg white uniform, with its gold commodore's epaulettes, which he was patently not entitled to wear. Da Souza invariably reminded Armitage of a seedy, shifty, South American bandit in an old Hollywood movie, trying to work out just how much he could sting the Gringo for. A final scratch of the armpit, a long sigh, then a regretful:

'I can only ask, Senhor Armitage. But I know the chief engineer won't like it. He loves those engines more than his own children, of which he has many. They are his friends. His babies. And if he thought they were being pushed too hard, well…' he shrugged, helplessly: 'There's nothing I can do about it.'

'Don't give me that, Jaime. You're the Captain. You can *order* him to increase the rate of knots. Especially if there's a few more dollars in it for you.'

Da Souza's eyes narrowed: 'How many?' he asked, swiftly.

For Armitage, it was vitally important that they got through British Territorial waters in the shortest possibly time, because of the distinct possibly of the British authorities deciding to inspect the cargo of every merchant ship known to be heading for the Port of Piraeus which, in the circumstances, they would be well within their rights to do so. He wondered if the *MV Athena* had been allowed to sail though the Straits unchallenged, but he doubted it. With all the publicity surrounding Athena Papadopoulos, her on-going crusade for the return of the Elgin marbles to Greece and the fact that her ocean-going yacht just so happened to be moored at Cowes, anyone with the faintest glimmerings of intelligence would have inevitably made the connection. Which is why, at the very last moment, he had decided to switch the cargos. Right from the start and entirely for her own safety, he had never wanted her to become involved in the operation itself, in any way whatsoever. She had so very much to lose. While he, Beynon and Messiter had so very little.

The altercation between the captain and the chief engineer, via the voice pipe from engine room to bridge, was loud, angry and included a string of Portuguese obscenities from the irate engineer that appeared to impress even Captain Jaime Carlos António José da Souza. A final obscenity was followed by a weary admission of defeat from the beleaguered maestro of the oil-can and, despite the vehement protests from his throbbing engines, by the time the *SS Rosetta* entered the Straits of Gibraltar, the ship was travelling at almost twice the speed of its more leisurely progress through the Bay of Biscay.

Armitage and Beynon were more than satisfied. They were a little less so when, as they were passing the Rock itself, the leaking, hissing, geriatric boiler finally called it a day and blew a series of main gaskets, in an explosion of scalding steam. The engines gratefully subsided; the vessel slowly came to a halt and without any means of propulsion, began to drift, quite helplessly, in the very middle of the Straits of Gibraltar, between the coasts of Spain and North Africa.

Halfway through his long convalescence at a luxurious private nursing home in the heart of rural Kent, Gavin Messiter eagerly checked the E-mail on his laptop computer. His late employer's private health insurance scheme was one of the few retirement perks to survive the hasty departure of the company's sticky-fingered Chairman, along with most of the staff pension fund and Messiter was intent on making the most of it. The screen disappointedly informed him that he had no unread E-mail and he switched to his mobile telephone, in the hope of finding a coded text-message from either Armitage or Beynon. The tiny screen was blank. With rising frustration, he leafed quickly though the morning's mail, which he'd arranged to be re-directed from his home address. But now having apparently been identified by numerous mail order companies as having joined the massed ranks of the old age pensioners, most of the envelopes contained nothing but junk mail, seemingly specifically targeted at the old, the naïve, the confused and the bewildered.

The unrepeatable bargains ranged from geriatric miracle pills that would cure his inevitable impotence, to leaflets promoting a whole range of stair-lifts, invalid carriages and genuine, handcrafted commodes. The personalised mail included a wide variety of congratulatory letters from various Amsterdam-based awards committees, informing him that he had definitely won a six-figure sum in their lottery draw, the cheque for which would be sent by return of post once he had signed and returned the claims form, accompanied by a standard fee to cover the cost of what was vaguely described as 'processing his award.'

Most irritating of all was a missive from a self-proclaimed psychic and cosmic astrologer from an address in Milton Keynes, inviting him to send her his date of birth, plus a small donation, presumably to cover the cost-per-minute rental when she went on-line with her crystal ball. Upon the receipt of his donation, she would have something really exciting to tell him – like, he supposed morosely, the news that both Beynon and Armitage had been arrested and that it was only a matter of time before they came to arrest him, too.

What, he wondered, for the umpteenth time, could have happened to his partners in crime? He had already scanned the day's morning newspapers for any reference to the Elgin marbles and again, he had drawn a complete blank. While he had ascertained that a certain Mr. Beynon and a certain Mr. Armitage had made several telephone calls to the hospital to check upon his condition during and immediately after his operation, why hadn't they contacted him – or even visited him – during the last couple of weeks? If they were now out of the country, where were they? In short, what in the name of heaven had happened since he'd last seen either of them? Surely, if they had been successful in removing the marbles from the British Museum as planned, by now, the event would have made the front pages of every national and provincial newspaper – and in a typeface of a size traditionally reserved for the possible outbreak of World War 3, the second coming of The Messiah – or the unlikely event of an English tennis player winning Wimbledon.

It was all very puzzling. And extremely worrying.

The Captain of the silently drifting *SS Rosetta* winced as another string of obscenities spouted from the voice pipe, in the furious tones of an obviously close-to-tears chief engineer.

'See what you've done, Senhor Armitage?' he said sadly, to the man standing silently beside him: 'By forcing me to push my vessel past its natural capabilities, you've wrecked a fine ship and broken the heart of my chief engineer. I hope you're proud of yourself,' he added, reproachfully. And as an afterthought: 'You do realise that the necessary repairs are going to cost you a great many dollars?' He reached for the ship-to-shore telephone: 'Not to mention the cost of being towed into Gibraltar by a salvage vessel.'

'Spare me the crocodile tears, Jaime,' said Armitage irritably: 'You know you can hardly believe your luck. A new set of engines for free? I won't renege on our deal, but I've got news for you, old friend. We're not going to be towed anywhere – least of all into Gibraltar. So put that phone down and just show me our exact position on the charts.'

'Why?'

'Just show me.'

Said Beynon, sotto, as the mystified da Souza disappeared into the adjoining chart room: 'What have you got in mind, John?'

'There's only one thing we can do; make our avaricious captain an offer he can't refuse, on behalf of our sponsor who, as you know, is prepared to pay anything for the return of the marbles.'

'Even though you told her it would be payment on delivery?'

'Unfortunately, it still will be, as far as *our* fee is concerned. But the situation's changed, Ken. It was hardly our fault that her tanker got clobbered in the English Channel. If it had turned up on time at the oil terminal, everything would have gone to plan and the marbles would have been safely back in Piraeus by now.'

'Even so,' said Beynon: 'How d'you know she'll agree to pay da Souza's asking price?'

'Because money means absolutely nothing to her.' And dryly: 'You can tell that by the way she spends it.'

Beynon was unconvinced: 'Let's hope you're right.'

Da Souza reappeared on the bridge from the chart room, with a dog-eared chart in his hands and the now equally mystified Beynon watched as the Captain traced a grubby forefinger across the Straits of Gibraltar, until it paused at a point just a few miles off the Rock itself:

'We're here, Senhor. More or less. We may have drifted a little, but give or take half a nautical mile, this is where we are.'

Said Armitage: 'How many metres to the sea-bed?'

Da Souza peered at the chart: 'Forty. Maybe fifty.'

Armitage was well aware that the draughts of even the biggest liners and cruise ships rarely exceeded fifteen to twenty metres and he gave a smile of satisfaction:

'Then it won't present a hazard to other shipping after we've scuttled her?'

Da Souza considered: 'I wouldn't think so, Senhor. Most of the big ships only have a draught of – scuttled her!' His mouth fell open in shock and surprise: 'You want me to scuttle my beautiful Rosetta?'

'In a word, yes. You'll be well compensated, of course.'

Da Souza shook his head in bewilderment: 'I do not understand, Senhor Armitage. Why do you wish to send my ship and your cargo to the bottom of the ocean?' He gave Armitage a thoughtful, speculative look: 'Just what is in this cargo of yours for which you are prepared to pay a great deal of money to destroy, rather than let it be open to inspection by the British authorities in Gibraltar?'

'That's our business,' said Armitage, quietly: 'Just name your price and if I believe it is not unreasonable, it's a deal.'

'And if I decide to be towed into Gibraltar?'

'As captain and sole owner of the *SS Rosetta,* you'll be held equally responsible for whatever the British authorities may or not find. The choice is yours.'

'What sort of choice is that?' demanded da Souza angrily. But cupidity ruled. He licked his lips: 'Very well, Senhor. Tell me what you think would be a reasonable price, then be prepared to double it.'

⸙

Athena Papadopoulos was dining *al fresco* on the *Athena's* upper deck, the last of the crated paving stones having been lowered into the after hold and the sub-lieutenant and his men having finally departed, each bearing a jeroboam of vintage champagne from the ship's grateful owner, by way of appreciation for their sterling efforts, over and above the call of duty. As the attentive Jefferson prepared to serve the first course, she glanced casually over the rail towards the jetty as three men, one vaguely familiar, one lithe and muscular and one short and stocky, strode purposefully along the dock towards the moored *MV Athena.*

She took a second look, then rose abruptly to her feet, causing her butler to take a sudden step backwards and drop the ladle from the soup tureen on to the deck, spattering his immaculate shoes and carefully-pressed striped trousers with *crème de champignon.*

'Oh fuck,' said the butler involuntarily.

'Language, Jefferson, language,' said his employer reprovingly, adding under her breath a string of colourful Greek expletives that would have put her butler's outburst to shame: 'It would appear we have a visitor. A Mr. John J. Armitage. In person.'

She tried to mask her surprise and delight at the sight of his sudden and quite unexpected appearance, determined that this time, she'd keep him at arm's length and would not be foolish enough to allow him to take advantage of her yet again – until, that is, he'd properly explained himself, or even better, made a grovelling apology for his total insensitivity in allowing her to believe that she had been caught red-handed, in possession of the Parthenon marbles.

☞

It had taken all of half an hour for the *SS Rosetta* to sink slowly out of sight in the middle of the Straits of Gibraltar, the air bubbling out of the opened stopcocks as if the old ship was quietly bleeding to death. Its slow decent to its final resting place was silently watched from the ship's only seaworthy lifeboat by an expressionless Armitage and Beynon, an oil-stained, openly tearful chief engineer, an inwardly smiling da Souza, who was about to become richer beyond his wildest, most fevered dreams and the other five, somewhat motley members of his crew.

Da Souza had promised each member of the crew a substantial redundancy payment on the condition that if asked, each would swear on oath that the ship had gone to the bottom of the ocean because of a massive explosion in its boiler room. He did not consider it necessary to tell then that as the sad and unfortunate demise of his magnificent vessel would then be deemed to have occurred due to natural causes – in a manner of speaking – he would then be able to claim a substantial sum from the marine insurance company with whom the ancient rust-bucket, as Senhor Armitage had so accurately described it, had been insured.

An hour or so later, the lifeboat had been beached on the shingle of a small, deserted cove, close to the Spanish town of La Linea and the crew members had gone their separate ways. Armitage, Beynon and da Souza walked the last couple of kilometres to the Spanish-Gibraltar border and made straight for the dockyard. As soon as he saw the still securely moored *MV Athena*, Armitage felt an overwhelming sense of relief at his decision to switch the cargos, albeit at the very last minute. His hunch, his instinct had been right and because of it, Athena Papadopoulos was still a free woman. But as the three erstwhile mariners made their way up the gangplank, Armitage, as he had half expected, was met by a cold stare from his unsmiling patron and an abrupt:

'Well?'

Said Armitage, pleasantly: 'Well what, Miss Papadopoulos?'

'What you doing in Gibraltar and who the hell are these two?'

'May I introduce Mr Kenneth Beynon and Captain Jaime Carlos António José da Souza?'

'No you may not.' She turned to the watching Jefferson, who appeared to find Armitage's sudden appearance both puzzling and interesting. His employer indicated Beynon and da Souza and snapped: 'Jefferson? Give these men whatever they want to drink.' To Armitage, she said: 'Mr Armitage? Please come with me.'

She rose to her feet and strode imperiously towards her stateroom. Armitage gave Beynon an enigmatic smile and followed. An apprehensive Beynon watched them go. From the grim expression on the face of their sponsor, it would seem that John J. Armitage was in deep shit. And Beynon had no wish to speculate as to what might happen when Armitage finally told her exactly where her beloved marbles had ended up, which he obviously had to do, if only because if he didn't, da Souza would never receive the promised pay-off. At a guess, the self-same deep shit would then hit the proverbial fan with the velocity of an incontinent African bull elephant.

She closed the door behind them, sat on the edge of the bed and nodded towards one of the two identical, voluminous armchairs. As he sank into the embrace of its marshmallow-like upholstery, she leaned forward towards him and demanded:

'Why didn't you tell me I was carrying nothing but paving stones?'

'Plus a full size replica of the Selene horse's head, don't forget – in the one crate with *The British Museum* stencilled all over it.' Armitage smiled: 'Rather a nice touch, we thought. We knew they'd go straight for that one.'

'But why didn't you *tell* me? When the British Navy came aboard, I nearly had to…how do you English say it? I nearly had to change my lingerie!'

'Because,' said Armitage: 'If you'd been in on it, you would have simply laughed in their faces and that would have spoiled everything. We needed you to be escorted into Gibraltar. We *needed* the extra time. And that's exactly what we got.'

'I could have *pretended* I was carrying the marbles.'

'Possibly. But that would have depended on how good an actress you were and as far as I knew, you could have been about as convincing as the back end of a pantomime horse. I just couldn't risk it.'

She bristled: 'Why the *back* end of a pantomime horse? Are you saying my bottoms are too big?'

Armitage sighed: 'Of course not.' As usual, the conversation was taking a turn for the bizarre. 'Look,' he said gently: 'We're very grateful for your help in all this. We couldn't have done it without you. But we've still got a great deal to do. That's why I'm here. In Gibraltar.'

'And the other ship? The one that's really carrying the marbles? Where is it by now? In Greek territorial waters?'

Armitage took a deep breath: 'Ah,' he said carefully: 'That's a very good question. Not in *Greek* territorial waters, no.'

'Then where is it? And where are the marbles?'

☞

Seated on the yacht's upper deck, enjoying the soft, balmy breeze wafting gently over the Straits of Gibraltar from the direction of the North African coast, Beynon took another sip of his single malt whisky and wondered if Armitage had got as far as telling their sponsor the admittedly not-so-good news. A pleasantly mellow Captain Jaime Carlos António

José da Souza, intent on making the most of their hostess's hospitality, took another gulp of his V.S.O.P. cognac and, in the absence of Jefferson's employer, generously invited the butler to join him for a drink.

Jefferson shook his head: 'Most kind sir, but I'm on duty,' he said virtuously. There was no point in incurring his employer's wrath when, the moment she had retired, he would have the run of her entire floating cellar, of which he had always made very good use. It was at that moment that a piecing shriek came through the open porthole of the Papadopoulos stateroom, followed by an equally loud:

'The marbles are *where?*'

The marbles, thought Jefferson? What on earth could she mean? He noted the sudden expression of alarm on the face of the man called Beynon and even the cheerfully befuddled Portuguese Captain seemed to prick up his ears with interest. A moment later, the open porthole was slammed shut and the voices from within the stateroom became almost completely muted.

Beynon took another, larger sip of his whisky. It would seem that his partner had finally managed to break the news.

Without realising it, Armitage was in the process of making the understatement of the millennium:

'All right,' he said, placatingly: 'I can understand you being a trifle upset about what has happened, but try to see it as merely a temporary set-back.'

Her eyes blazing and almost incoherent with rage, Athena Papadopoulos looked at him with total incredulity:

'Are you mad? Are you crazy? Are you loco? You have my marbles thrown overboard and expect me to be just a little upset? I'm not just a little upset, John J. Armitage; I'm *bloody, bloody, bloody* upset. You've destroyed my marbles, you've destroyed our relationship and you've destroyed me.'

She was obviously close to tears. Said Armitage softly:

'Listen to me, please. I didn't have the marbles thrown overboard; I had the ship scuttled with the marbles still inside it. And even though they *are* at the bottom of the Straits of Gibraltar, they won't come to any harm.'

'How can you say that? You must know what the seawater will do to them. They'll be ruined. Each and every one of them.'

Armitage shook his head: 'Not true. The containers were hermitically sealed – the British Museum always does that, to protect their exhibits against possible climatic changes in storage or during their transportation and Ken Beynon and I checked out every crate, just to make sure. So when the time comes for us to bring them up again, you'll find them completely undamaged, that I promise you.'

She was silent for a moment. It was a lot of information to digest. Her anger gradually ebbed away as she said:

'And when will that be?'

'In three or four weeks – when the British Museum finally accepts that the marbles have gone for good and calls off its hounds. That's the time to call in a team of deep-sea divers, who'll locate the ship, hitch cables to the cargo and have it winched up to the salvage vessel.'

'And where will you find such a team and such a salvage vessel?'

'In Greece, preferably. I'd rather not arouse the curiosity of the British deep-sea diving community by trying to hire a diving team and a salvage vessel to go with it.'

Another long silence, then a thoughtful: 'And in the meantime?'

'First, I'd like to accompany you to Greece and start looking for a salvage ship and the right diving team.'

'I see.'

For the first time that evening, Athena Papadopoulos almost smiled. The prospect of having John J. Armitage by her side for the next three or four weeks suddenly had a great appeal.

'And your friend?'

'Ken Beynon? He plans to take the first plane back to the U.K. to see the third member of our team, who has not been in the best of health.'

'What about the other man?'

'Ah yes,' said Armitage: 'I'm afraid I had no option but to take your name in vain.'

'In what way?'

'Well, not to put too fine a point on it – do you happen to have a cheque book handy?'

'Why?'

Armitage produced a hand-written bill of sale: 'Because you are about to become the proud new owner of the *SS Rosetta*, including its precious cargo – provided you make out a cheque in favour of a certain Captain Jaime Carlos António José da Souza.'

She looked at him searchingly. He met her gaze with his usual calm equanimity and reassured, she gave an abrupt nod and reached for her handbag.

☙

As the *MV Athena* nosed back into the Straits of Gibraltar, later that evening, Armitage watched the lights of Gibraltar receding into the distance and reflected that he had been correct in his assumption that Athena Papadopoulos would be prepared to pay anything that facilitated the eventual return of the Parthenon marbles. Immediately and without demur, she had signed a cheque in favour of Captain Jaime Carlos António José da Souza, for the sum that he and Armitage had finally agreed. Then, despite Armitage's protests and with a generosity that surprised him, she had also insisted upon signing a another cheque, this time in favour of a Mr. John J. Armitage, for his out of pocket expenses to date.

'The deal was three million quids, plus expenses, John J. Armitage,' she reminded him.

'The deal was also payment on delivery.'

'How much working capital do you still have?'

'Not a lot,' admitted Armitage: 'After your tanker had to go into Cherbourg for repairs, our running costs went through the roof.'

'There you are then,' she said triumphantly, the phrase she always used to end a discussion and to get her own way. And that had been that.

At least, thought Armitage, the cheque would be enough to stay the hands of the banks and their bailiffs for a few more weeks and enable him to complete the job. The door of the stateroom opened behind him and Athena Papadopoulos she was framed in the doorway, dressed in a long, diaphanous peignoir and looking, thought Armitage, incredibly beautiful.

'What are you doing, John J. Armitage?' she asked softly

He looked at her in appreciation, smiled and said: 'It's been a very long day. And I intend to go to bed.' He nodded towards the doorway: 'Care to join me?'

Her brow wrinkled in anger: 'You're doing it again, aren't you? Taking me for granted. Who d'you think you are? You really think you can just walk back into my life again, into my bedroom, without so much as a hallo my darling?'

Sighed Armitage wearily: 'Look, like I said, it's been a very long day, so are you coming to bed or aren't you?'

She glowered, pouted, then slipped her arm under his.

'English asshole. I think you never ask.'

The stateroom door closed behind them.

☞

It wasn't until his plane was touching down at London Heathrow that the British Museum's temporary acting Head of Security noticed the fellow passenger sitting immediately in front of him, immersed in a copy of *The Gibraltar Chronicle*. While he had yet to see little more than the back of the man's head, he did seem to be vaguely familiar. Throughout their relatively short journey, the dejected Anderson had been trying to think of a way of informing the Museum's Director of Operations that all he'd actually managed to achieve from his abortive expedition to one of the last remaining outposts of the British Empire, was total humiliation. After his confident dockside telephone call to London, the admission that he had returned home empty-handed would, he knew, not go down very well with the Museum's somewhat explosive Director and did not bode well for the future.

The aircraft came to a halt, the exit doors were opened and he rose to his feet – as did the man in front of him. Without even a glance in Anderson's direction, Ken Beynon grabbed his hand-baggage from the overhead locker and made his way down the gangway. At the first glimpse of his face, the blood drained from Anderson's cheeks. Holy shit! After the strain of the last few hours, he was obviously beginning to lose the plot. Just for one fleeting moment, he could have sworn that his fellow passenger looked just like that scruffy bastard he'd once seen in the British Museum – and how could that be? The fucking marbles had obviously scrambled his brain and he was beginning to see things that couldn't possibly be there. The next thing he knew, he'd be coming face to face with someone who resembled a *Selene* horse's head. Ashen-faced, he sank back into his seat and by the time he'd managed to calm his nerves and rise unsteadily to his feet again, the aircraft was decanting the last of its passengers and the apparition had vanished as quickly as it had appeared. There and then, a twitching Anders of the Yard decided to seek the services of an appropriate medical specialist – and at the earliest possible opportunity.

6

ASSISTED BY AN ATTRACTIVE young nurse, Gavin Messiter finally finished packing his suitcase, prior to his discharge from the convalescent home. Physically, he felt better now than he had for many months but mentally, with still no word from his absent partners, he felt a growing concern that threatened to send him into a pit of dark despair. As he closed his suitcase he asked himself, yet again, what on earth could have happened to them?

'Hallo Gavin,' said a familiar voice from behind him.

Messiter whirled around to see a contrite Ken Beynon standing in the open doorway, bearing a bunch of flowers and an apologetic smile. Messiter gave a long sigh of relief. Then angrily:

'So you're back. Better late than never, I suppose. What the hell's been happening? I've been worried sick about you. You deserve a kick up the arse, young Ken. And that goes for John Armitage, too.' And to the nurse: 'Please excuse my intemperate language, my dear, but as you will gather, I'm extremely pissed off with him.'

The nurse gave the seemingly shy, but rather nice young man a dazzling smile and said: 'I'll leave you both to it then, Mr Messiter.' She was looking directly as Beynon as she said, softly and invitingly: 'If there's anything you want, please let me know.' Another smile and she was gone.

Messiter looked after her and grunted: 'Seems you've cracked it. Must be the suntan. Where have you been – round the bloody world and back?'

Beynon grinned. It was good to find that Messiter was once again the cantankerous, short-tempered, bloody-minded old fart he knew and loved. Well, at least, the old fart he had a strong liking for.

Though relatively small, the privately owned island of Thiros was, thought Armitage, quite beautiful. Though heavily wooded, it was still ablaze with colour from the exotic wild flora found only in that part of the Aegean. From the top of the sheer cliffs on the North side of the island, the terrain gradually sloped downwards to the Southern shore, with its horseshoe-shaped bay and gleaming white sands, lapped by the crystal clear, azure-blue waters of the Aegean. To one side of the bay was a purpose-built jetty, against which the *MV Athena* would soon be moored. As the yacht nosed its way gently into the bay, Armitage stood in the prow of the vessel to get a clearer view of the equally gleaming white *Villa Athena* that was perched dramatically halfway up the upper regions of the island, commanding a view that would undoubtedly prove to be quite breath-taking.

It was apparently reached, Armitage noted with some amusement, by its very own cable car. Obviously no expense had been spared, but from where he was standing, the villa's architecture seemed a little too ostentatious for his own personal taste. As he had half expected, the villa's architectural style was in the best traditions of classical Greek, with soaring columns that bore more than a passing resemblance to the Parthenon itself. But to each his own, he conceded. Or in this case, *her* own.

'It is very beautiful, no?' asked Athena Papadopoulos softly, as she came up behind him and slipped her arm under his.

'It is very beautiful, yes,' said Armitage, diplomatically.

'My father bought Thiros for me as an eighteenth birthday present and as a way of thanking him, I had the villa designed and built in a style which I was sure would please him.' She looked up at the villa and gave a sad little smile: 'Poor papa. Unfortunately, he died before it was finished. Even so, I look upon it as not just another residence, but a shrine, a monument to his memory.' She was silent for a moment, then almost half to herself: 'I loved him very much, John J. Armitage.'

'I'm sure you did.'

'Almost as much as I love you.'

Armitage's jaw tightened, but he said nothing.

'Did you hear what I said?'

'I heard.'

'And?'

Thought Armitage wearily: And *what*, for Christ's sake? While he had thoroughly enjoyed the last few days in her company, on her yacht, in her bedroom, why did the woman have to complicate matters? Why couldn't she just enjoy their relationship for what it was – a short term affair by two utterly disparate people from two utterly different worlds who had come together, as it were, out of a mutual need, a mutual loneliness? Afterall, what had they really got in common?

While he had to concede that over the last few days, he had discovered that she was not only most attractive, but was also highly intelligent, well read and had a surprisingly comprehensive knowledge of the arts. He also couldn't deny that there was a great sexual chemistry between them and that again, on reflection, he found her mercurial temperament both stimulating and amusing. But what else had they going for them?

Admittedly, that was a great deal more than he'd ever had going for him when he'd married his now thankfully estranged wife and even though he felt drawn more towards Athena Papadopoulos than any other woman he'd ever known, that was still hardly a sensible basis for a long-term relationship, surely? Afterall, what had he got to offer a woman who already had everything? Even with a million of her quids in his bank, to a woman like her, it would mean sweet damn all.

'I haven't got *you*, John J. Armitage.'

My God, thought Armitage. She's even beginning to read my mind. It seemed that she now knew him even better than he'd realised.

'Listen to me, Athena,' he said wearily: 'The fact is –'

She laid a gentle finger across his lips:

'No. Please. Every time you say listen to me Athena, in that tone of voice, I hear something I do not like. So you listen to me. I know you English find it very difficult to talk about such things, but I want you to know that the last few days with you have been the happiest days of my life.' She took his hand and pressed it: 'It was as if we were on our honeymoon – even though we are not man and wife.' She walked away from him, back to her stateroom, to complete her packing for their sojourn on the island of Thiros, adding, under her breath: 'Not yet, anyway.'

He called after her: 'What did you say?'

A wide-eyed smile and an innocent: 'Nothing of any importance, John J. Armitage.'

She disappeared through the doorway. The *MV Athena* edged slowly towards the jetty. The engines fell silent and the crew leapt ashore. As Armitage finally escorted Athena Papadopoulos down the gangway, he little realised that the next few weeks were to prove to be the most eventful in his entire existence.

∗

As he had glumly anticipated, the meeting between temporary acting Head of Security Charles P. Anderson and the British Museum's Director of Operations had not been a happy one. The moment he had walked through the door, Hamish Munro had greeted him with a beaming smile and an outstretched hand:

'Well done, Anderson. I always knew I could rely on you. The Duveen Gallery has now been completely renovated and the entire staff is eagerly awaiting the return of the marbles to their rightful home.' He indicated resident architect J.C. Caldwell, who was leaning languidly against the wall, close to the open office window overlooking the main forecourt.

'All Mr. Caldwell and I need to know is when we might expect them.'

There was a long silence. Then Anderson had forced a smile and said the only word that had come into his head:

'Ah.'

The Director had raised a single eyebrow: 'Ah?'

'Well, the thing is, Director, after I'd telephoned you from Gibraltar, things didn't work out quite as I'd anticipated.'

The raised eyebrow turned into a puzzled frown: 'Quite as you'd anticipated?'

Jesus, thought Anderson, why does he have to repeat everything I say? He was beginning to sound like a constipated budgerigar. There was obviously only one thing to do. Take a deep breath and dive in off the deep end:

'Well, the thing is, Director…' He tried again: 'Well, let me put it this way – '

The Director's howl of anger and outrage was clearly heard through the open office window and, after bouncing around the forecourt, because of the British Museum's mausoleum-like acoustics, it then echoed around the entrance hall, the mezzanine and the Duveen Gallery itself:

'Fucking paving stones? You're telling me that all you found was a load of fucking paving stones?'

Behind her counter in the Museum's souvenir shop, Julie Baker looked in perplexity at a suddenly smiling Barry Lucas and said:

'What was that all about?'

Said Lucas, happily: 'At a guess, it means that our temporary acting Head of Security, having tried to shaft me, has simply shafted himself.' He grinned: 'A classic case of the biter bit. Seems there really is a God. I might even go and light a candle to St. Nerd.'

'St. Nerd?'

'The patron saint of people like me.'

Julie Baker frowned: 'There you go again. Running yourself down. You're not a nerd, Barry. Who said you were a nerd?'

'You did.'

'Ah. Yes, well, that was some time ago. But since I've got to know you a little better…'

'Nice try, Julie – but we both know what I am. See you.'

As he left the shop, Julie Baker looked after him thoughtfully. A little while later, when she caught sight of the resident architect walking through the foyer, she came out from behind her counter and with a ravishing smile, called towards him:

'Mr. Caldwell? D'you think I might have a word with you?'

Said Caldwell: 'So what are you going to do about him?'

'About who?' asked Hamish Munro, irritably.

'Whom,' corrected the architect smoothly: 'Our temporary acting head of monumental cock-ups. Thank God we never told the press what was going on, least of all Anderson's supposed fellow crime-busters at New Scotland Yard. The British Museum – and you in particular – would have ended up as   a laughing stock.'

It felt good to rub it in. The Director glared at him. Once again, he sensed that the arty-farty Sassenach bastard, with his superior manner, poncey purple shirts and his spotted bow ties, was actually enjoying the situation.

'Even so,' said Munro, through gritted teeth: 'I now have no option but to call in the police. If we can still keep the press out of it, so much the better – but we just can't sit back and wait for the inevitable ransom demand.'

'I quite agree, Director. But I do think that calling in New Scotland Yard's Finest may still be a little premature.'

The straw was offered. The Director of Operations snatched at it:

'What's the alternative?'

'First, I would suggest that you promote Anderson sideways, to a position where he can do the least harm. Afterall, as he has proved to be quite incapable of protecting exhibits of the size and weight of the Elgin marbles, doesn't that suggest that all our other exhibits are equally unsafe and insecure and present an open invitation for their removal by every passing rogue, rascal or miscreant?'

'You're suggesting that I close down the Museum until Stanley Bracegirdle returns from New York?'

The resident architect held up his hands in mock horror: 'Heaven forbid, Director. How could one possibly explain that away to the press, the public and above all, The Powers That Be?'

He pronounced the words as if with capital letters and in tones of deep reverence, nodding significantly towards the administrative block that housed the Museum's governing body:

'Those eminent people who hold in their hands the future of each and every one of us,' he added pointedly and was gratified to see that Munro appeared to be on the point of developing a nervous tic.

It would seem that the Director had yet to inform the Governors that the marbles were not, as they'd thought, in safe keeping while the Duveen Gallery was being repaired, but that they had somehow gone astray, in transit.

'There's no need to replace Anderson,' continued Caldwell: 'I gather Bracegirdle will be back in a couple of weeks or so. But in the meantime, we do need someone to examine all the evidence we have on the theft of the marbles and to suggest what would be the next logical step in trying to trace them. Someone rather younger than our somewhat frayed-at-the-edges ex-policeman. Someone discreet, enthusiastic and certainly brighter.'

'And who – whom would that be?' He corrected himself quickly.

'Who,' smiled Caldwell: 'You were right the first time. I suggest you should have a quiet word with Anderson's assistant, Lucas. I gather from the charming young lady in the souvenir shop that it was he who first made the connection between Athena Papadopoulos and the disappearance of the marbles. But when he pointed this out to Anderson, the man immediately dismissed it out of hand – then came straight to your office, claiming the thought as his own.'

Munro was silent for a moment as he digested the information, then he nodded, slowly: 'At the time, I did think his theory was surprisingly perceptive, coming from a man like him. But even so, it still turned out to be a dead end.'

'Not quite. From what Anderson told us, Athena Papadopoulos has to be up to her neck in it. And I believed him when he said that after the *MV Athena* was stopped and boarded in the Straits of Gibraltar, from the way she reacted, she really thought that she *was* carrying the marbles. And I suggest what is needed is someone with a clear head on his shoulders to try and discover what has really happened to them.'

The architect neglected to mention that in his considered opinion, the Elgin marbles were a lost cause and that by now, they were probably well on their way to Greece, or to someone's private collection – possibly that of the Greek shipping heiress herself – and that Barry Lucas had as much chance of tracing them as he had of finding Elvis Presley alive and well and working as a traffic warden in East Finchley. But he had promised the girl that he'd have a word with the Director to put the facts straight and that is what he had done.

Said the Director: 'I agree that Anderson has turned out to be total disaster, but what makes you believe this young man will do any better?'

'He could hardly do much worse, Director.'

Munro thought for a moment, then nodded and pressed a button on his intercom. To his secretary, he said:

'Ask Mr. Lucas of security to come to my office, will you, Mrs Henshaw?'

The architect smiled to himself. Young Lucas owed him one. Even more to the point, so did the charming and extremely attractive young lady from the souvenir shop. He had long deliberately cultivated an image of a charming, if somewhat louche, unattached male, still searching for his sexual identity. As he had hoped, this had prompted more than one earnest young woman to 'save him from himself,' as they had invariably put it. And saved he had been. Frequently. And most pleasurably.

Over the next few weeks, Armitage spent most of his mornings on the telephone, assisted by a bi-lingual, Papadopoulos Shipping Line senior executive, who had been flown in from Athens by helicopter. The often-laborious negotiations to assemble a team of Greek deep-sea divers and charter a specially equipped salvage vessel, took time and a great deal of patience. While, for obvious reasons, he would have preferred to have the use of a Papadopoulos Line vessel, none of its fleet proved to be suitable for his needs and, much to his chagrin, he was informed that in Greece, such salvage vessels were few and far between and that it would be several weeks before one would become available.

At the insistence of his hostess, his afternoons were spent in her company, mostly by the side of the large, kidney-shaped swimming pool, in the centre of a discreetly wooded copse behind the villa where, away from the prying eyes of the servants, their privacy was assured. Which was just as well as, once at the pool, Athena Papadopoulos would invariably throw modesty to the winds and take to the water *au natural.* What was more, from time to time, she would also wickedly encourage him to make love to her *al fresco.* Which is probably why, he mused, that when he informed her of the considerable delay in the salvage operations, the news seemed to please her greatly:

'So, it means we will be stuck with each other for most of the summer, yes?'

Armitage nodded: 'Seems like it, yes. Sorry about that.'

She gave him a sharp, searching look: 'You're sorry about it? Why are you sorry about it? You do not like the idea of being stuck here with me for the next few weeks?'

Armitage sighed. The negotiations that morning had been particularly frustrating, but knowing how vulnerable she was beneath her volatile exterior, he should have put it a little more tactfully. It was obviously time to poor oil on troubled waters:

'I love the idea of being stuck here with you, Athena, but I like the idea of bringing up the Parthenon marbles even more – and as quickly as possible.' And for good measure, he added a virtuous: 'We made a deal and I won't be happy until I've finished the job you hired me to do.'

Another searching look, then: 'You're full of craps, you know that, John J. Armitage? But I like it. You want to oil my back?'

She slipped out of her bathrobe to reveal that as usual, she had eschewed even the most miniscule of bikinis. She stretched herself face down on the soft, poolside towel with a sinuous grace that never failed to make a considerable impression on him, which was doubtlessly what she'd intended.

He gave an inward chuckle, well aware that the question 'you want to oil my back?' was merely her euphemism for what would then inevitably develop into an uninhibited bout of amorous gymnastics and he had to admit that it was an offer he'd always found very difficult to refuse. He grinned and reached for the bottle of suntan oil. It was a demanding job, he reflected, but someone had to do it.

ɛ⌒

'I can hardly believe it, lad,' said the temporary acting Head of Security morosely, as he took a bite out of his sticky bun, in the British Museum's staff canteen. He liked sticky buns. They were one of the few things that seemed to cheer him up:

'I make one little mistake,' he continued, bitterly: 'A mistake that anyone could have made – and I end up in charge of the night staff, with a particular responsibility for the car park, the Duveen Gallery – which has got bugger-all in it – and the public conveniences.'

And serves you bloody right, thought Barry Lucas, with grim satisfaction, as he cradled his cup of coffee. If the man sitting opposite him hadn't pinched his idea and they'd both got on to it right away, they might have been able to nail the Papadopoulos woman before she'd had a chance to switch cargos, which she – or someone else – had obviously done.

'What I'd like to know,' continued Anderson morosely: 'Is who's going to take over from me? They *need* someone like me as their security *Numero Ono.* They need my expertise. All my years at New Scotland Yard, fighting the good fight against the criminal fraternity, has honed my investigative powers into a razor-sharp intellect second to none.' He took another bite out of his sticky bun: 'Believe me, lad, I know how the criminal mind works and, given the chance, I'll find those marbles – and finger the low-life scum what nicked them.'

Good grief, thought Barry Lucas. The man lived in a world of his own. He was either into galloping self-deception, or a prospective candidate for his own, personal, padded cell. The problem was, because of Anderson's demotion – which is patently what it was – it effectively meant that he, as his assistant, had been demoted along with him. Why did life, he wondered despondently, seem to have this habit of doing it on him – and from a bloody great height?

Anderson glanced at his watch, swallowed the last of his sticky bun and rose to his feet: 'Coffee break over. We'd best get on.'

Lucas nodded, drained his cup of coffee and followed Anderson towards the exit. They were stopped in the doorway by the Director of Operation's somewhat severe-looking, middle-aged secretary:

'Ah,' said Mrs Henshaw: 'I've been looking all over for you. The Director wants you in his office right away.'

Anderson visibly brightened. Hamish Munro was obviously having second thoughts about his top security man being seconded to other, less important duties.

'I'll be there directly, madam.'

'Not you, Mr Anderson. Mr. Lucas.' She turned on her heel: 'Please come with me, Mr. Lucas.'

Thought Lucas unhappily, he might have known. It was guilt by association. Because of Anderson, he was for the chop. Anderson obviously thought so, too.

'Ah well lad, you can't win 'em all. I'll try to put a good word in for you, of course, but I doubt if it will make much difference.'

Mrs Henshaw called from across the mezzanine: 'Mr Lucas?'

'Coming.' To Anderson, he said: 'See you later.'

Anderson sighed: 'I sincerely hope so, son.'

Lucas followed Mrs Henshaw towards the administrative block. Anderson hesitated, then went back into the staff canteen for another sticky bun. Life, he acknowledged sadly, could be a bitch. And he wouldn't like to be in his erstwhile assistant's shoes.

As on previous evenings since their arrival at the *Villa Athena*, Armitage and Athena Papadopoulos were ending their day with an after-dinner cognac on the front terrace that overlooked the little harbour and for the first time in many months, Armitage felt at peace with the world. He could, he thought, get to like this way of life. Which is when she said, quite casually:

'Tomorrow night we will have a party. To celebrate.'

'To celebrate what?'

'To celebrate *us*. I want to show you off to my friends. You'll like them, John, I promise you. And I want them all to know that Athena Papadopoulos now has a man about the house.'

He sighed. Oh God. Not again: 'Now listen to me Athena –'

She shook her head, stubbornly: 'No. I told you. I will not listen to you when you talk in that tone of voice.' Then softly, pleadingly: 'Please, John. It is all arranged. Let us not quarrel about this. What is so wrong in me holding a party in your honour?' She gave a tremulous little smile: 'You might even enjoy it.'

Armitage glowered, inwardly. And pigs, he thought, might loop-the-loop. One-to-one tête-à-têtes with a beautiful Greek heiress was one thing, mingling with God knows how many members of the international jet set, with him being exhibited as a rich socialite's latest plaything, was another.

'Please,' she said again, in that familiar, little girl voice, seemingly close to tears. He took a deep breath. Jesus. He hated it when she did that.

It always made him feel like a Victorian workhouse master, denying Oliver bloody Twist another helping of gruel. But what the hell? As she had said, where was the harm in it? And if it meant all that much to her…

'Very well,' he said finally, reluctantly: 'Just this once.'

She gave him a radiant smile: 'Thank you, John J. Armitage. You make me very happy.' She rose to her feet and held out her hand: 'Now I will make you very happy.'

He took her hand, rose slowly to his feet and with a totally spurious sigh of weary resignation, muttered: 'Your wish is my command, thou smooth-talking, silver-tongued, daughter of Zeus and shameless seducer of mere mortals. But please. Be gentle with me.'

She gave a snort of laughter: 'You really are full of craps, John J. Armitage, but I say again – I like it.'

Hand in hand, they walked back into the villa.

☞

'Can you credit it?' said a delighted Barry Lucas: 'I not only kept my job, I actually got promoted.'

'Is that a fact?' said Julie Baker, diffidently: 'I'm so pleased for you, sunshine.'

'What I don't understand is *why*. Because of Anderson, I was quite sure I was about to get the Ancient Order of the Boot.'

'Now why should you think that? I always knew you had it in you. The trouble with you, Barry, is that you always underestimate yourself and when you put your mind to it, you can be quite bright. Well, most of the time.'

Lucas was partly mollified: 'Well, maybe you're right. The Director and the architect feller – what was his name now? – they certainly seemed to think so.'

'Julian Caldwell.'

'What?'

'The architect. That's his name.'

'Oh, right,' said Lucas vaguely: 'But the thing is, now I've still got a job and a pay rise to go along with it, why don't I take you out tonight? To a really decent restaurant this time. I mean, it would make a nice change from the Chinese chippy or our usual cheap-and-cheerful spaghetti house, right?'

She shook her head and said quickly: 'I'm sorry, sunshine. Can't make tonight. I'm already going out.'

He frowned: 'Oh? You never told *me* you were going out tonight.'

'Yes, well, I don't have to tell you everything, do I?'

The green-eyed monster within every man slowly awoke from its slumbers.

'Where are you going?' demanded Lucas.

'Oh, just here and there.'

'Who with?'

She avoided his gaze: 'That's none of your business. Now if you don't mind, I've got work to do.'

Lucas's heart sank. He might have known it wouldn't last. Just as he was beginning to think he was really getting somewhere with her, she'd finally discovered what a boring little twat he really was and that it was time for a parting of the ways. And who could blame her? His shoulders slumped and he gave a wry little nod:

'None of my business. Yes, right.' He tried to force a smile: 'Been nice knowing you, Julie. See you around, okay?'

He turned to go. She sighed. Trust the poor, pathetic, *lovable* little idiot to get hold of the wrong end of the stick. She'd decided not to tell him about her brief chat with the resident architect, because she'd wanted him to think he'd won his promotion all by himself. Ah well. As he walked out of the shop, she called after him:

'I'm being taken out by Mr. Caldwell.'

He froze in mid-stride and turned back to her: 'The architect?'

She nodded: 'I asked him to put in a good word for you with Mr. Munro and that's what he did. So when he asked me out, I could hardly refuse, could I?'

Lucas considered: 'So it was you who was behind my promotion.'

'Sort of. In a way. Yes.'

'I see.' He considered again: 'I suppose I ought to say thank you.'

'For what? Like I said, I knew you were up to the job and all I did was to point it out to Mr. Caldwell.'

The green-eyed monster became fully awake: 'And now it's payback time, right?' And with suspicion writ large: 'May I ask just how you propose to show your gratitude on my behalf?'

Another sigh: 'Sometimes, I really don't know why I bother with you. If you mean what I think you mean, you should be ashamed of yourself.'

'He's a very good-looking bloke,' said Lucas stubbornly: 'Fine head of hair, nice dresser and obviously worth a few quid.'

'He's also an old man – must be at least forty – and what's more, he also happens to be gay.'

Lucas blinked: 'Gay? Are you sure?'

'That's what I've heard. And you must admit that what with those awful purple shirts of his and his funny bow ties, he's not exactly God's gift to women, now is he?'

Lucas shook his head, bemusedly: 'Then why has he asked you to go out with him?'

She shrugged: 'How would I know? Maybe he wants me on his arm as a sort of window-dressing – to try and convince everyone that deep down, he's as butch as Conan the Barbarian.' She giggled: 'Fat chance.'

Lucas took a deep breath, then after a long pause: 'Yes, well, that's all right then. Seems I owe you one, Julie.'

She crooked a finger: 'Come here,' she said softly.

'What?'

'I said come here.'

He moved back to the counter. She looked swiftly around the shop, then leaned over the counter to plant a firm, lingering kiss on his lips, before pushing him away with a peremptory:

'Now hop it. Like I said, I've got work to do.'

'Hop it, yes, right,' repeated Lucas happily: 'Will do. But how about tomorrow?'

'You're on.'

Lucas was actually whistling when he finally walked out of the shop. It seemed that St.Nerd was now working overtime on his behalf.

⟨ ⟩

To his surprise, Armitage quite enjoyed the evening. Well, at least, almost all of the evening. The guests had flown in by helicopter, motor launch and private yacht from, as far as he could make out, all parts of the globe. An invitation to an Athena Papadopoulos party was, it seemed, more of a royal command than a request and one to be missed at one's own social peril.

To Armitage, the term 'filthy rich' had always been a bit of an oxymoron. Rich, the guests certainly were, but filthy? Bathed, perfumed and pampered by a retinue of personal crimpers, beauticians and *haute couture* dress designers, they had emerged from their yachts and helicopters superbly attired, the women in a haze of expensive perfumes and the men in immaculate white tuxedos, exuding equally-expensive after-shaves – glittering proof, thought Armitage, of the power of money.

The party, with its food, its wines and the small army of servants, presided over by a suitably deadpan Jefferson was, without doubt, the most sumptuous function Armitage had ever attended. Perhaps predictably, most of the men had immediately gathered together in small groups, to discuss high finance, business trends and the latest fat stock prices, while their women greedily savoured the latest tit-bits of international gossip with a malicious relish that Armitage found a trifle disagreeable.

But at the same time, he was both flattered and amused to observe that many of the female guests were also intent on weighing-up Athena Papadopoulos's new man about the house with an equally malicious intent, some sending out signals that should he ever tire of his Grecian paramour, there was more than one willing port in a storm. Clinging proprietarily to Armitage's arm, Athena introduced him to her friends one by one, flashing warning glances at any particularly young and desirable female guest whom she considered to be getting a little too close to her guest of honour.

The evening ended with the guests being invited to follow their hostess out on to the prettily-lit main terrace, high above the harbour and the twinkling lights of the visitors' moored yachts, to dance to the music of the small orchestra, especially flown-in from Athens for that evening's entertainment. It was in the early hours of the morning when, as they danced the last waltz, Athena Papadopoulos slipped out of Armitage's arms, stepped up on to the small bandstand and whispered into the orchestra leader's ear. The leader raised his baton, led his musicians into a loud fanfare and Athena Papadopoulos addressed the microphone.

'Dear friends, I have an announcement to make.' Armitage had a sudden premonition, which was immediately reinforced when she turned towards him, shot him a ravishing smile, then continued, breathlessly: 'You have now all met Mr. John J. Armitage, my partner for this evening and I'm sure you have found him to be as charming, as handsome and as clever as I did. As I *do*.'

Oh shit, thought Armitage. Now what?

'I have finally decided,' she continued: 'That the time has now come for me to stand down as Chief Executive of Papadopoulos Holdings, the parent company of my late father's many business interests.'

There was a ripple of interest among the assembled guests. Their interest quickly became knowing smiles when, with another look in the direction of the apprehensive Armitage, she said softly:

'Now I know this will come as a great surprise to him, but I intend to appoint Mr. Armitage as my successor, to take immediate effect.' She turned towards him, with an obviously heartfelt: 'Welcome aboard, John. We at Papadopoulos Holdings are very lucky to have you.' She indicated the microphone: 'Now, if you would care to join me and say a few words…'

A suddenly stone-faced Armitage did indeed care to join her and say a few words. But once he began to address the assembled guests, it soon became evident that his few words were not quite the few words Athena Papadopoulos had expected or had wanted to hear, even though many of the guests found them highly amusing. To their delight, the party had ended on an unexpectedly high note and would prove to be a topic of scandalous conversation for a long time to come.

§

'Where did he take you?' asked Barry Lucas: 'Somewhere nice and incredibly expensive, I hope?'

'Nice, yes,' said Julie Baker, as she unlocked her cash till: 'Expensive, no. He prides himself on his cooking, so we went back to his flat in Chelsea where he cooked us dinner.'

Lucas's eyes narrowed: 'You went back to his flat? So it was just you and him, alone in his flat?'

'Of course not. Apart from the two of us, there were half a dozen Chelsea old-age pensioners, a couple of Jehovah's Witnesses who just happened to ring the doorbell and the odd double-glazing salesman. Of course it was just me and him, you idiot. So what?'

Lucas considered, then: 'Yes, you're right. As you say, so what? Afterall, him being gay and all…'

'Oh, he isn't gay. On the contrary.'

'He isn't? But you said –'

'I only said what I'd heard. But it seems it's just an act. A lot of men do that. It's a ploy, to get silly young women who haven't got the sense they were born with, to end up sharing his interior-sprung mattress.'

Lucas bristled: 'The bastard. If he laid a finger on you –'

'Calm down, sunshine. I marked his card right away. I wasn't born yesterday, you know.'

'Even so, if he came on strong –'

'Of course he came on strong, what did you expect? But he really is a good cook and after such a nice meal, I hadn't the heart to do what I usually do in such circumstances.'

'And what's that?'

'Let's just say that I have a knee and he has a groin. No, I just told that I had to leave right away, as I had an early appointment for a check up at the local special clinic.'

'Special clinic? But isn't that what they call the place where they treat people for..?' He reddened: 'Well, you know...'

'That's right.'

Lucas's mouth dropped open: 'You told him you had a..?' He almost choked on the words: 'An anti-social disease?'

'Of course I didn't. That would have been gross.' She gave a little giggle: 'I just sort of...hinted at it. And he couldn't get me out of his flat and into a taxi fast enough. Now unless you got something important to say, hop it. I have to open up the shop.'

Lucas looked at her with open admiration. What a remarkable girl she was. So confident, so street-wise and obviously quite capable of handling any situation with a style and panache he would never be able to emulate. Which was why he valued her opinion so highly.

'Yes, as it happened I do have something important to ask you.'

'Oh?' She paused in mid-motion: 'And what might that be, then?'

'I've been doing a bit of research on what could have happened to the Elgin marbles and it appears that of all the ships listed as having sailed from a British port and through the Straits of Gibraltar over the last few weeks, only one of them seemed to fit the bill as a possible carrier of the marbles.'

She sighed inwardly. So it was that sort of question. For a moment, she'd thought he was about to ask her something of a more personal nature. Something which, to her surprise, she now knew she would be more than happy to consider. But sadly, he obviously had other things on his mind.

'The ship was called the *SS Rosetta*, out of Guatemala,' continued Lucas: 'And its movements and sailing dates are all spot-on. The thing is, does that in itself justify me putting my head on the block by advising the Director of Operations to send down a diver to check it out? Because knowing the Director, if I'm wrong, it'll be goodbye the British Museum and hallo the jobs centre.'

Julie Baker blinked: 'Sorry, sunshine, you've lost me. Send down a diver to where?'

'The bottom of the Straits of Gibraltar. It seems that the ship went down a few weeks ago and that its owner is now claiming on his marine insurance.'

'How could you humiliate me like that, in front of all my friends?' demanded a furious Athena Papadopoulos, after the last guest had long departed: 'How could you tell me to stuff my appointment where – what did you call it? – where the monkey stuffs his nuts?'

'For your information, it's an old English expression and though admittedly not in the best possible taste, it did, however, sum up my feelings precisely.' He gave a weary gesture of despair: 'Haven't you got the message yet, Athena? I am not for sale.'

'But I thought it would make you very happy to be my chief executive.'

'Without even asking me if I wanted the bloody job?'

'Of course you want the bloody job. You have to have the bloody job. You think that Athena Papadopoulos is going to marry a small-time English businessman who hasn't got two pences to rub together?'

As soon as she'd said it, Athena knew she'd scored an own goal.

'Not that I expect you to marry me,' she added hurriedly: 'Unless you really want to. But I did feel that over the last few weeks, having become so close, so intimate, I thought perhaps that you and I…'

She left the question floating in the air.

Said Armitage coldly: 'My only commitment to you is to deliver those fucking marbles to the port of Piraeus and that's all I intend to do. Do I make myself clear?'

She looked at him in genuine bewilderment: 'What is it about you Englishmen? Why do you find it so difficult to show what you really feel? Because I know what you really feel about *me*, John J. Armitage. A woman always knows. And I just don't understand how you can throw what I am offering you straight back into my face, without so much as a thank you, my darling.'

Said Armitage, equally quietly: 'Have you finished?'

'Not quite. I know you are a proud man. Just as my father was. And to me, that is one of your attractions. But why is it that men like you and my father always feel they have to wear the pantaloons in a relationship – and that accepting a helping hand from a woman threatens their masculinity?'

'It's not quite as simple as that.'

'It could be. If you would let it.' She gave a gesture of helpless resignation: 'There. Now I have finished.'

'I do hope so,' said Armitage, enigmatically: 'We need to get our priorities right. And first thing tomorrow, I fly to Gibraltar to meet Ken Beynon. The divers and the salvage ship are already on their way and will arrive in the Straits in a few days time. Now if you'll excuse me, I need to get some sleep.' He gave her a brief nod: 'Goodnight, Athena.'

He walked off into the darkness. She looked after him sullenly. Damn the man. He was as stubborn as her late father. Almost as stubborn as she herself. Her brow wrinkled in thought. Then she gave a sudden little smile and called softly after the departed Armitage:

'Finished? You think we are finished, John J. Armitage? Then you don't know Athena Papadopoulos as well as you thought you did.'

☞

It was in the early hours of the morning when, watched by Armitage and Ken Beynon, the three Greek divers went over the side of the salvage vessel in their first attempt to pinpoint the exact location of the scuttled *SS Rosetta*. While Armitage had made sure that its position had been carefully plotted on the charts, he knew that a sinking ship didn't always go straight down to the bottom. Prevailing tidal currents could have carried the *Rosetta* for some considerable distance, before finally allowing it to come to rest on the seabed.

It was another twenty minutes or so before one of the divers broke the surface of the water just a short distance away from the ship and gave them a triumphant thumbs up. Armitage was pleased. If the under-sea currents had been really strong, they could have spent half the morning trying to locate the *Rosetta* and the object of the whole exercise was to find it quickly, recover its cargo and get the hell out of the Straits, before a British Royal Navy patrol boat was sent out from Gibraltar to discover just what they were up to.

The salvage vessel re-started its engines and moved to a position directly over the wreck. The motors of the heavy lifting derrick burst into life, its operator sending the cables and steel-mesh lifting nets down to the waiting divers on the deck of the sunken ship. It was some time before they managed to break open the hatches, but when the cover of the main hold was finally slid open, the first of the divers lowered himself down into the darkness. After a surprisingly short time, a signal from the diver sent the crane into reverse. An eager Armitage and Beynon leaned over the ship's rail, waiting expectantly for the sight of the first of the sealed crates to break the surface. But there was no crate in the lifting net – just one of the divers clinging to it. Once back on board, the diver spoke animatedly to the ship's captain, in a strong Greek patois that, even if the Englishmen had possessed a working knowledge of the language, the conversation would still have been quite incomprehensible.

'What did he say?' demanded Armitage.

'He say,' said the captain: 'That there is no cargo. The other two are searching the rest of the ship, but it seems that the holds are empty. It would appear, my friend, that someone has got here before you.'

7

FROM THE TERRACE OF GIBRALTAR'S Rock Hotel, overlooking the harbour, Armitage and Beynon silently watched the salvage ship, its divers and its crew finally sail out of sight, heading back towards Greece. The vessel had not been at anchor in the Straits long enough to raise any eyebrows – either from the Royal Navy or Her Majesty's Customs and Excise. Not that it would have mattered, thought Armitage resignedly. Without any cargo to salvage – illegal or otherwise – the whole question had become totally academic. As he had anticipated, the somewhat puzzled Greek captain had been openly curious as to what Armitage had expected to find aboard the sunken *Rosetta,* but Armitage had sidestepped his queries, paid him off with a cheque pre-signed by Athena Papadopoulos and requested that he and Beynon be put ashore in Gibraltar.

'What,' said Beynon after a while: 'Are you going to tell our sponsor?'

'Nothing, at the moment. The first thing we have to do is find out who beat us to it – and that shouldn't be too difficult. The only other person who knew the exact location of the *Rosetta* was our old friend Captain Jaime Carlos António José da Souza. So who else could it have been?'

Beynon considered. Then nodded: 'You're right.'

'And what's more,' continued Armitage: 'Having been handsomely paid for the loss of his ship, he had more than enough money to hire a salvage vessel and the divers to go with it – probably out of Portugal.'

'But he couldn't have known he was carrying the Elgin marbles.'

'He didn't need to know. He obviously reckoned that if Athena Papadopoulos was prepared to pay that amount of money to scuttle a rusting old hulk like the *Rosetta*, then there must have been something extremely valuable on board.'

'So he nicked them. How dishonest can you get?' demanded an angry Beynon. The fact that it was he and Armitage who had stolen them in the first instance was, to Beynon, quite irrelevant. They'd made a deal and after all, there was supposed to be honour amongst thieves. But da Souza had still gone ahead and screwed them. He couldn't wait to catch up with him and when he did…he unconsciously flexed his fingers.

Armitage sighed: 'Knowing da Souza as I do, I suppose I should have anticipated that he might renege on our deal – but I never thought he'd move so quickly. It's as though he was tipped off that we were on our way.'

'Tipped off? By who?'

'No idea. It's just a feeling, that's all.'

Said Beynon: 'And now he knows exactly what he's got, what d'you think he'll do with them?'

Armitage shrugged: 'Try and do a deal with the British Museum, I suppose.'

'Not Athena Papadopoulos?'

Armitage smiled grimly: 'Not directly. Having crossed her once, I don't think he'd dare. She'd have his balls for breakfast.'

'But how would he explain to the British Museum, let alone the police, how he came to be in possession of stolen property – whether or not he was the one who was actually behind the theft?'

'I don't think he'd even try to. He'll probably use a go-between to negotiate a no-questions-asked, cash-for-marbles handover, then sail off into the sunset. I know that's what I would do.'

Beynon thought for a moment, then nodded in agreement: 'Makes sense. So now what?'

'We go back to London to see if my hunch is right. And if da Souza hasn't already had them delivered them to the British Museum, we'll still be in with a chance.'

'But if he has, bang goes our three million quid.'

It was a depressing thought. All that work, that planning, that hardship, all having been for nothing. And, thought Armitage, God only knew how the tempestuous Athena Papadopoulos would react when she finally found out what had happened to her damned, elusive marbles. But one thing was certain. Having screwed up once again – from her point of view at least – he would no longer be in the running for the position of chief executive of Papadopoulos Holdings, whether he wanted the appointment or not or, for that matter, in the running for any of the fringe benefits that would have gone along with the job – Athena Papadopoulos in particular. And that had to be some consolation, he supposed. Then why, he suddenly wondered, did the thought of losing her depress him even more?

☞

On her return to the island of Thiros, after a short shopping trip to the Greek mainland, Athena Papadopoulos was sunning herself on the patio when she received an urgent and unexpected telephone call from the senior executive whom she had instructed to assist John Armitage in his negotiation for the salvage vessel. He informed her that he had just had a message from the ship's captain, to tell him that the operation had been unsuccessful and that the ship and its team of divers were returning to Greece empty handed.

His employer had listened silently and quite without expression. She had then replaced the telephone and shouted angrily for her butler. He appeared from within the villa with the speed and imperturbability of a jack-in-the-box.

'You bellowed, madame?'

'Don't be impertinent, Jefferson. During my visit to Athens, has there been any communication from Mr. Armitage that you have neglected to tell me about?'

'No madame. Not a word.'

'I see. Then please make the necessary arrangements for our return to London.'

'By land, sea or air, madame?'

'The quickest.'

He brightened: 'The quickest, madame? Yes, right. That'll be by air, then.'

'Just get on with it, Jefferson.'

Get on with it. Yes. Right. With pleasure. Leaving the sodding island of Thiros much earlier than he'd expected, had a great appeal. Thanks to the blistering, all-day-long sunshine, he not only sweated cobs from morning to night, but he had ended up with a painful rash of prickly heat. What's more, he thought happily, they wouldn't be returning in her frigging boat either; with him puking up his guts all the way back to the UK.

Before he walked back into the villa to arrange their journey, he was pleased to see, from her rigid expression, that she was not a happy woman. At a guess, he thought, she was pissed-off with her fancy feller again. He was beginning to like her fancy feller. If only because when she was pissed-off with John Armitage, she always forgot to get pissed-off with him.

Yes, things were certainly looking up. With a bit of luck, they'd be back in time for him to spend one of his few nights off at Mrs. Hennessey's charming Victorian residence in the leafy North London suburb of Muswell Hill, just off The Broadway. The ever-warm and welcoming lady in question ran a discreet little establishment where a bevy of pretty and obliging young ladies were always more than willing to entertain gentlemen who fully appreciated the finer things in life and were prepared to pay for them. For the first time in many weeks, he found he was actually humming to himself, in eager anticipation of what was to come.

☞

The notice outside the British Museum's main doorway was short and to the point:

THE ELGIN MARBLES.
The Duveen Gallery
Will re-open on Monday,
4ʰ August, at 9 am.

Precisely at 9am the following Monday, Armitage, Beynon and a frail but mobile Gavin Messiter, leaning on a walking stick, entered the main gates and made their way towards the gallery entrance. They gazed despondently up at the marble exhibits that adorned the walls and plinths throughout the gallery.

'So we're too late,' muttered Beynon.

'Seems like it,' said Armitage.

'Ah well,' said Messiter with a philosophical resignation he didn't really feel: 'It seemed like a good idea at the time. Let's get out of here.'

They moved towards the doorway, passing the little girl in her father's arms who was stretching out her hand towards the massive piece of sculpture described as *Horses Reigning In.*

'Nice horsey,' said the little girl.

'Don't touch, Jennifer,' said her father quickly. But he was too late.

'Giddy-up, horsey,' said the little girl and gave the rump of the nearest horse a resounding slap. The slap echoed hollowly around the gallery. The little girl turned to her father in surprise and disappointment:

'The horsey's all empty, daddy.'

The trio pause in the doorway and turned back towards the exhibits.

'Jesus,' whispered Beynon: 'I don't believe it. They wouldn't. They couldn't.'

'They bloody have,' said Messiter, after a closer inspection: 'Polyester-fibre replicas. The lot of them.'

'Well, well, well,' said Armitage, with a grim smile: 'Who would have thought that the fusty, dusty old British Museum would have had the nerve to try and deceive the British public like this? They should be ashamed of themselves.' He chuckled: 'Isn't it marvellous?'

Said Beynon: 'It means we're still in with a chance. And the first thing we have to do is track down da Souza – and quickly.'

In the event, it was da Souza who tracked them down.

'Well, I don't think it's right,' said Barry Lucas; 'It's just not honest. And I'm sure that if we'd sent a diver down like I suggested, we'd have the real marbles back in the gallery by now.'

Julie Baker dusted down the replica *Selene* horse's head and began re-arranging the racks of souvenir cards into their proper order. Why, she wondered crossly, did her customers always seem to take them out of their proper rack, have a quick shufty, then put them back into the wrong rack? She had enough to do without having to spend half the morning shuffling the cards from frigging rack to another.

Said Lucas morosely: 'The Director seemed to think that by putting up the replicas, it would buy us more time in trying to find the real ones.'

'Is that a fact?' said Julie Baker, absently.

Perhaps, she mused, if she put the cards into the wrong racks in the first place, the punters might then put them back into their proper racks, without even knowing it. Could be worth a try.

'But even though the marine insurance company gave me the exact position where the *Rosetta* went down, he still wouldn't let me hire a local diver to check it out.'

'Really?' said the preoccupied Julie Baker: 'That's not right, is it?'

'Seems that Anderson's trip to Gibraltar and the way he called in the Royal Navy cost the Museum an arm and a leg,' continued Lucas: 'And because of it, there was nothing left in the kitty for that sort of thing and – are you listening to me, Julie?'

'Um? Yes, of course I am.'

The truth be known, she was getting fed up to her pretty back teeth with him constantly going on about the rotten old Elgin marbles. Why didn't everyone face up to the fact that they were well and truly gone forever – over the hills and far away – and let everything get back to normal? Life was too short for her lovely little feller to allow himself to get so worked up over a pile of broken bits and pieces. There were far more important things to think about – like when would he finally find the bottle to ask her to go away with him for a romantic weekend?

If they did eventually agree to make it legal, she first had to find out if he was up to the job, in a manner of speaking. She had no intention of ending up with the sort of feller who was more interested in cars than acquiring carnal knowledge (as her mother called it). The sort of feller who always wore long underwear and went to bed with his socks on. The sort who'd prefer to spend his spare time fiddling with his fretwork set – rather than ravish her at very regular intervals.

What was the matter with him, for God's sake? He was supposed to have the hots for her, but over the last few weeks, even though she'd sent out more signals than an admiral of the fleet, he'd been about as responsive as a neutered ginger tom.

'So where do I go from here, Julie?'

She heaved a sigh: 'How about the staff canteen, where you can buy yourself a coffee? Please sunshine, you can see I'm very busy, and if you really want to have a chat, you'll have to wait until I shut up shop, all right?'

A nod of resignation and a morose: 'All right. I'll pick you up at five-thirty.'

A despondent Barry Lucas drifted out of the souvenir shop in the direction of the staff canteen. He was so preoccupied with his problems, he did not initially register the three men who passed him in the entrance hall and who were walking towards the main entrance. Then a tiny bell tinkled. He stopped and looked after them. Even though they all had their backs to him, there was something familiar about two of the three men, something that struck a chord. The two men and the older man with the walking stick had already disappeared through the doorway when the chord suddenly became a deafening cacophony. Good grief, it was them. The last time he had seen them, they had been wearing uniforms and driving a pantechnicon.

By the time Lucas burst out of the front entrance, Armitage, Beynon and Messiter had already reached the main gates. Struggling to push his way through the crowds of visitors, Lucas tried to shout above the roar of the traffic to the security men at the gates to stop them. The security men reacted quickly, but with so many visitors passing in and out of the gates, it was difficult to ascertain the 'them' to whom Lucas was referring. Quite unaware that they were being pursued, the trio walked along Museum Street towards Centrepoint. As they waited for a break in the traffic, to enable them to cross the road, a black taxicab came to a sudden halt in front of them. The passenger door swung open to reveal a grinning Captain Jaime Carlos António José da Souza.

'Hey Amigos. Been looking for you everywhere. You wanna buy some marbles?'

Armitage managed to restrain Ken Beynon from dragging da Souza out of the cab and on to the pavement and, at da Souza's invitation, they joined him in the rear of the taxi. As it moved away from the kerb, a panting, red-faced Lucas ran out of the Museum gates and looked wildly about him, but the cab was already accelerating towards Southampton Row. His howl of frustration echoed around the main concourse and along Museum Street:

'Shit, shit, shit! I've lost them!'

'Watch it, son,' warned a passing policeman: 'People don't like to hear that sort of language.'

Why is it, thought Lucas miserably, the only time you see a policeman is when you don't want one?

The Portuguese restaurant in London's Soho was small and intimate. In a discrete corner alcove, Armitage, Beynon and Messiter faced da Souza across the table with an open animosity that was almost palpable. When the waiter had poured their coffees and departed, da Souza looked back at them with an expression of hurt surprise:

'Please don't look at me like that, gentlemen. I have as much right to those marbles as you do.' To Armitage he said, sadly and reproachfully: 'You were not honest with me, Senhor. You did not tell me that you were using my ship to transport stolen property. Had we been apprehended, even if I had managed to convince the courts that I had no knowledge of what I was carrying, it would still have ruined my professional reputation. Something that is without price and very precious to me.'

Grunted Armitage: 'Spare me the outraged virtue, de Souza. I've known you for far too long. How did you know where to find me?'

'I rang the telephone number you gave me the last time we did business together and your charming cleaning lady told me you had gone into London.' He grinned: 'It was not difficult to work out why. You wished to find out if the marbles were already back in the Museum, yes?'

'Perhaps.'

'So now you know. And it is *because* we are very old friends, Senhor, that I have decided to give you the opportunity to make me an offer for the Elgin marbles, before I do contact the British Museum.'

'I think I'm going to strangle him,' growled Beynon.

'You strangle me, Mr. Beynon and no one will ever see the marbles again. They will be gone forever.' To Armitage, he said: 'So. How much would you be prepared to pay for them?'

'You've already been paid. We made a deal.'

'For my beautiful *Rosetta*, yes. But not for what was inside it. Had I known what a valuable cargo I was carrying, I would not have settled for such a small sum. Afterall, Miss Athena Papadopoulos has so much, while I have so little.' He smiled, revealing a jagged row of cheroot-stained teeth: 'It was not until we went on board her elegant yacht in Gibraltar that I began to put two and two together. And as I had a contact in the Portuguese salvage business, I decided to investigate further.'

Said Beynon: 'How did you know our salvage ship was already on its way?'

Da Souza chuckled: 'My partner told me.'

Beynon and Armitage exchanged a look: 'Who is your partner?'

'I am afraid I'm not at liberty to say.' He rose to his feet and to Armitage, he said: 'I will give you three more days to discuss the matter with Miss Papadopoulos, then I will contact you again.' He pointed to the menu: 'As it is approaching lunchtime, I suggest you read the menu. The food here is very good. Traditional Portuguese. Adios, amigos.'

They watched him walk out of the restaurant. It was Messiter who broke the silence:

'Know what? The bastard didn't even pay for the coffee.'

'Know something else?' said Armitage thoughtfully: 'I don't think he knew that the Museum has re-opened the Duveen Gallery.'

Beynon shrugged: 'So? They're only replicas.'

'But pretty convincing ones – especially to the untrained eye.'

Messiter thought for a moment, then nodded: 'I think you could be on to something, John.'

⸙

For the second time that day, ex-Chief Inspector Charles Anderson inspected each and every vehicle in the staff car park, in the hope of apprehending an illegally parked vehicle. The only satisfaction he got from his new, mind-numbingly boring duties, was calling for a wheel-clamping crew to render the vehicle immobile or, in extreme cases, for a truck to remove it altogether – and then waiting for its owner to turn up and to happily witness his fury and distress.

Since his return from Gibraltar, he had bitterly pondered upon the fate of the marbles and their actual whereabouts. Even though his idiot assistant's suggestion that they were aboard her yacht had proved to be wide of the mark, he was still convinced that somehow, the Papadopoulos woman was up to her expensively bejewelled neck in their disappearance. His biggest mistake was taking on board Lucas's suggestion that someone should fly out to Gibraltar and confront the woman. Devious little sod. He probably did it to get back at him, just because of his fatherly interest in the girl from the souvenir shop.

But as the marbles weren't on the *Athena*, where were they? Could it be, he wondered, that they had not been shipped anywhere and were still in the country? Carefully stored away in some warehouse, or even in a place that no one would even think of searching? And, he mused, if he were Athena Papadopoulos, where would *he* store the damn things – until all the fuss had died down and they could then be shipped quietly out of the country? Somewhere not too far away. In or around London, perhaps – at her country estate, if she had one.

He paused. One thing she did have was a bloody great house in one of the best parts of London, with enough space to store the Elgin marbles several times over. He'd read about it in the newspapers. Godammit, even her private ballroom was probably bigger than the Duveen gallery itself. The more he thought about it, the more animated he became. He was on to something. He knew it. Her mansion in the heart of Belgravia was the most obvious place to stash the marbles until the time came for their removal.

They'd need a search warrant of course. But that would mean bringing in the police, which the damn-fool Director still didn't want to do. And in any event, after the unfortunate Gibraltar cock-up, even though it had hardly been his fault, he very much doubted if the Director would even listen to him. But it had to be checked out. It was his last chance, his only chance, of getting his career back on the rails again.

The only problem was *how* to check it out. Without a search warrant, it would be quite impossible. He could hardly ring her front doorbell and ask her if she wouldn't mind him taking a quick gander around the house to see if she was sitting on a pile of stolen property. Come on Anderson, he told himself, think. There had to *some* way of getting into that house and giving it a quick once-over. For the next few minutes, his brow was wrinkled in agonised cogitation. Then suddenly, wonderfully, the answer became crystal clear. Yes. Of course. That was it. It was as simple as that. He hastened across the car park and entered the Museum, with an eagerness he hadn't felt for weeks.

As he had promised, the telephone call from da Souza came on the morning of the third day. Armitage and Messiter were sitting at his living room table as Armitage placed the receiver into an amplification cradle, to enable both he and Messiter to hear what was said.

Said da Souza cheerfully: 'So, Senhor Armitage, did you talk to Miss Papadopoulos, like I suggested?'

Armitage glanced at Messiter, then barked towards the receiver: 'Are you trying to be funny, de Souza?'

Da Souza was obviously surprised by Armitage's tone of voice: 'I do not understand you, my friend. All I wish to know if the lady wishes you to make me an offer for the return of the marbles. And if so, how much?'

Snapped Armitage: 'And *I* don't understand *you*, da Souza. D'you think we're stupid? How can you expect us to do a deal when you know full well that you've already done a deal with the British Museum?'

'What are you talking about?'

'I'm talking about…'Armitage's angry tone of voice suddenly became as surprised as da Souza's. He looked pointedly towards Messiter, leaned towards the receiver and said carefully and clearly: 'My God, Gavin. He doesn't know. He really doesn't know.'

'What is it that I do not know?' asked the genuinely puzzled voice through the loudspeaker.

'That the Elgin marbles are back on display at the British Museum?'

'What? Are you loco, Senhor? How could that be? Three days ago, you saw for yourself that – '

'That was three days ago. They're now back up again, right Gavin?'

Armitage glanced again at Messiter, who nodded and spoke into the receiver:

'Don't take our word for it, da Souza. Go and see for yourself. The Duveen gallery has now re-opened.'

'Impossible. I have done no deal with the Museum.'

'Then perhaps someone else has.' Messiter waited for his words to sink in, then said softly: 'This partner of yours, Senhor da Souza. Are you sure he can be trusted?'

There was a long silence, followed by the sound of a telephone being slammed down.

Said Messiter to Armitage: 'Do you really think it's going to work?'

'No idea. The rest is up to Ken.'

☞

Beynon was watching through the window of the Museum Street public house, immediately opposite the Museum's main gates when, as he'd hoped, a taxicab drew up at the entrance and disgorged an obviously agitated Captain Jaime Carlos António José da Souza. Beynon did not follow him into the Museum. He had no wish to run the risk of coming face to face with either the temporary acting Head of Security or his assistant. He did not have long to wait. A furious da Souza, his face flushed in anger, reappeared in a matter of minutes and after storming across the concourse and out through the gates, he hailed the first passing taxicab.

Beynon slipped out of the pub and hailed the second. As he climbed in, he pointed towards the cab ahead of them and said crisply:

'Follow that cab.'

He smiled grimly to himself. He'd always wanted to say that.

It was just as well that Beynon had decided not to follow his quarry into the British Museum. Had he done so, he would have walked straight into both Anderson and Lucas, who were making their way across the entrance hall in the direction of the staff canteen.

Said Lucas: 'You want to talk to me about what?'

Anderson glanced about him and lowered his voice: 'Not here, son. Walls have ears.'

Once at a discreet corner table of the staff canteen, he spooned six lumps of sugar into his coffee, took a bite out of his sticky bun and, in a quietly confident voice:

'I reckon I know where she's hidden the marbles.'

'Who?'

'The Papadopoulos woman – who else? You said yourself that you thought she was behind the whole thing and I've got it all worked out. Oh yes. I've finally sussed her.' He tapped his forehead: 'Had the old grey matter working overtime, as that frog detective used to say – Hercules Parrot, wasn't it?'

'Hercule Poirot.'

'Well, whoever. Now I know this might come as a bit of a surprise to you, lad – but there's really only one place they could be. And d'you know where?' He paused for dramatic effect: 'Her house in Belgrave Square.'

He nodded with smug self-satisfaction and leaned back in his chair. Lucas looked him in utter disbelief. Good grief. It wasn't just the British Museum that had lost its marbles; Anderson had obviously lost his, too. The man was insane.

'In her *house*?' he repeated: 'How d'you make that out?'

'Because if I'd been in her position, that's just what I would have done.'

Yes, I'm sure you would, thought Lucas, but then, you're barking mad. And she isn't.

'Have you mentioned this to the Director?'

'Not yet, no,' said Anderson evasively: 'If I'm right and that's where we'll find them, why should we let him take all the credit? No, lad, if we pull this off, we'll be set for life.'

Lucas had a sudden, unwelcome sense of foreboding: 'If *we* pull it off?'

'Me and you. We're a team, right?'

Wrong.

'And I can't do this on my own.'

'Do what?'

'Get inside her place and check it out.'

'After applying for a search warrant, you mean?'

'I'm afraid that's not as easy as you might think. No, we'd have to do it sort of…unofficially.'

Lucas's mouth fell open: 'Now let's get this straight. Are you actually suggesting breaking into her house and searching it from top to bottom?'

'Of course not.' This time, he tapped his nose: 'This old fox is a little too clever for that. To gain entry, we'll need to use a little guile. And this is what I want you to do.'

He crooked his finger and as Lucas leaned across the table, he whispered into his ear. Anderson's erstwhile assistant's expression slowly changed from total bewilderment into open incredulity.

'Are you serious?

'Deadly, son. Deadly. If I could do it myself, I would. But as I came face to face with the woman, in Gibraltar, she'd recognise me. And so would her butler.'

Lucas shook his head, firmly: 'Sorry. But it's just not on. It's too risky. You'll have to get someone else.'

'There is no one else. No one else I'd trust, anyway. And you owe me. You wouldn't be here if it wasn't for me. I got you your job, right? '

'Well yes, but – '

'And you could be in and out of there in a couple of shakes, without anyone being any the wiser. And like I said, if I'm right, it could be the making of you. Of both of us. So what d'you say?'

He looked at Lucas with such pathetic eagerness, Lucas felt his heart sink. Oh God. The man was like an aging, unwanted, frayed-around-the edges mongrel in the Battersea Dogs' Home. Poor old bastard. Since he'd been forced to take early retirement from Scotland Yard, he couldn't have had much of a life. And even though he was in no doubt that Anderson would still shaft him soon as look at him, Lucas knew he couldn't turn the man down. Oh shit, he thought resignedly. I'm a fool to myself. Always was. Always will be.

ɛ ś

As da Souza's taxi came to a halt in the leafy London square, Beynon climbed out of his cab, paid-off the driver and positioned himself behind one of the several large parked cars; a four-wheel-drive people-carrier. Though more suited to navigating rural farmland than narrow inner-London residential streets, it seemed that many well-heeled local residents unaccountably chose such off-road vehicles simply to transport their children to and from their nearby private schools.

God knows why, thought Beynon. Most of the off-roaders probably hadn't been anywhere near so much as a cowpat since leaving the showrooms. Must be a status symbol thing. But they did provide him with a safe and suitable vantage point. Da Souza was standing on the pavement on the other side of the street, looking about him, as if checking the house numbers. His gaze steadied on one particular house and he then marched purposefully up the short flight of steps to the front door and rang the doorbell. After a few moments, the door swung open and a man was framed in the doorway.

Without a word, da Sousa reached out and grabbed the startled Jefferson by the throat, pushed him violently back inside the house and kicked the door shut behind him. Beynon reached for his mobile phone, punched in a number and put the phone to his ear.

'John? I think we need to meet up – and as fast possible. I think we've found da Souza's partner.'

Almost half an hour went by before a grim-faced da Souza reappeared in the doorway and was ushered out of the Papadopoulos residence by a somewhat dishevelled Jefferson, who hastily closed the door behind him. It would seem that the butler had finally been able to persuade his irate partner that he'd been deliberately mis-led by the devious Armitage and that the marbles in the Museum were merely replicas. The watching Beynon did not attempt to follow the Portuguese, who again hailed a passing taxi and was driven off in the direction of London's West End, presumably to have a second look at the exhibits, if only to satisfy himself that Jefferson had been telling the truth. As Armitage had said, it was a question of priorities and their first priority was to come face to face with da Souza's partner in the presence of his employer, without da Souza being aware that they now had a direct link to him – and the marbles.

During his surveillance of the house, a silver Rolls-Bentley limousine had drawn up at the front door and an elegantly attired Athena Papadopoulos had descended imperiously to the pavement, followed by her uniformed chauffeur, loaded up to his chin with shopping bags, all bearing the logos of *haute couture* establishments and presumably containing even more elegant attire.

It was lucky for Jefferson, thought Beynon - and indeed for them – that his employer had not been at home when an angry Portuguese sea captain had apparently attempted to throttle her butler. The woman was no fool and would have immediately made the connection. And when the moment came to confront her employee, both he and Armitage wanted to be there.

It was another hour before Armitage, travelling by train and mini-cab, was finally able to join him in Belgrave Square. They exchanged a few words, crossed the road, climbed the few steps up to the front door and rang the doorbell.

☞

'You're going to say you're from *where?*' asked a startled Julie Baker.

'The gas company,' said Barry Lucas glumly: 'That was Anderson's idea and the trouble is, what does a gasman look like? I mean, does he wear a uniform and have a peaked cap – or does he just wear jeans and a duffle coat and carry a clip-board?'

'You're barmy, you know that? And as for that silly old fool who calls himself Anders of the Yard, he must have a brain like a flat battery. You're not going to go along with him on this are you?'

'I've no choice, Julie,' said Lucas helplessly: 'Like he said, he did get me the job at a time when I was really desperate and if he hadn't, I would have never met you, would I? And that would have been awful. So I owe him. That's why I've got to do it.'

She looked at the troubled Barry Lucas with a sudden, almost maternal rush of warmth and affection. So he was only doing it because of her. What a lovely thing to say. He really was a nice, kind, loyal little feller. And it was about time had someone did something nice for *him*. She glanced around her, leaned over the counter and said softly:

'What are you doing on Friday?'

'What with all that's been going on, I haven't really thought.'

'Then think. And what about Saturday and Sunday?'

'I dunno. Why d'you ask?'

'My mum and dad are going away for the weekend and the thought of me having to be in the house all on my own for three whole nights…' She looked at him with an expression that she hoped would indicate her totally bogus feelings of fear and anxiety: 'Well, it is a bit scary, Barry. Anything could happen. I mean, I'm only a slip of a girl,' she added, with an equal lack of veracity. In truth, she felt as fit as a butcher's dog: 'But if you were there to protect me…'

Said Lucas, without hesitation: 'Say no more. I'll look after you.' He almost flexed his muscles. It was good to feel wanted: 'Now. What do *you* think I should wear?'

She gave him a wide-eyed, innocent little smile: 'Anything – as long as it doesn't include black socks and long underwear.'

'Pardon?'

'Granted. See you Friday.'

'See me Friday. Yes. Right.'

Black socks and long underwear? Had he missed something? He shrugged, shook his head bemusedly and walked out of the souvenir shop. He'd never understand women. On the other hand, why bother? The prospect of spending a whole weekend with the lovely Julie Baker had a much greater appeal than what he usually did in his spare time – building a scale model of St. Paul's Cathedral, out of used matchsticks.

When he opened the door to Armitage and Beynon, if Jefferson was surprised, or even a trifle apprehensive to see them, he certainly did not show it. He merely conducted them into one of the main sitting rooms and invited them to be seated, while he informed his mistress of their arrival.

Beynon glanced around the room with interest, taking in the antique furniture, the lavish décor, the obviously valuable oil paintings that adorned every wall and the floor-to-ceiling, woven silk curtains. So this was how the other half lived. Perhaps they should have asked for more than a meagre three million for the return of the marbles. Even so, it felt good to know that, with da Souza not yet having done a deal with the British Museum, they could still be in with a chance of collecting even the odd three million. A small chance, admittedly. But a chance, never the less.

As Armitage had said, the first thing they had to do was convince their sponsor that it was only because of her toe-rag of a butler that they'd lost the marbles in the first place. Had Jefferson not tipped-off the equally mendacious da Souza that their salvage ship was on its way, they would have got to them first and by now, the marbles would have been safely unloaded at the Port of Piraeus. The door swung open and Athena Papadopoulos was framed in the doorway.

'Where the hell have you been?' she demanded, without any preamble: 'And even more importantly, what has happened to the Parthenon marbles?'

Without a word, Armitage rose swiftly to his feet, walked over to the door, grasped her by wrist, pulled her roughly into the room and closed the door firmly behind her.

She wrenched her arm away, her face flushed with anger: 'What do you think you're doing? I do not hear a word from you for days and then you walk straight into my house and without so much as a good afternoon, Miss Papadopoulos, you assault me.' She examined her reddening wrist: 'Have you gone loco?'

Said Armitage quietly: 'I had to close the door quickly, because the less your butler overhears, the better.'

'Jefferson? What's he got to do with it?'

'Everything.'

'What are you talking about?'

'I'm talking about the marbles. And since you ask – no. We don't know where they are – but your butler does. Or at least, his Portuguese partner does. And if we play our cards right, we might well be able to get them back again.' He returned to his seat and indicated the nearest chair: 'Now d'you want to listen to what we have to say, or don't you?'

It took some considerable time to brief Athena Papadopoulos on the series of events that had led up to the disappearance of the sunken marbles. To Beynon's surprise, she neither interrupted nor questioned Armitage at any point during his discourse. She just listened to him, seemingly hanging upon his every word, as if desperately *wishing* to believe what he was telling her. Good grief, thought Beynon, somewhere along the way, Armitage must have got lucky. The woman was obviously besotted with him. And even though Armitage had never actually spelt it out, since they'd boarded her yacht in Gibraltar, he'd had a feeling that something had been going on between them.

For a moment, he felt a twinge of envy. But only for a moment. The volatile Athena Papadopoulos was obviously quite a woman – but unless he was mistaken, she was also quite a handful. A ball-breaker, in fact. The sort of woman who always had to have her own way in a relationship. Any relationship. But that was Armitage's problem and Beynon was amused to see that by the time he had completed his explanation, her open hostility had turned to one of total understanding, as if he had taken a great weight off her mind. And in more ways than one.

'So tell me, John J. Armitage,' said Athena Papadopoulos, softly: 'What do you wish me to do?'

'For a start, ring for the ever-attentive, eaves-dropping Jefferson and let us hear what he has to say.'

'And then what?'

'That depends on *what* he has to say.'

Athena Papadopoulos nodded and reached for the nearby bell-pull. A couple of minutes later, the door opened and a professionally stoney-faced Jefferson moved into the centre of room and intoned, somewhat predictably:

'You rang, madame?'

As Beynon rose and locked the door behind him, Armitage looked the butler up and down and said: 'Indeed she did. A classic case of for whom the bells tolls. And it tolls for thee, Jefferson.'

Jefferson raised his eyebrows and turned to his mistress with a puzzled: 'Madame?'

'In other words, Jefferson,' said Athena Papadopoulos: 'You are a disloyal, ungrateful little bastard – and you are up to your ears in what I believe you English colloquially call deep shit.'

Jefferson's eyebrows were raised even higher: 'Might I ask why, madame?'

'In a word, Captain Jaime Carlos António José da Souza.'

'With respect, madame, that's seven words. And I have no idea what you are talking about. So unless there is something else…?'

'Just this. What have you and your crooked Portuguese partner done with the Parthenon marbles?'

There was a long pause while Jefferson carefully digested what had been said. Then nodding towards the nearby couch, he said:

'May I take a seat?'

'No.'

'In that case, madame, in equally colloquial English, you can get stuffed.' To Armitage he said: 'I've been wanting to say that for years. She can be a right cow, you know. God knows what you see in her, apart from her money.'

Said his employer: 'I trusted you. I treated you as one of the family.'

'You treated me like donkey droppings. And if it wasn't for the fact that you paid me over and above the odds, I would have walked out on you from day one.'

Said Armitage: 'All right. Now you've got that off your chest, are you going to tell us where the marbles are – or is my ex-SAS friend here going to have to persuade you?'

Jefferson allowed himself a slight smile: 'Even though I admit I'm a devout coward with a very low pain threshold, I don't think you'd resort to violence to get what you wanted. If you did, the only thing that would stop me going straight to the police would be for you to whack me, as the Americans say. And somehow, I can't see you going quite that far. Neither you nor young Rambo here. You're both so terribly, terribly English. Wouldn't be cricket, right?'

Said a seething Athena Papadopoulos: '*I'm* not terribly, terribly English, Jefferson. Neither do I play cricket.'

'Oh, I wouldn't put my premature demise past *you*, madame – or past one of your hired flunkeys. But in any event, you won't have to take me out, as they say. I'll tell you exactly where the marbles are – for a price.' He licked his lips: 'So how much are you prepared to pay for their return?'

Athena Papadopoulos looked at Armitage who nodded, almost imperceptibly. Jefferson's reaction had been more or less as they'd anticipated. She gave Armitage an apologetic shrug and said:

'I am prepared to pay what I had agreed to pay these gentlemen. Three million pounds cash.'

Jefferson thought for a moment. Three million pounds? It was a good start. 'In US dollars?'

'US dollars? As you wish. But payment on delivery. To the island of Thiros.'

'To Thiros?' repeated Jefferson. He shook his head: 'Come now, madame, as you yourself said, you're neither English nor do you play cricket – and Senhor da Sousa and I have no wish to end up as fish fodder, at the bottom of the deep blue sea. No. We make the exchange here. In the UK. And how you get them back to Greece is your problem.'

'You're saying they're back in the United Kingdom?'

'That is for me to know and for you to find out.' He turned towards Beynon: 'Now, if you'd be good enough to unlock that door, I would like to contact Senhor da Souza.'

Said his employer: 'I hope he realises that it will take time to get three million pound's worth of US dollars together, in cash. Even for me.'

'Of course, madame. My partner and I are not unreasonable. Shall we aim for the exchange to take place within a couple of weeks, or so?'

'As you wish.'

At Armitage's signal, Beynon unlocked and opened the door. The butler stalked majestically through the open doorway, turning for an equally majestic:

'And by the way, madame, I hereby give you the required one month's notice.'

That should give him enough time to find a suitable apartment on the promise of all the wealth to come. The door closed behind him.

'Well now,' said Armitage: 'That was all rather interesting.'

'What was?' said a grim-faced Athena Papadopoulos: 'He didn't tell us a thing.'

'On the contrary, we at least know that the marbles are relatively close

to hand – either still aboard the Portuguese salvage ship, which could be hovering somewhere off the English coast, waiting for delivery instructions – or even more likely, aboard an ocean-going fishing trawler that could sail into any British fishing port without attracting too much attention. Remember, da Souza's been in the shipping business for a very long time and he knows all the angles.'

Said Beynon: 'You're saying they could already have been smuggled back into the country?'

'That's what Jefferson implied. And it does make sense.'

'So now what do we do?' asked Athena Papadopoulos.

'We wait for de Sousa to contact us again. There's not much else we can do,' said Armitage, adding enigmatically: 'At the moment.' He rose to his feet: 'We'll be in touch.'

'Wait,' said Athena Papadopoulos quickly: 'I have a proposition for you.'

I'll bet you have, thought Beynon, with an inward grin. And why not? Now she and Armitage had kissed and made up, she obviously wanted to make up for lost time.

'Yes, well,' he said diplomatically: 'I'd best be off. Gavin Messiter needs to know the score.'

He gave Armitage a knowing smile and made for the door. Armitage looked after him, sourly. God, was it that obvious? He wondered why Beynon hadn't given him a broad wink and a big nudge-nudge, while he was about it. To Athena Papadopoulos he said:

'May I use your telephone?'

'Of course.'

She nodded towards pearl-coloured receiver on the coffee table.

'No, not that one. The one Jefferson normally uses.'

'The servants have their own dedicated line. When he's not in his room, Jefferson usually makes do with the one in the hall. But why on earth do you –?'

'Later. This won't wait.'

He walked quickly to the door and out into the hallway.

ɪ ꜱ

'Are you sure this is what gas company officials wear?' asked Lucas dubiously, indicating his bright yellow donkey jacket and peaked cap: 'I feel more like a traffic warden.'

As he had half-anticipated, the whole exercise had descended into total farce. In Lucas's opinion, Anderson's plan was utterly insane and doomed to failure. Who would think for a moment that he was a genuine gas inspector?

'Trust me,' said Anders of the Yard: 'You look fine. And besides, it's your ID that's important – a quick flash of that badge and you could fool anyone.'

Anderson had gone to a great deal of trouble to fabricate the false identity card dangling from Lucas's lapel, having reported a gas-leak at his own home in East Croydon and insisting upon examining the gas inspector's ID in great detail. It is true that the gas company's representative had looked more like an off-duty accountant than a horny-handed son of toil, but Anderson was a great believer in the power of the uniform and had insisted upon Lucas dressing for the part. As they secreted themselves behind a parked car in Belgrave Square, said Anderson, for the umpteenth time:

'Now lad. You know what you've got to do?'

This was it, thought Anderson. His big moment and he struggled to keep his rising excitement under control.

'I think so,' said Lucas.

'Then let me hear it. Just one more time.'

As if by rote, Lucas wearily repeated what Anderson had instructed him to say:

'I go across the road, ring the doorbell and say good afternoon, sir or madame, as the case may be, then I say I'm from the gas company and that we have had a report of a leak and that I need to inspect the premises forthwith. So may I came in?'

'And? *And?*'

'Um? Oh yes. Please refrain from igniting any naked flame until I have finished my inspection – such as a candle or a cigarette."

155

'That's it. Gives your spiel a ring of professional authenticity. All right, son. Off you go.'

Anderson held his breath as Lucas started to make his way across the road, but before he reached the imposing mansion on the other side of the street, the front door was abruptly opened and a vaguely familiar figure was framed in the doorway. Without giving him a second look, the man ran down the short flight of steps and walked briskly in the direction of Hyde Park Corner. Lucas froze in his tracks. It was him! The younger of the two removal men! For a moment he just stood there, debating his next move, oblivious to the odd car and taxi having to swerve around him, with blaring horns and angry abuse. Should he follow him or not? From behind him, he heard Anderson's equally angry shout of:

'What the fuck are you doing?'

Lucas turned and walked quickly back to the ex-policeman and told him. Anderson looked after the disappearing Beynon and almost danced a little jig.

'That's it!' said the elated Anderson: 'Just as I thought! They're all in it together and that's where the bloody marbles are! Go in and check it out, lad!'

'Don't you want me to follow him?'

'No, no, no. The Papadopoulos woman will know where we can find him and his partner and we'll have them picked up later. Just go and finger the marbles and as soon as you have, I'll phone the police and tell them to come mob-handed and seal off the entire Square. Off you go, lad.'

The lad went off, as instructed. He crossed the road, climbed the steps and rang the front doorbell. Anderson watched with eager anticipation as the door opened and a man he immediately recognised as the Greek woman's butler, appeared in the doorway. As Lucas intoned his pre-arranged script, Jefferson gazed coldly at the nervous young man in his yellow donkey jacket and peaked cap, then shook his head. Lucas obviously began to argue with the man, who merely said a few words and closed the door in Lucas's face. Somewhat taken-aback, he retraced his steps to the equally surprised Anderson.

'What happened? Why wouldn't he let you in? He has to. By law.'

'Even if the house is all-electric?'

'What?'

'That's what he told me. I did try to argue with him but he just told me to piss off.'

Said Anderson furiously: 'Damn, blast and bugger it. Just my luck. Of all the houses in Belgrave Square, this is probably the only one without so much as a Bunsen burner. We'll just have to think of something else.' He thought for a moment, then snapped his fingers: 'Got it.' He turned: 'Come on lad, we've got to get you kitted out.'

'Kitted out? As what?'

'Trust me son. We'll get inside that place one way or another. And I know just how to do it.'

Lucas trudged after the erstwhile temporary acting Head of Security with weary resignation. The whole lunatic operation was getting more and more bizarre by the minute. And he felt sure it was all going to end in tears.

8

ARMITAGE WAS GENUINELY PUZZLED. And as Athena Papadopoulos handed him his first drink of the day, he repeated his question:

'What sort of business proposition?'

She poured herself a generous gin and tonic from the nearby decanter and joined him on the couch. She sipped her drink and grimaced. The mix was much too strong. But then, she was not used to doing things for herself and even though Jefferson would still be around for the next seven days or so, her bitter sense of betrayal still rankled and she couldn't bear to look at the odious little man. She could, of course, have kicked him out there and then, but as Armitage had said, it was better for them to know just where he was at all times, just in case da Souza decided to make a personal appearance.

'Now listen to me, John J. Armitage,' she said, choosing her words with great care: 'And please do not interrupt. First, do you still insist upon abiding by the terms of our original deal – that is payment only on delivery of the marbles, back to Greece, by you and your associates?' She looked at him speculatively: 'Even if I was prepared to pay twice over for their return? Once to you and once to Jefferson and da Souza?'

Said Armitage firmly: 'A deal's a deal. It's up to us to get them back without you having you to pay those bastards one, single penny.'

She frowned. Damn the man and his principles. It was like trying to negotiate with a boy scout. Why couldn't he see it was only money? But there more ways than one of threading a camel through the eye of a cobbler's needle, as her late father used to say.

'I thought that might be your answer, so I've been giving the matter some very serious thought,' she continued: 'And I have come to the conclusion that you really deserve *something* for all your efforts. After all, had it not been for the three of you, the marbles would still be safely locked up inside the British Museum. That is why I wish to put to you a purely business proposition – and no,' she added quickly: 'Not an executive position within the Papadopoulos group of companies. A position where you would be your own master, answerable only to yourself.' She took a deep breath: 'I would like to re-finance your business.'

Armitage gave a grunt of amusement: 'What business? The creditors are already queuing up to take the shirt off my back, as well you know.'

'I also know that *Armitage Transport International*, which you built up from scratch, was once one of the biggest companies in its field and could be again. With you running it and with the banks off your back.'

'And you owning it? No thanks.'

'Not owning it, John. Just investing in it. As a shareholder. With you holding fifty-one percent of the equity.'

She took another sip of her gin and tonic and watched his face. If that didn't ensure that he'd always be around and enable them to continue their relationship – with his admirable, if misplaced, English sense of decency and fair-play still totally intact – she didn't know what would. It was her only hope. He stared thoughtfully into his glass.

'I am a businesswoman,' she continued evenly: 'Not a charity. I only invest in businesses that I believe will show me a profit. And with you in charge and no cash-flow problems, a revitalised Armitage International could well prove to be a very sound investment.'

He took another sip of his drink and, after a long pause: 'I have to admit, it's a very interesting proposition.'

At least, he reflected, if they did fail to out-smart de Souza, which would mean them losing their three million quid, they would still come out of the affair with something to show for their time and trouble. Once he had the business up and running again, he would be able to help out Messiter in his hour of financial need and provide Beynon with well-paid, gainful employment.

'Thank you, Athena,' he said, finally: 'That's a very generous offer. And because I believe that you would be making a sound investment, I accept.'

'Good. And I hope you will also accept an invitation to dinner.'

Armitage smiled: 'It would give me great pleasure.'

Almost as much pleasure, thought Athena Papadopoulos, with a secret little smile, as he would soon be giving *her*. Immediately after dinner.

⬧

'I cooked this myself,' said a fetchingly domestic Julie Baker, in a pretty apron and matching oven-gloves, but with a total disregard for the truth. She placed the impressive steak and kidney pie on the dining room table and invited her house-guest to take a seat. The truth be known, her mother had prepared more than enough food for the entire weekend and all her daughter had had to do was take it out of the refridgerator and put it into the oven, on gas mark regulo seven. As an only child, happily over-indulged by her doting parents, she had never felt the need to acquire even the most basic of culinary skills, a fact which she had decided was not something she should readily admit to a possible partner for life – at least, not until after their nuptials. The Possible Partner for Life was staring gloomily into his glass of warm white wine, which his domestically-challenged hostess had neglected to chill.

'I also peeled and mashed the potatoes,' she volunteered, with an equal lack of veracity: 'And shelled the peas.'

161

Both vegetables had, in fact, been microwaved from frozen, but her guest did not need to know that. In the event, Barry Lucas didn't really care if she'd also organically grown the vegetables in her back garden and personally slaughtered the beast that had provided them with the ingredients for the steak and kidney pie. For despite being alone at last with the living, breathing, quite exquisite creature who had become the focal point of his affections, Lucas was not a happy man.

'D'you know what he wants me to do this time?' he asked his hostess: 'Impersonate a feller from the water company.'

'Oh yes?' said his hostess, vaguely, wondering just how one carved a steak and kidney pie. Her father always carved the Sunday joint, but this wasn't a joint, was it?

'Why don't you do it?' she said suddenly, holding out the large knife and fork towards him.

'Do what?'

'Carve the steak and kidney pie.'

'Don't you mean dish it up?'

'Dish it up, yes.'

'All right. But I'll need a big spoon. And a metal slice for the pastry.'

'Of course you will. I was just about to get them.'

She disappeared back into the kitchen. Her Possible Partner for Life actually seemed to know what he was doing. It was all rather promising. She wondered if he could cook, too. An hour or so later, after he had cleared the table and stacked the dishwasher, he joined her in on the living room couch, where she was sipping a *Tia Maria* and watching television.

'That was very nice of you, Barry. Thank you.'

'Not at all,' said Lucas, still not quite sure just how he had ended up in the kitchen, wearing rubber gloves and an apron, scraping leftovers into a bin and wiping down the working surfaces. At her invitation, he helped himself to a liberal shot from her father's cherished decanter of single malt whisky and joined her on the couch. The images on the flickering television screen were those of a fictional policeman, in the act of arresting a baleful malefactor for some sort of transgression or other.

Impersonation of a utilities company official was also against the law, he reminded himself morosely. And what would happen to him if he was nicked in the act? What if the butler, despite him now being in the guise of an official from the water company, recognised him as the very same person who'd claimed to be from the gas company, a couple of days earlier? But Anderson had just brushed his question aside with an airy:

'That had occurred to me, too, lad. So on went my thinking cap and the answer came in a flash. Trust me. He won't suspect a thing. And why? Because you'll be wearing a false moustache, that's why.'

A false moustache, for Christ's sake! What if the bloody thing came unstuck and fell off, halfway through his inspection? The whole plan was becoming more and more lunatic by the minute. So why didn't he just call it a day and tell Anders of the Yard that he couldn't go through with it? He already knew why. Because no matter what, he felt so sorry for the pathetic old fart, he just hadn't the heart to let him down. Julie Baker studied his troubled expression, took his arm, draped it around her shoulders, snuggled up to him and said:

'What's worrying you, sunshine?'

He told her. In great detail. She felt a sudden rush of genuine concern for her nice, kind, put-upon, Possible Partner for Life. Like he'd said, he was a fool to himself. But he was also extremely stubborn and she knew that nothing she could say or do would make him change his mind and tell the idiotic Anderson to take a running jump.

She kissed him gently on the cheek. This was it. The moment of truth. The one that would finally put their relationship to the test. A test upon which their whole future life together would depend.

'Tell you what,' she said softly: 'Why don't we both sleep on it? Things always seem much better in the morning.'

She rose from the couch, took the somewhat surprised but not unwilling Lucas by the hand and led him out of the room and towards the stairs, fervently hoping that before the night was over, even if he hadn't exactly made the earth move for her, he would at least have rattled the odd window-frame.

[s]

'Let's run through what we know,' said Gavin Messiter, as they sat around his living room table.

'Not a great deal,' admitted Armitage: 'Except that the marbles are almost certainly back in the UK and probably stored in some remote warehouse or other, awaiting collection.'

Said Messiter: 'Getting down to the practicalities, how do they intend to make the exchange?'

'Jefferson has told Athena Papadopoulos he'll be expecting the money to be handed to him in a suitcase and as soon as he's counted it, he'll phone de Souza to tell him it's okay to reveal the exact location of the marbles – which we'll then be able to go and pick up.'

'Providing,' said Messiter: 'That when you do eventually turn up at the warehouse, or wherever, with one of your pantechnicons, the marbles will still be there. If they were there in the first place.'

'The whole thing stinks,' grunted Beynon: 'We could end up with bugger all, while Jefferson walks off into the sunset with our three million quid under his arm.'

'Which,' suggested Messiter: 'Would then enable them to do a deal with the British Museum, right?'

Armitage shook his head: 'No. Da Souza knew we'd never go for that and he has agreed that Jefferson would stick around until we telephoned Athena and told her we were in possession of the marbles and that they were the genuine article. Of course,' he added casually: 'If we find out where they are being stored in advance of the exchange, she won't have to pay them a penny.'

Said Messiter: 'And how do we do that?'

'That may not,' said Armitage slowly: 'Be as quite as difficult as it might seem.'

Said Beynon dryly: 'Convince me.'

Armitage sipped his coffee and said: 'Da Souza had to have Jefferson's phone number to stay in contact and it suddenly occurred to me that as there's a completely different telephone system in Portugal, de Souza might not have been familiar with the British system that allows you to keep your own number secret – by punching in one-four-seven, before dialling out.'

'And?' asked Messiter.

'And so, over the last couple of days, while going through the re-financing deal with Athena Papadopoulos and her lawyers, I took time out to made regular one-four-seven-*one* last-caller checks on all incoming calls on her servants' line. And one particular number came up time after time.'

'Da Souza's?' said Beynon.

Armitage nodded: 'His mobile. I recognised his voice immediately.'

Said Messiter: 'By the same token, are you sure he didn't recognise yours?'

'Pretty sure. I just muttered a 'sorry, mate, wrong number' in a cor-blimey accent and put the receiver down.'

'But how does that help us?' asked Beynon.

'I'm hoping it will help us to arrange a meeting between Da Souza and Jefferson – and find out just where they're holding the marbles.'

'Bit of a long shot, isn't it?' said Messiter dubiously: 'Da Souza's no fool. He'd smell a rat immediately.'

'Unless he took a call from Jefferson saying he had to see him urgently.'

'You've lost me. John. Why should Jefferson do that?'

'Jefferson wouldn't. But one of us would. Which one of us, would obviously depend upon who can do the best imitation of an extremely agitated British butler.'

Beynon and Messiter exchanged a look.

'Oh come on,' said Beynon: 'You mean impersonate Jefferson's voice on the phone? We'd never get away with it.'

Messiter agreed: 'We do seem to be entering the realms of science fiction.'

Intoned Armitage, in a passable imitation of the butler's measured enunciation: 'With respect, sir – or entirely without it – have you got a better idea?'

The following Monday morning, in a state of some excitement, the British Museum's Director of Operations called Barry Lucas into his office and handed him a letter. In doing so, Munro felt that his softly-softly approach to the theft of the marbles and his decision to keep the police out of it had been totally vindicated. Right from the start, he'd maintained that it would only be a matter of time before the Museum would be contacted by the thieves – and the letter proved it. The ransom note was short and to the point. It read:

The Elgin Marbles are now up for auction. An opening bid of three million pounds has already been received. If you would care to make an improved offer for their safe return, kindly indicate your willingness to do so by running up the flag of St. George on the main British Museum flagpole. If you are successful in your bid, you will then be contacted to arrange how, when and where the exchange will be made. Do not bring in the police or you will never see the Marbles again. I will telephone you in exactly one week's time.

'The letter could be a fake, of course,' said the Director: 'But even if there's the slightest chance of us regaining the marbles, it must be checked out. That's why I want you to find a flag of St. George and run it up the flagpole.'

Barry Lucas studied the note with some difficulty. After spending an entire weekend in the company of the quite wondrous and exceedingly energetic Julie Baker, he was so weary, he could scarcely keep his eyes open. He had come to work in a state of dazed euphoria. It would appear that right from the start, she had intended the long weekend to be a sort of dummy run for what might be ahead of them and, even more importantly, it seemed that he'd successfully negotiated the amorous obstacle course to her complete satisfaction. In a manner of speaking. He re-read the letter and shook his head bemusedly:

'It doesn't make sense, sir. If Mr Anderson is right and Athena Papadopoulos is in possession of the marbles, why should she wish to put them up for auction?'

'Anderson? What's he got to do with it?'

'He believes he knows where they're hidden.'

'And where's that?'

Lucas told him.

'Then why didn't he tell me?'

'He wasn't sure you'd believe him.'

Munro nodded in agreement: 'I'm not sure I would, either. The man's a complete buffoon. But even though I think it's highly unlikely that the marbles are hidden somewhere inside the Papadopoulos mansion, we can't dismiss it out of hand. We'll have to check that out, too.'

'And how would we do that, sir?'

'I'll have a discreet word with a certain Metropolitan Police Chief Superintendent.'

'But I thought you wanted to keep the police out of it.'

'Officially, yes. But the Superintendent also happens to be a fellow Freemason and member of my Lodge. If I ask him to inspect the premises, on some vague sort of pretext or another – a security check, for instance, at the request of and behalf of the local neighbourhood watch – I'm sure he won't find that a problem. That's what the Grand Order of Freemasons is all about.'

All Lucas knew about the mysterious world of Freemasons and their Masonic Lodges was that it was some sort of all-male international secret society, where its members allegedly entertained each other by rolling up their trouser legs and hitting each other's knee-caps with little hammers. Or so he'd read, somewhere or other. Even so, he could hardly conceal his elation. He'd done it. He'd got out from under. No dressing up as a water board official with a dodgy mustache, supposedly searching for a leak. And if Anderson proved to be right, the temporary acting Head of Security would still get all the credit. Well, some of the credit. The Director would undoubtedly demand *his* pound of marbles.

'But what if it turns out that the marbles aren't inside the house?'

The Director gave a thin smile: 'Then Mr Anderson will have scored yet another own goal.'

'You told the Director?' said an outraged Anderson, as they walked into the staff canteen: 'How could you do that to me, lad? It was my idea – not his. Now he'll get all the kudos.'

'Not necessarily,' said Lucas, reassuringly: 'If you're proved to be right, I'll make sure everyone knows whose hunch it was. And you have to admit that a genuine Chief Superintendent from the Metropolitan Police with authentic credentials makes much more sense than a young bloke with a stick-on mustache, pretending to be from the water company.'

Anderson sighed and chewed miserably on his sticky bun: 'I suppose you're right. But dammit all, son, I've put a lot of time and trouble in arranging your water company identity card, getting together the official clobber and finding the right mustache – and what am I going to do with it all?'

Lucas was severely tempted to tell him, but resisted the impulse. Like Hamish Munro, he also believed that it seemed highly unlikely that Athena Papadopoulos would be foolish enough to fill her house with artefacts illegally removed from the British Museum. But they'd soon know. The Chief Superintendent had promised to report back later that day and the least Lucas could do was try and prepare the temporary acting Head of Security for yet another disappointment.

Said Lucas gently: 'Look, chief. There is a strong possibility that he may not find a thing.'

'D'you think I don't know that, lad?' snapped Anderson: 'And if he doesn't find anything – d'you know why? Because the marbles will have already been shifted out of the house and put aboard some ship for transportation to Greece.'

'If they were in the house in the first place.'

'Oh, they were there all right, son. Take my word for it. And if we'd gone in there from day one like I wanted, they'd be back in the British Museum by now.'

In other words, thought Lucas wearily, don't confuse me with the facts. The man was impossible. He tried again:

'Then if the marbles are still in the possession of Athena Papadopoulos, why did the Director get a ransom note?'

Anderson's nose quivered like a mouse scenting cheese: 'Ransom note? What ransom note?'

'Of course, you don't know about that, do you? Someone sent the Director a note saying the marbles were now up for auction. And if Athena Papadopoulos is sitting on them, she'd hardly be offering to sell them back to the Museum, would she?'

Anderson paled. Bloody hell. If the ransom note turned out to be genuine, then his theory was shot to pieces. If the damned woman did prove to be in the clear, he was going to look a right berk. It wasn't right. It wasn't fair. He was positive that she was involved in the heist, in one way or another. Dammit, even Lucas had thought he'd seen one of the two men who'd driven off with the marbles, coming out of her house. It just didn't make sense. But no matter what, it seemed that once again, everything had gone pear-shaped, lemon-shaped, banana-shaped, every fucking shape.

Lucas noted his sudden dejection with a touch of pity 'Don't let it get you down, chief,' he said gently: 'You can't win 'em all.'

Anderson heaved a sigh: 'I don't want to win 'em all, son. Just one.' He rose to his feet: 'Just one.'

He walked gloomily out of the canteen. Lucas watched him go. Poor old sod. Another day, another slap in the face for one of life's walking wounded.

*

As both the Director and Lucas had anticipated, the search of Athena Papadopoulos's house had revealed nothing. The Chief Superintendent's credentials had been accepted without question and the mansion had been thoroughly checked out from top to bottom. Athena Papadopoulos, on one of her many shopping excursions to the fashionable emporiums of Knightsbridge and Bond Street, had not even been aware of the inspection, until well after the event and had accepted it for what it was – or, more accurately, for what it wasn't.

A little while later, a flag bearing the simple red cross of St. George of England was stirring leisurely in the gentle summer breeze at the top of the Museum's main flagpole. From his vantage point in Museum Street, Jefferson had watched its jerky elevation with deep satisfaction. So far, so good. He was going to enjoy informing Athena Papadopoulos that she might well have to improve her offer of a measly three million quid. It had been his idea to play one against the other. Neither he nor da Souza gave a damn as to who eventually ended up with the marbles and why settle for three of a kind when you could well end up with a royal flush? And in spades?

All they had to do now was take the money and run. Life was good. And it could only get better. Afterall, what could possibly go wrong now?

Watched by Beynon and Messiter, Armitage first dialled one-four-seven, then punched in the number of da Souza's mobile. The traffic outside the carefully chosen telephone booth close to Charing Cross Station was loud and unremitting. Da Souza answered the call on the second ring.

'Listen to me, Senhor da Souza,' said Armitage urgently, in the sonorous tones of his accomplice: 'This very important and I have to make it quick. Things have gone very wrong and I need to see you urgently.' He held the phone away from his ear a da Souza's alarmed voice squawked from the handset: 'I do apologise most profoundly for the noise but I'm phoning from a telephone box in the West End. Pardon me? Because all the phones in the house are being tapped – so you must not try to telephone me there.' Another squawk. 'No. I'll tell you when I see you. Just tell me where.' Armitage listened carefully: 'At what time? Very well. See you then.'

He slammed down the receiver before da Souza could say another word and opened the door of the phone booth. To the anxiously waiting Beynon and Messiter, he said, dryly:

'John J. Armitage. Man of a thousand voices.'

Said Beynon: 'He bought it? He actually bought it?'

'Seems so. The traffic noise did seem to help.'

'So where and when?' asked Messiter.

'Liverpool Street station. Platform eight. He's getting the first train from Lowestoft. It should get in around seven o'clock this evening.'

'Lowestoft?' repeated Beynon: 'That's a fishing port, isn't it?'

Armitage nodded: 'On the East Anglian coast. Close to Southwold and Alderburgh. With long stretches of pretty deserted coastline in between.'

Said Messiter: 'Seems you were right, John. It would be an ideal place for a drop-off.'

Armitage glanced at his watch and said: 'As I happen to know a rather pleasant little Italian restaurant within walking distance of Liverpool Street station, I suggest we get over there, order a halfway decent bottle of Chianti and a little pasta. It's going to be a long night.' He looked at Messiter with some concern: 'Especially for you, Gavin. You're the only one of the three of us who da Souza has yet to meet. But of course, if you don't feel up to it...'

'Oh, I'm up to it,' snapped Messiter: 'I want to nail those bastards even more than you do. Now stop fussing and let's get over there.'

Armitage raised an arm and hailed a passing taxi. Despite his reservations, he knew better than to argue with a bloody-minded old age pensioner who, having been effectively divested of his pension by a now fugitive, once captain of industry, had devoted the last few months of his life to getting even and who had no intention of giving up now.

•

As skipper and sole owner of the now sunken *SS Rosetta*, Captain Jaime Carlos António José da Souza was well acquainted with the Port of Lowestoft. Significantly, Lowestoft was not only one of England's designated fishing ports, with a centuries old fish market, it was also a thriving centre for bulk container and general cargoes – and da Souza's itinerant tramp steamer had been regularly chartered to transport a wide range of equipment and topside deck structures into Lowestoft, destined for the various North Sea off-shore gas and oil fields.

Because of this, da Souza knew every inch of the shoreline along most of that part of the East Coast and the surrounding countryside. After spending several days, sometimes weeks at sea, having to dine on an unappetising diet of rather less than *cordon bleu* fare, provided by the somewhat unhygienic ship's cook, on reaching Lowestoft, he had used his days ashore to explore the busy little seaside town and its environs, in search of food, wine and rather more convivial company than his equally unhygienic crew. And he had rarely been disappointed. To his surprise and pleasure, it seemed that the normally demure and reserved English female holidaymaker, when far away from home and well out of sight of her friends and neighbours, often cast all her inhibitions to the wind. Which is why he'd long had a great affection for what Lowestoft had to offer and on this, his latest visit to the town, he was looking forward to it being not only most pleasurable, but extremely profitable.

That evening, in anticipation of the riches to come, he had struck up a conversation with a plumply pretty, middle-aged lady in one of the town's most fashionable bars in the nearby Kirkley, the up-market esplanade just south of the town. He had been about to order a bottle of vintage champagne, to be followed by an invitation to accompany him back to his rented accommodation for a euphemistic night-cap, when his mobile telephone had shrilled out its unwelcome message. Despite the background noise of the London traffic, the urgency in his business associate's normally sonorous tones had been most pronounced and had forced him to make his apologies to the lady by his side and take the first train into London Liverpool Street. She had looked after the departing da Souza with genuine regret. It wasn't often that a lonely, middle-aged widow attracted the attention of a charming foreign sea captain who, despite his somewhat grubby uniform, was obviously affluent enough to order vintage champagne.

The train arrived at Liverpool Street station exactly on time and da Souza emerged through the barrier of platform eight into the bustling forecourt. He scanned the station for the first sign of the diminutive English butler, who would be immediately distinguishable by his measured tread and permanently doleful expression. Indeed, Jefferson's entire demeanour had always reminded da Souza of his local Portuguese undertaker who, when walking majestically down the village street, leading a funeral procession in which the dear departed occupied the traditional, horse-driven hearse, he always managed to look far more miserable than the po-faced professional mourners hired especially for the occasion. The undertaker's air of gloom and despondency was almost palpable and would send the grieving relatives of the deceased into a frenzy of anguish, dabbing their eyes to stem the flow of sometimes real, but mostly crocodile, tears.

And whether he was aware of it or not, the English butler, with his depressingly woeful expression, was born to be an undertaker and had obviously, if unknowingly, chosen the wrong profession. Be that as it may, reflected da Souza grimly, Jefferson's barely intelligible telephone call demanding an urgent meeting had ruined what had promised to be a most rewarding social occasion and if his journey proved to be quite unnecessary then, he promised himself, the butler might well require the services of his own local undertaker.

'There he is,' said Armitage, from the top of the distant escalator: 'The man in the black jacket, epaulets and the gold-braided peaked cap.'

From the upper floor of the once dingy, soot-encrusted Victorian railway terminus, but now transformed into a modern, gleaming shopping mall and central concourse, Armitage, Messiter and Beynon gazed down at the figure far below them. Messiter peered over the rail and said:

'Does he always go around dressed like someone straight out of a touring version of *HMS Pinafore?*'

Armitage grinned: 'Most of the time, yes. And he's all yours. We've got to keep out of his way.'

'Just one question. What if he gets fed up with waiting for Jefferson to turn up and despite the warning, decides to try and phone him – or even go directly to Belgrave Square?'

Armitage tapped his pocket: 'That's when the Jefferson sound-alike will phone *him*.'

'But whatever happens, Gavin,' said Beynon: 'Make sure you stick to da Souza like sugar to a blanket.'

Messiter gave a sniff of disapproval: 'What an inelegant phrase, young Ken. But even though I'm not ex-SAS, I'll do my best.'

He made for the elevator and began to descend to the lower level, where he bought a magazine from the nearby bookstall and took up a position below the electronic train departures indicator, almost immediately opposite platform eight. A few yards away, da Souza paced up and down in front of the platform eight barrier and was already beginning to glance impatiently at his watch. From their position on the upper level, Armitage and Beynon looked down at the distant da Souza and the discreetly anonymous Messiter – and the waiting began.

&

Jefferson was well aware that like most national institutions, it would take time for the British Museum to raise the sort of sum that he and da Souza were obviously expecting and, with da Souza's agreement, he had waited several days before telephoning the Director of Operations from the anonymity of a public telephone box. The Director's response had been sadly predictable, with a craven and misguided plea to the butler's better nature. Didn't the idiot understand that in a situation such as this, with so much at stake, no one could afford the luxury of a better nature?

'Good God, man,' the Director had pleaded: 'We're not the Royal Mint. We have very limited resources and while we'll do our best to make a matching offer, as an Englishman – and from your voice, I assume you are English – how could you even contemplate selling one of England's national treasures to a third party? Haven't you an ounce of decency left in you?'

Jefferson had give the question his due consideration and replied:

'Can't say that I have, no. Now please dispense with the muted violins and talk business. Otherwise, you won't hear from me again. Shall we start off with an opening bid of five million, which I'll then put to the other party?'

Hamish Munro looked at Lucas, Anderson and resident architect J.C. Caldwell, who were now gathered around the extension speaker attached to the telephone and made a gesture of despair.

'Very well,' he snarled into the mouthpiece: 'I don't know how I'm going to be able to raise that sort of money but...'He paused: 'Hallo? *Hallo!*' He replaced the receiver: 'He rang off.' To Anderson, he said: 'Did you manage to record it?'

Anderson fiddled with the telephone answering machine, which he had been ordered to purchase from an electrical shop in the nearby Tottenham Court Road and said:

'I think so, Director. Not that it'll be much use. He sounded as if he was talking with his mouth full of marbles.'

As soon as he'd said it, from the way the Director glared at him, he realised his unfortunate choice of words had hit a nerve.

'What I mean,' he said hastily: 'Is that he muffled his voice.'

'That was bloody obvious,' snapped the Director: 'So you're saying there's no point in trying to get a voice print.'

Anderson shook his head: 'Or trying to trace the call. He'll be long gone by now.'

The Director sighed: 'God only knows where we're going to get the money from. We'll get no sympathy from the Minister for the Arts and all we'll get from the National Lottery Board is the finger. They prefer to lash out on such worthy causes as Gay Accountants Against the Bomb.'

J.C. Caldwell gave an inward smile. Such anger. Such bitterness. Such incompetence. It was time to increase the little man's angst.

'Don't you think, Director?'he inquired innocently: 'That we should now inform the Museum's powers-that-be of the situation? Perhaps they could come up with an answer.'

Hopefully, the first one being to rid themselves of a Director of Operations they should never have appointed in the first place and replace him with someone far better qualified to run the Museum with the efficiency it deserved. Some one such as himself, for example – and at an annual salary far in excess of what he was currently being paid as chief resident architect. But by the way Munro pointedly ignored his suggestion, it would appear his hope was in vain. It was Barry Lucas who broke the silence.

'If the whole thing is not just a very elaborate scam,' he said thoughtfully: 'What I'd like to know is the identity of the so-called other party.'

'We already know who it is,' grunted Anderson, stubbornly: 'The Papadopoulos woman.'

The Director looked at him with rising irritation: 'We've already been through that and fallen flat on our faces on both occasions.'

'With respect, sir,' interposed Lucas quickly: 'I still think Mr. Anderson might have a point. Afterall, who else would be prepared to pay a small fortune to get her hands on the marbles and who also has the money to do it?'

Hamish Munro digested the thought, then said: 'If you are correct, what do you think we should do about it?'

'It may seem to be rather obvious, sir, but I think we should stake out her house in Belgrave Square and see who comes and goes. As Mr Anderson knows, I was pretty sure that the last time we were there, one of her visitors was the man who drove the truck that went off with the marbles.'

Munro gave the suggestion further consideration. Then after a pause:

'Very well, Mr. Lucas. Go to it.' To Anderson he said: 'You too, Anderson. There's little else we can do at the moment.'

Anderson ignored the pointed reference to himself as merely Anderson and his erstwhile very junior assistant as *Mr* Lucas and turned towards the door. As they walked across the concourse towards the main entrance, he muttered a grudging:

'I owe you one, lad.'

Or two. Or three, thought Lucas. Bailing the old fart out once again did have its drawbacks. How was he going to tell his beloved that he'd be spending most of his days and nights in a London square, sitting in his battered old banger of a car outside Athena Papadopoulos's house and that their social life would have to be put on hold? With great difficulty, he told himself despondently. He could only hope that if he were to be deprived of the pleasure of her company for a very extended period, his frustration would not be the cause of him developing a nervous tic. Afterall, he was not made of plastic, was he? And, he had recently and happily discovered, neither was the delightful Julie Baker.

☞

Da Souza paced the station concourse in front of platform eight for almost an hour, before giving a gesture of resignation and reaching for his mobile telephone. With the phone in his hand, he hesitated, obviously concerned about his business partner's supposedly dire warning not to telephone him at home, which gave the watching Armitage the opportunity to quickly punch in his number.

As the phone shrilled in his hand, da Souza looked at it suspiciously, and then put it to his ear. Watched by Beynon from the upper floor and by the nearby Messiter, da Souza listened silently as Armitage again adopted the butler's sonorous, if agitated, tones to whisper that he believed he was being followed and that he didn't want to lead whoever it was to their meeting place. There was a sudden, loud click from the station's Tannoy system and Armitage gave a silent curse as the station announcer's voice flooded the concourse with travel information.

He switched off his phone immediately, praying that da Souza had not latched on the fact that the announcer's voice had also come out of his telephone – and realise that his caller was actually in the immediate vicinity. He breathed a sigh of relief when da Souza just stared at the silent

177

telephone, shaking his head in puzzled frustration. He then replaced it in his pocket, glanced up at the electronic indicator board and walked slowly back through the barrier of platform eight, obviously intent on catching the next train back to Lowestoft, where presumably and when it was safe to do so, Jefferson would again try to contact him.

Messiter put his magazine into his raincoat pocket, glanced up at the watching Beynon and Armitage and gave them a slight nod. He then followed the Portuguese captain through the barrier of platform eight and climbed on to the waiting train. The two men on the upper floor made their way down the escalator to the main concourse, where they headed for the underground station to start their journey back to Kent. Gavin Messiter was now all on his own and all they could do was hope that he would have the good fortune and, above all, the stamina, to discover exactly what they all were all desperately eager to know.

9

IT WAS LATE IN THE EVENING when the train finally pulled into Lowestoft station. The journey had been quite uneventful, if rather slow, the remaining passengers having had to change trains at Norwich for the final leg. There were few other passengers at that time of night and while he had followed da Sousa into the same coach at Liverpool Street, Messiter had been careful enough not to get too close to his quarry. He had taken a seat at one end of the compartment, well away from, but within sight of, the Portuguese captain, who spent most of the journey gazing blindly out of the window, his body language that of a confused and troubled man, struggling with difficulty to make sense of what was apparently happening to him and his business associate.

After they had arrived at Norwich, Messiter again followed da Souza on to an adjoining platform, where they both boarded the small local train that would take them the final thirty-five miles or so to the Lowestoft town centre. The town was at the end of the line and as the train pulled into the station, da Souza shook himself out of his uneasy reverie and stepped out on to the platform, his shambling sailor's gait taking him towards the station's main exit. Messiter followed at a discreet distance, which was just as well, for, without warning and for no apparent reason, da Souza paused at the entrance to the ticket hall and turned to scan the platform behind him, as if checking the faces of the remaining passengers for some signs of familiarity.

Rather than get any closer to his quarry, without thinking, Messiter found himself dropping on to one arthritic knee to tie his perfectly knotted shoe lace, at the same time angrily chiding himself for not simply walking past the man who would have had no reason whatsoever to suspect that he was being followed by a somewhat fragile geriatric who, at that time of night, really belonged in bed with a cup of nourishing *Sanatogen*. SAS material, Messiter grimly told himself, he obviously wasn't.

By the time he had finished his unnecessary task and pulled himself painfully to his feet, da Souza had disappeared into the hall and, when Messiter finally emerged from the station and into the small forecourt, the captain was already climbing into a taxi. The taxi moved smartly out of the station, followed by the two remaining vehicles which had already been commandeered by a couple of fellow travellers. Messiter muttered a furious expletive and looked around him, in some agitation. The little forecourt was empty of any other form of transport and, Messiter told himself bitterly, by the time another taxi turned up, da Souza would have long disappeared into the night for a place or places unknown. He sank down on the nearest bench and cursed his own stupidity. He'd blown it. He'd lost his quarry. And the three million pounds that went with him. He fumbled in his pocket for his mobile telephone and, with a deepening sense of depression, punched in John Armitage's number. Curiously, Armitage seemed to take the news in his stride:

'You did your best, Gavin. But it's not over yet. Did you get the taxi's number?'

'No.'

'No matter. All you have to do is hang around the station and wait until it returns to the taxi rank and ask the driver where he took his last fare.'

Said Messiter angrily: 'How can I do that when I don't know which bloody taxi he took?'

'Calm down. Gavin. You'll ask the driver of every cab as it comes in, obviously. And when you describe the man you were supposed to meet – but sadly missed – you'll soon know if you've found the right cab. Afterall, whoever drove off with him couldn't have had all that many customers dressed up like a comic-opera admiral, straight out of Gilbert and Sullivan.'

Messiter thought for a moment, then admitted grudgingly: 'You could be right, John. I'll get back to you.'

He switched off his phone, just as a now empty taxicab drove into the station forecourt and came to a halt in front of him. Messiter rose to his feet, adopted the totally spurious air of a confused and bewildered senior citizen and said, plaintively:

'I wonder if you could help me?'

☞

'I'll leave you to it, lad,' said the temporary acting Head of Security as he opened the passenger door of Barry Lucas's rusting Ford Fiesta: 'I'll take over in the afternoon. And remember – '

'I know, Chief,' said Lucas wearily: 'Constant vigilance.'

Anderson nodded and walked smartly out of Belgrave Square, in the direction of the nearest underground. Lucas settled down in his seat, already having grave doubts about the wisdom of teaming up again with his erstwhile superior. For a start, it had not been easy to convince his beloved that volunteering to put Athena Papadopoulos's house under surveillance over the next few days was a good career move. For him and therefore, for her.

Julie Baker had pouted and said: 'But I thought we were going away for the weekend. I mean,' she continued crossly: 'It could be weeks before my parents spend another few days away from home and how can we be sure if we're really suited after just a single, one-night stand?'

'Two nights,' said Lucas automatically: 'And a half,' he added, recalling with pleasure an unexpected early morning awakening by his enthusiastic *amoureuse*.

'Well, whatever – and even though so far, I've no complaints in the nooky department, how can I be sure that you're the right feller for me, if those crummy marbles are far more important to you than I am?'

'Of course they're not. The thing is, if I can pull this off –'

'Because I'll tell you this, sunshine,' she went on fiercely: 'I've no intention of ending up like my Auntie Cissie, married to a man who turned out to be far more interested in squatting in front of the television, a can of lager in one hand and a bag of cheese and onion crisps in the other – when he should have been taking his wife to bed for a little bit of TLC.'

'TLC?'

'Tender Loving Care,' she elucidated patiently, before taking his hand in hers and saying earnestly: 'Marriage is far too important to me, Barry. And I'm not going to make the same mistake she did.'

Lucas had felt quite touched. It was, for her, quite a speech and obviously came straight from the heart.

'Look,' he said softly: 'You won't have to. I promise you, when this is all over, I'll really make it up to you. We'll have so much fun, you won't know if you're coming or going.' He reddened and added hastily: 'I meant in a manner of speaking.'

She had looked at him over the counter of the souvenir shop and burst into laughter:

'You big, daft, soft, lump. You do make me laugh. Off you go then. But if you do end up with the marbles, have someone else do all the heavy lifting. You'll be no good to me with a double hernia.'

Her laughter had followed him out of the souvenir shop. Things could have been worse, he reflected. There was a tap on his car side window. The traffic warden was polite but firm:

'You'll have to move on, sir. This is a residents' parking bay only.'

'I'm not parked.' He nodded towards the Papadopoulos mansion: 'I'm waiting to pick someone up.'

The warden glanced at the house, then took in the battered Ford Fiesta. In a clapped-out tin can like that? A likely story.

'You'll still have to move on, sir.'

Lucas sighed, switched on the engine and drove off around the square. Which is why he failed to see John J. Armitage disembark from a black cab and climb the few steps to Athena Papadopoulos's front door.

☞

Said Athena Papadopoulos angrily, as her housekeeper poured the coffee: 'I've been trying to call you – but even though I know you picked up my text messages, you never phoned me back. As usual.'

'Yes, well,' said Armitage: 'I've been pretty busy.' He waited until the housekeeper left the room and closed the door firmly behind her: 'I've got some news for you.'

'And I've got some news for you. Jefferson's price has gone up. It seems that the British Museum has offered five million pounds for the return of the marbles.'

'Ah,' said Armitage slowly: 'So he's playing each one of us off against the other, is he?' He sighed: 'Can't say I'm surprised. What was your response?'

'I told him I'd have to discuss it with you. If and when I was able to get in touch with you,' she added pointedly: 'Now what have you got to tell me?'

'Simply this. We've found out that da Souza's renting an old farmhouse, about seven or eight miles south of Lowestoft, going towards Aldeburgh.'

'Lowestoft?'

'Suffolk. It's right on the coast – and the farmhouse just so happens to be in a pretty lonely spot. It used to be a working farm and most of the outbuildings are still there, but since the floods of some years ago, it's been rented out as a holiday home.'

'An ideal place to bring the marbles ashore, presumably.'

'Especially at night. And the outbuildings would provide ample storage space. I initially thought that they would have been brought in via the Port of Lowestoft itself, but it makes much more sense to have used a barge or tender to load the marbles from a freighter a little way out to sea

– and bring them ashore there. According to Gavin Messiter, who checked the place out, there is a deep water inlet that goes directly to the farm's private beach.'

She looked at him, thoughtfully: 'What do you propose to do next?'

'Stall for time until I can really find out just what we'll be up against if we drive out to the farm and try to grab the marbles.'

As Beynon had pointed out, for all they knew, they could be guarded by a possibly armed bunch of da Souza's hairy-arsed Portuguese crewmembers. And in the meantime, it was now obviously essential to keep a very low profile, for at the first sign of trouble, Jefferson and da Souza would doubtlessly try to close a deal with the British Museum.

'Is Jefferson still around?' he asked suddenly.

'Unfortunately, yes. Even though he's had the sense to keep well out of my way and send in my housekeeper.'

'Call him in.'

'What?'

'I want you to grit your teeth and raise your bid for the marbles, which will mean he'll have to go back to the Museum again. And that should give us all the time we need.'

Athena Papadopoulos thought for a moment, then nodded.

'That's just what my father would have done. You know, John J. Armitage, you're growing more and more like him every day.'

Armitage shifted uneasily in his seat. I do wish, he thought wearily, she wouldn't keep saying that. She gave him a ravishing smile and reached for the bell push.

ɩ ꜱ

It was almost eight thirty in the evening when John Armitage emerged from the Papadopoulos mansion and climbed into the Rolls-Bentley limousine waiting for him at the kerb, its engine ticking over as quietly and smoothly as a sewing machine. The uniformed chauffeur waited until his passenger was comfortably seated before closing the door behind him, with the familiar and agreeable clunk synonymous with the marque since Mr Rolls first met Sir Henry Royce in the lobby of Manchester's Midland hotel and had then decided to go into business together. Armitage had accepted the invitation to dine but had refused the additional offer of accommodation for the night. As he had pointed out to his disappointed hostess, he needed to return to Kent as soon as possible to organise a plan of action which would hopefully enable them to retrieve the marbles. At the same time, he had gratefully accepted the offer of the use of her chauffeur-driven limousine to get him there.

Minutes before and true to his word, Anderson had joined Barry Lucas in the passenger seat to enable him to have a break and find somewhere to eat. Lucas nodded wearily. It had not had a very good day. Under the eye of the polite but watchful traffic warden, he had been forced to drive aimlessly around the square and the surrounding streets until the time of the evening when the residents' only parking facilities became available to the general public – and the traffic warden had finally accepted defeat and gone off duty. He was about to get out of the car, when Armitage had appeared in the doorway. Lucas recognised him immediately and could hardly believe his luck.

'It's him, Chief!'

'Eh?'

'Him getting into that big car. The other feller who was driving the pantechnicon!'

'Then don't just sit there, lad! Get after him!'

'Get after him. Yes. Right. Will do.'

Lucas mouthed a silent prayer and switched on the ignition. Please, you clapped-out rust-bucket, don't let me down now – or as God is my witness, first thing in the morning, I'll dump you in the nearest knacker's yard. The threat obviously hit a vehicular nerve, as the Fiesta not only immediately burst into life, but also drove away from the kerb with an unaccustomed alacrity that enabled them to catch up with the Rolls-Bentley within a matter of seconds. Anderson leaned forward in his seat, eyes gleaming:

'Don't lose 'em son. Not too close now, but for Chrissake, don't lose 'em.' He bared his teeth in a voracious smile: 'Didn't I tell you the Papadopoulos woman was up to neck in it? Didn't I tell you?'

Lucas fixed his eyes on the vehicle ahead and sighed: 'I do believe you did, Chief,' adding under his breath: 'Even though I thought of it first, you sneaky old bastard.'

The limousine took the road that led to the Blackwall Tunnel.

The Fiesta followed.

§

They gathered in Messiter's cottage the following morning.

Said Messiter, as he poured the coffee: 'Once I'd found the right taxi and the driver had told me where he'd taken da Souza, I decided to stay the night in a local B&B and check the place out first thing in the morning.'

Armitage spread out the road map across the living room table and asked: 'Where is it exactly?'

Messiter put on his reading glasses: 'Between Kessingland and Southwold.' His finger stabbed the paper: 'Just there. Along the A12 then on to the B1127, towards South Cove. The farm is at the end of a long, unmade road, which is not even on the map.'

Beynon followed Messiter's finger: 'Looks pretty remote.'

'It is pretty remote,' said Messiter: 'And after the taxi driver dropped me off at the beginning of the road, it took me all of fifteen minutes on foot to get up to the farm.'

He passed Armitage a sheet on paper, on which he'd drawn a neat architectural plan of the farm and its outbuildings:

'That's roughly the layout and, as far as I could make out, there are three men staying at the place. De Souza himself and a couple of rather scruffy young men in jeans and tee-shirts who seem to spend most of their time watching television.'

Armitage nodded: 'Da Souza would have needed at least a couple of men to help him get the marbles ashore. But how did you find out there are only three of them?'

Messiter dropped a couple of sweeteners into his coffee: 'When I felt it was safe to do so, I crept up to the house and looked through the window.'

'Jesus,' said Beynon: 'That was a damn fool thing to do. You could have been spotted.'

'Not really,' said Messiter evenly: 'When I say I crept up to the house, I meant I crept up *close* to the house. The place is surrounded by sand hills and it gave me a clear view right into the living room, without any danger of being seen. Old as I am, young Ken, I'm not completely devoid of commonsense.'

Asked Armitage: 'Did you have a chance to check the outbuildings?'

Messiter shook his head, firmly: 'Now that *would* have been asking for trouble. I would have in full view from the kitchen windows. But the old barns are certainly big enough to store the marbles.'

'The sand hills could be a useful cover,' said Armitage thoughtfully. Had the surrounding terrain been open land, their approach to the farm would almost certainly have been observed as soon as they'd left the main road.

Beynon seemed to read his thoughts: 'Not if we went in at night.'

'True. But they'd certainly *hear* us coming.'

'In that case,' grunted Beynon: 'We'll first have to go in on foot. And if Gavin's right and there are only three of them to deal with…'

'But all possibly armed, remember.'

Beynon shrugged: 'So?' The ex-SAS man felt the all-too-familiar surge of adrenaline, prior to every operation and said, dryly: 'Be just like old times.'

'So we're going to go for it?' asked Messiter, eagerly.

Said Armitage: 'Ken and I are going to go for it. You're going to wait in the truck until the place has been secured, all right?'

'Oh for God's sake, John. I'm not that infirm. Why should you two have all the fun?'

Said Beynon grimly: 'I'd hardly call it fun, Gavin. It's crunch time. And it could all get rather nasty.'

They finished their coffees in silence, before locking up the house, climbing into Armitage's car and driving off down the High Street. Preoccupied with their own thoughts, neither Armitage, Messiter nor Beynon noticed the battered Ford Fiesta parked on the other side of the village green, directly opposite the cottage. Its two unshaven, bleary-eyed occupants nudged each other awake and the Ford's engine hiccupped into life.

ᘜ

As they reached the Essex Industrial Estate and drove up to the entrance of the huge *Armitage Transport International* depot, Armitage noted with satisfaction that the *For Sale or Rent* sign had been taken down, which indicated that Athena Papadopoulos had wasted no time in investing in what she believed to be a good business proposition. For their part, the banks and other creditors could hardly have believed their good fortune when her representatives had approached them to settle the company's outstanding debts, which sent their latter-day usurers scurrying back to their counting houses to re-write their ledgers.

Messiter and Beynon had been genuinely pleased, if a trifle envious, of Armitage's success in negotiating such a deal. They had been even more pleased when he'd invited them to join his company, should the Elgin marbles operation come to nought.

'I'm not into charity,' he'd told them: 'I need people I can rely on to help me through the long and arduous process of re-establishing a once prosperous business. In other words, I'm not doing you any favours. For the first few months, we'll all have to work our arses off.'

But it was a financial lifeline and they'd both grabbed it, gratefully.

The car nosed its way through the door of the depot and a few minutes later, the original pantechnicon was driven out of the hangar-like depot and on to the forecourt. After the heavy steel door had slid back into place, the truck moved back to the main road and headed for the A.12, which would take them all the way up the East Coast, towards Lowestoft and its environs. It was to be a long haul and each of the men agreed to take their turn at the wheel. Even Gavin Messiter, who predictably, had insisted upon it:

'I've always wanted to have a go at driving one of these things, John, ever since I was a kid. And now's my chance – all right?'

Armitage exchanged a look with Beynon who shook his head:

'Without an HGV driving license? I don't think so, Gavin. It's not like

driving a family saloon, you know.'

'I know that, for God's sake. But you could at least let me try.' He indicated the deserted Industrial Park: 'A couple of laps around the block with you sitting next to me should prove it I can do it, one way or the other.'

Armitage again looked at Beynon, who shrugged.

'All right, Gavin,' said Armitage resignedly: 'But you will spare us the boy-racer bit, won't you?'

For the first time in many days Messiter gave a broad smile: 'Trust me, John. Now move over.'

Armitage moved over and the vehicle accelerated along the empty access roads. A little while later, with an eager Messiter still at the wheel, it moved out of the estate and headed for the A12. The little Ford Fiesta, which was being driven in the same direction, was tucked neatly out of sight behind a large furniture van.

Anderson shifted uneasily in his seat: 'Let's hope they have to pull in somewhere soon to fill up. I'm bursting for a slash.'

Oh God, thought Lucas. Trust the poor old bugger to have problems with his personal plumbing. But whether he liked it or not, Anders of the

Yard would just have to grit his teeth, cross his legs and hope for the best. Lucas had no intention of losing the pantechnicon now.

☙

It was already dusk when the vehicle, with Beynon at the wheel, turned off the A12 and took the B1127 towards South Cove. Under Messiter's directions, it finally came to a halt half a mile or so past the start of the unmade road that wound through the sand hills and ended up at the farmhouse. Through the rear mirror, Beynon could see the twinkling lights of the Port of Lowestoft itself, a few miles across the bay, behind them. At Armitage's suggestion, he turned the truck around and parked in an off-road lay-by, its nose pointing back towards the A12.

'Mobile switched on, Gavin?' asked Armitage, as he and Beynon prepared to descend from the cab.

Messiter nodded.

Said Beynon, dubiously: 'And you're sure you'll be able to handle this thing without us sitting beside you, holding your hand?'

'Up yours, young Ken,' said Messiter coolly: 'I may not hold an HGV driving license, but if you can drive a British Army personnel carrier, you can drive anything.'

'Since when did you drive an army personnel carrier?'

'When I was in Korea – fighting to defend the likes of you from the communist hordes that threatened our British way of life. Now piss off and do what you have to do. And good luck.'

Beynon grinned and climbed out of the cab. He and Armitage then made their way back along the road towards the start of the track that would take them to the farmhouse. Both were quite unaware that they were being followed a temporary, acting Head of Security and his erstwhile assistant who, on seeing the pantechnicon come to a halt, had hastily parked their car in a nearby field, out of sight of the main road.

'Where the hell are they going?' grunted Anderson, as Beynon and Armitage walked off into the darkness: 'This place is the back of the beyond.'

'We'll soon know,' whispered Lucas: 'And keep your voice down, Chief. We don't want to blow it now.'

Captain Jaime Carlos António José da Souza was a troubled man. Since his return from his fruitless visit to Liverpool Street railway station, he had heard no word from his business partner and the deafening silence was beginning to concern him. He wondered what could have happened to him. If, as Jefferson had claimed, his telephone was being tapped, that was obviously the work of Athena Papadopoulos and her associates. But as for the butler's belief that he was also being followed, what in the name of Vasco de Gama would be the point of doing that? Armitage would have known that Jefferson would never be stupid enough to lead them to the location of the marbles. And in any event, as he still resided, albeit in isolation, at the Papadopoulos mansion, they already knew where the butler was, almost every hour of the day.

No, if Jefferson was correct in his belief that someone was watching his every move, there had to be someone else involved. The British Museum, perhaps? In his negotiations with the Director of Operations, might the butler have let something slip that had somehow identified him as the go-between? It was all very puzzling and very worrying. And despite the butler's claim that his telephone was unsafe, he decided to go into Lowestoft and, rather than use his mobile telephone which, according to Jefferson, might conceivably be traced, he would try to contact him from one of the town's public telephone booths.

To the two seamen, he said abruptly, in Portuguese: 'I'm going out. I'll be back within the hour, so if you're thinking of getting rat-arsed on my scotch whisky as usual, forget it. I need you to remain alert and sober. Si?'

'Si, capitano.'

As soon as he'd said it, he knew his admonishment would not have the slightest effect on the pair of lazy drunken matelots, neither of who were over-burdened with intelligence. Their presence at the farmhouse was purely functional. Without their muscle, he could never have handled the loading and unloading of the marbles, now stacked up in the main barn, alongside the hired fork-lift truck. He emerged from the house via the back door and climbed into his rented car, parked in one of the smaller outbuildings.

Armitage and Beynon were almost halfway along the bumpy track when they first saw the car headlight coming towards them. They immediately dived sideways and flattened themselves in the sand hills, peering through the sparse grass towards the approaching vehicle. As it passed them, Armitage gave a grunt of satisfaction:

'One down, two to go. That was da Souza.'

'I wonder where he's off to at this time of night?' mused Beynon.

Armitage smiled: 'The fleshpots of Lowestoft, perhaps?'

'I didn't know there were any.'

'You never can tell, Ken. Behind the plastic lace curtains of little old Lowestoft, could be a snake-pit of original sin.' He rose to his feet: 'Come on. We've got a job to do.'

It was another ten minutes before the dark shape of the farmhouse came into view. As Messiter had said, from the top of the sand hills, it was possible to look straight through the uncurtained windows into the illuminated living room. The two rather scruffy young men, as Messiter had accurately described them, were sitting at opposite ends of the long leather sofa, each sipping a glass of what appeared to be scotch or brandy, which they topped up at regular intervals. On the flickering television screen, the characters in *Coronation Street* were doing their best to confuse the non-English-speaking Portuguese seamen with their Northern patois – and succeeding. One of them reached for the remote control and began to flick through the channels. As he leaned forward to do so, Armitage caught a glimpse of the handgun, tucked into the broad leather belt of his jeans. Beynon saw it too:

'Oh shit. Now we'll have to do it the hard way.'

⟨☞⟩

'What are you talking about?' asked Jefferson, blankly: 'I never said this number was being tapped. And even if it was, what difference does it make? We've never said anything to each other over the phone that they don't already know.'

'Then why did you ask me to meet you at Liverpool Street Railway Station?' demanded da Souza into the telephone, above the rumble of the Lowestoft High Street traffic: 'And then at the very last moment, call it off?'

'I did what?'

'You fucked up my whole evening, Senhor.'

'Now listen to me,' said Jefferson urgently: 'Whoever telephoned you, I can assure you it wasn't me. For one thing I don't know your mobile number. You've never given it to me. For reasons of security, we agreed that you should always contact me, remember?'

There was a long silence. Then a puzzled: 'But it sounded just like you.'

'Hold on. Let me think,' snapped a suddenly suspicious Jefferson.

Just what the hell was da Souza up to? Partners they might be, but he had no illusions about him. From the way he'd shafted Armitage, the man was obviously as slippery as a handful of sprats. Had he cooked up this damn fool story as part of a secret agenda to renege on their deal to split the money right down the middle? It all smelled as fishy as the Billingsgate Market. Well, whatever the devious bastard had in mind, he wasn't going to get away with it. In a totally spurious show of friendly reassurance, he said into the telephone:

'Listen to me, amigo. I've no idea what this is all about, but whoever got your number, unless you told them where you're holed up – '

Da Souza bristled: 'Of course I didn't, Senhor.'

'Well there you are then. Nothing to worry about. And while you're on the line, as far as the auction is concerned, everything's going according to plan and we should have a deal within the next two or three days, or so – all right?'

A still unconvinced Da Souza heaved a sigh and said: 'If you say so, Senhor.'

The captain replaced the receiver and headed for the nearest bar. Despite what the butler had said, he needed time to think the situation through for himself and a couple of cognacs would be a great help in oiling his thought processes. Could it be, he pondered, that the shifty little Englishman's phone calls were simply the first step in a very clever plan to somehow cheat him out of his share of the money? He wouldn't put it past him. From the moment he'd first set eyes on him, he'd seen him for what he was – an underhand, conniving, treacherous little bastardo. A man totally devoid of any moral principles whatsoever. A man after his own heart.

It would, he mused, be a pity if it transpired that the butler *was* trying to cheat him, as, with Jefferson's natural talent for deceit and dishonesty, they would have made an ideal team. And working together, they could have gone on to even greater things. There was only one way to find out what the butler was up to – meet him face to face and beat it out of him. Not that he was a violent man by nature but, as the English were prone to say, needs must when the devil drives. He finished his cognac and made for the door. What he needed now was a good night's sleep to prepare himself for the possibly extremely disagreeable day that lay ahead. A few minutes later, he was behind the wheel of his rented car and heading back towards the farmhouse.

☞

It had taken all of five seconds for Armitage and Beynon to silently enter the farmhouse through the unlocked back door, burst into the living room and confront the two, now happily well-oiled guardians of the Elgin marbles. Even if they were aware of what they were supposed to be guarding – which Armitage doubted – it would have made very little difference. For with an ease born of long practise, Beynon had swiftly disarmed them before they'd even realised what was happening and, with their hands and feet securely taped, the Portuguese seamen were then roped to a couple of hooped-back chairs, brought in from the adjoining kitchen.

'Adios, amigos,' grunted Beynon, as the two men regarded him through an alcohol-induced haze, too befuddled to even protest at their predicament. Armitage reached into his pocket for his mobile telephone phone:

'We're ready for you, Gavin.'

A mile or so away, Messiter switched on the parked pantechnicon's engine and drove it out of the lay-by, heading towards the track that led to the farmhouse. From their hidden observation point in the sand hills, Anderson and Lucas, who had just witnessed, with total astonishment, the dramatic sequence of events in the farmhouse living room, were even more astonished when the pantechnicon suddenly appeared out of the darkness and, directed by Armitage, came to a halt outside one of the several outbuildings. It was Beynon who operated the fork-lift truck that began loading the series of crates, some large, some small, out of the old barn and into the back of the vehicle, while Armitage and Messiter man-handled them into position. Armitage glanced at the heavily breathing Messiter with some concern:

'You all right, Gavin?'

'Don't fuss. I'm fine.'

As always, Messiter was determined to play his part, no matter how fragile his health and, watched by an excited Anderson and an apprehensive Lucas, he continued to wrestle with the crates.

'That must be them. The marbles,' muttered an excited Anderson.

Whispered Lucas anxiously: 'Then hadn't we better call in the police?'

Anderson shook his head, violently: 'And let them get all the glory? No way, son. This one's going to be down to me – to us,' he corrected himself hastily: 'Just do what I tell you, all right?'

Like what? thought Lucas. Make a citizen's arrest and, like the two men in the house, end trussed up like a couple of chickens – possibly followed by a burial at sea? The man was barking. He really did see himself as Anders of the Yard. It took another five minutes to complete the loading and Beynon finally stepped down from the forklift truck. Messiter and Armitage climbed out of the rear of the pantechnicon and closed the heavy doors behind them. As they all paused for a moment to regain their breath, Messiter gave a little groan and sank to his knees, fumbling in his pocket for his medication.

'I knew you were overdoing it, Gavin,' muttered a worried Armitage. To Beynon, he said: 'A glass of water, Ken. And quickly.'

Beynon nodded and ran back towards the farmhouse. Armitage wrenched the bottle of pills from Messiter's pocket and began to unscrew the cap.

'Now's our chance, lad!' snapped Anderson: 'Follow me!'

With Beynon out of the way and Armitage totally occupied with the ailing Messiter, Anderson, followed by a silently protesting Lucas, made a crouching run through the surrounding sand hills, looping back towards the front of the truck and, completely unobserved, they climbed into the cab, locking the doors behind them. It wasn't until the engine roared into life and the truck lurched forward towards the exit track that Armitage realised that they'd been hi-jacked. Beynon came running out of the farmhouse, a glass of water in his hand. Without a word, he handed the glass to the kneeling Armitage, who administered the pills to the gasping Messiter and Beynon then took off, on foot, after the accelerating pantechnicon.

It was an unequal race. The truck had had too much of a head start on its pursuer and Beynon was finally forced to concede defeat, throwing himself down on the ground with a howl of rage and frustration.

'We've done it lad, we've done it,' crowed a jubilant Anderson, as the truck swerved from one side of the track to the other, with the temporary acting Head of Security wrestling with the unfamiliar steering wheel.

'Are you sure you know how to drive this thing?' asked Lucas nervously: 'And do you need to go this fast? No one's following us.'

'Not at the moment, perhaps. But we'll only be safe when we get back on to the A12. Then it'll be a straight run to London and the good old British Museum, where, if there's any justice, they'll all be waiting for us, to shake us by the hand and give us a round of applause. It's going to be the greatest moment of your life, lad – and never forget that it's me you have to thank. Right? Right.'

Da Souza's car came out of nowhere – its headlights illuminating the cab and completely blinding its driver, who unwisely took his hands off the wheel to shield his eyes.

'Bloody hell,' moaned Lucas as the truck veered off the track and headed into the sand hills, narrowly missing the oncoming car by inches: 'I told you not to go so fast.'

'Don't panic lad. Don't panic,' panted the shaken Anderson as he grabbed the wheel again and steered the truck towards the ocean: 'We'll soon get where we want to go. I know a short cut.'

Why, thought Lucas morosely, as he desperately clung to his seat, do those words suddenly fill me with dread? Short cut? What sodding short cut? Anderson had never been in this part of the word before in his life. Anderson elucidated:

'When we were driving along the coast road, I noticed that the tide had gone right out and once we hit the beach, it'll be an easy run across the sand to the next exit road.'

Why, wondered Lucas again, does his explanation also give me so very little comfort? His apprehension increased as, a few minutes later, the truck lurched out of the sand hills, on to the beach and crunched its way over the shingle, before hitting the smooth, packed sand.

'See what I mean, lad?' asked Anderson: 'Another ten minutes and we'll be home and dry.'

Lucas peered ahead and tapped his driver's arm, urgently: 'Watch out, Chief. You're going straight for a signpost of some kind.'

'Signpost? What signpost? I can't see anything.'

With a dull crunch of splintering wood, the truck's front wheels flattened the tall signpost with its white lettering, into the sand.

'That signpost,' said Lucas wearily.

'Did you see what it said?'

'I hardly had time to,' pointed out Lucas: 'You must have hit it at fifty miles an hour.'

'Ah well, no matter. It was probably pointing the way to the next exit.'

The truck continued to thunder alongside the ocean, towards the distant lights of Lowestoft, across the bay. It left behind it a now demolished signpost, its inscription pointing skywards, with the words *DANGER, QUICKSANDS*, disfigured by the tyre tracks of an eight-wheeled pantechnicon.

10

'HOW COULD YOU do this to me, Senhor?' asked Captain Jaime Carlos António José da Souza, bitterly: 'I thought you were a man of honour.'

'You've got a bloody nerve,' muttered Beynon: 'After what you've done to us.'

The two Portuguese seamen, after having had to endure a tongue-lashing from their employer, had been securely locked up in one of the outbuildings and, in the relative comfort of the farmhouse living room, Armitage poured himself a glass of what remained of da Souza's malt whisky. The now fully recovered Gavin Messiter was sipping a cup of well-sugared tea, while a dejected Beynon looked down into his beer.

Armitage settled back in his chair and said: 'Sadly, we've done nothing to you, da Souza. We were merely trying to retrieve what was rightfully ours – well, ours and the British Museum's – until someone beat us to it. Any idea who it might be?'

Said the captain sullenly: 'I know who did it. My so-called friend and business partner, Senhor Jefferson.'

Afterall, who else could it be? Da Souza promised himself that at the first opportunity and no matter how long it took to find him, the perfidious English butler would pay the ultimate price for his treachery.

Armitage sipped his whisky and considered the situation. The possibility that the hijacking of the marbles was the work of Athena Papadopoulos's duplicitous butler, just didn't add up. For one thing, he could hardly have handled the operation entirely on his own. He would have needed help. And for another…

'How did Jefferson find out where you were hiding the marbles?' he asked the disconsolate da Souza: 'I assume you didn't tell him.'

The captain shook his head: 'He didn't want to know, Senhor – in case you, or more likely, your friend here – ' he nodded towards the grim-faced Beynon – 'decided to beat it out of him.'

'In that case,' said Armitage thoughtfully: 'It must have been down to a third party. Which takes Jefferson right out of the picture.'

He reached into his pocket, brought out his mobile telephone and punched in a number. The call was picked up within seconds. Said Armitage into the phone:

'Athena? Our old friend Captain de Souza and his partner in crime are no longer in possession of the marbles, so no matter what Jefferson tells you, there's no point in continuing to negotiate with him.' He held the phone away from his ear until her angry, machine-gun like response had abated and continued: 'At the moment, we've no idea who's got them or even where they are, but be prepared for a phone call from person or persons unknown, proposing a deal.' He clicked off the phone to avoid further discussion and then turned back towards da Souza: 'You've cost us a great deal of time and money, da Souza and, like your partner, I'm afraid you're in deep shit.' To Beynon, he said: 'Right Ken?'

Beynon nodded and rose slowly to his feet, to tower menacingly over the suddenly apprehensive Portuguese captain, who was cringing back into his chair. Said Beynon softly, his fists clenching and unclenching:

'It's payback time, amigo. Had it not been for you, by now, the Elgin marbles would have been back where they belonged and me and my partners would have joined the ranks of the idle rich.'

'In other words, you bastard,' said Messiter, angrily: 'We've had it up to here with you and that little turd of a butler – and we want compensation.'

'So bring out your cheque book,' said Beynon: 'And as soon as we've emptied your bank account of every euro you conned out of Athena Papadopoulos, we might even let you and your two orang-utans leave here in one piece. Comprendo?'

Said da Souza piteously: 'Every *euro*, Senhor? Cannot we come to a more equitable arrangement? After all, I did save you a great deal of money by salvaging the marbles at my own expense and bringing them back to England for you.'

'Jesus,' said Beynon: 'You're unbelievable.' His tone became even more menacing: 'Your cheque book, da Souza.'

The captain was close to tears as he felt in his inner pocket and reluctantly pulled out a cheque book. He knew that with a certified cheque, his bank account could be emptied within a matter of hours. And while he did not believe that a man like Armitage would resort to physical violence, he had not the slightest doubt that his muscular, beetle-browed partner, whom he understood to have once been a member of the British Army's legendary SAS – reportedly a group of highly-trained, professional psychopaths – would not have the slightest hesitation in battering him to a pulp. Even the aggressive geriatric, glowering at him from across the room, would doubtless want to put the boot in, too.

It was all Jefferson's fault. No matter what Armitage had said, he was sure that the bastardo of a butler was involved in it up to his soon-to-be cauliflowered ears. He gave a gesture of despair, of defeat and, with a feeling of utter helplessness, he took Armitage's proffered pen and began to write.

Quicksands are not a peculiarly English phenomenon, but they do occur at a considerable number of places along the entire British coastline, some small, some large, but all extremely hazardous. Over the centuries, the mud flats of the infamous Morcambe Bay, on Lancashire's West Coast, have claimed the lives of many unwary fishermen and have quickly swallowed coaches, horses and their passengers, with a speed and avidity that gave them no chance of survival. Due to a lethal combination of sudden high tides and the treacherous sinking sands, many of those who had the temerity to venture across the bay at the wrong time of the day, were never seen again.

Until that first terrifying moment, Anderson and Lucas had little or no knowledge of the vagaries of attempting to drive a loaded pantechnicon across one of Suffolk's most notorious natural hazards. Within seconds, its wheels began to sink into the soft mud and the vehicle came to a sudden and shuddering halt.

'I think,' shouted a distraught Barry Lucas: 'That the signpost was trying to warn us that there were quicksands ahead.'

'Oh my God! Let's get out of here!'

They managed to open the doors and haul themselves out on to the roof of the cab, where they sat, shaking with fear, as the truck began to sink slowly but inexorably, into the sands.

'What the hell are we going to do?' howled Anderson hysterically: 'Think of something, lad, or we're going to go down with it.'

'We'll just have to make a run for it – no, not a run, a crawl, keeping as flat as we can.'

Lucas vaguely remembered a piece of advice he had gleaned as an eager young Boy Scout, when studying for his life-saving badge: spread the body-weight as wide as possible.

'Follow me, Chief. Do what I do.'

And as the sand came up to within a foot or so of where they were crouching, he launched himself on to the sticky, swirling wet surface and began to wriggle towards firmer ground, pulling himself along by his elbows, swaying from side to side like a demented tadpole, with the muddy waters sucking hungrily at his body. Anderson gave a whimper of fear, then followed him. By the time he'd successfully crawled out of glistening mud flats, Lucas was totally drained. Anderson was even more exhausted. He had come to a halt a few yards from the edge of the quicksands and was lying there, like a beached whale.

'It's no good. I can't go any further. Help me, lad. Please. I'm sinking.'

Lucas took a deep breath, crawled back towards him and held out his hand:

'Take my hand. Come on. Now hold on.'

He didn't know how, but inch by inch, he managed to drag the older man out of the grip of the voracious sand and pull him to safety. Then together, they watched in silence as the pantechnicon sank completely out of sight below the surface of the mud flats, just as the approaching tide began to ripple into the bay.

Said Lucas, forlornly: 'That's that, then. How are we going to tell them?'

'Tell them what, for God's sake? That due to circumstances beyond our control, their sodding marbles are buried ten feet down, somewhere off the Suffolk coast?'

'What d'you mean, *somewhere* off the Suffolk coast?' said Lucas indignantly: 'We know exactly where they are. So why can't they just dig them up again?'

Anderson gave a mirthless laugh: 'Dig them up from where?' He nodded towards the incoming tide which now completely covered the mud flats: 'You're still quite sure where they went down, lad?'

Lucas followed his gaze: 'Oh bloody hell. We should have marked the spot.'

'With what? A white hanky on a stick?'

'Oh bloody hell,' said Lucas again.

'So if you want to keep your job, none of this ever happened, right? Besides,' he rationalised desperately: 'Those plastic replicas look just as good as the real thing. No, better. And they're not a security problem any longer, are they? So all in all, you could say we've done the Museum a favour.'

'Do you really think they'll see it like that?' asked Lucas dubiously.

'Possibly not, son. Possibly not. Trouble is, people like them have no imagination. Not that I give a toss either way,' he continued morosely: 'After what I've been through tonight, I'm going to jack it all in. Hang up my truncheon and take early retirement.'

What, again? Thought Lucas.

'I'm just too old for this sort of caper,' continued Anderson wearily. He tried to brush some of the wet mud from his jacket and trousers, but without success: 'Come on, lad. Let's go home.'

He turned and trudged miserably off into the sand hills. To Lucas, he looked a broken man and, with a reluctant feeling of pity for one of life's born no-hopers, who'd elevated professional inadequacy to a fine art, Lucas gave a sad shake of his head and trudged after him.

After Armitage's phone call, a bitterly disappointed Athena Papadopoulos had thought long and hard, before ringing for her housekeeper.

'Ask Jefferson if he could possibly spare me a few minutes, will you Maria?'

'Of course, madame.'

A few minutes later, the diminutive butler gave a smile of satisfaction at the phrasing of his ex-employer's request. Could he possibly *spare* her a few minutes? He liked that. To have humbled the rich bitch simply because he and his partner were in possession of a few crates of broken masonry was intensely gratifying. How the mighty had fallen and how much he was looking forward to watching her face when she finally had to hand over the ransom money. Or alternatively, witness her utter desolation, should the British Museum top her final offer. He opened the library door without knocking and, in the absence of an invitation to do so, sank into the nearest armchair and nonchalantly crossed his legs.

'I believe you wish to see me,' he said to the woman sitting opposite him. He glanced pointedly at his watch: 'I'm extremely busy at the moment, but I can spare you five minutes or so.'

God, that felt good. He glowed with an inner contentment. How was it, he mused, that one could derive so much pleasure from so few words?

'You're very kind, Mr. Jefferson,' said Athena Papadopoulos, with unaccustomed humility: 'But this will only take a couple of minutes or so.'

Mr. Jefferson. He liked that, too.

'I very much regret to have to inform you,' she continued sadly: 'That I can no longer continue to negotiate a price for the return of the Parthenon marbles.'

The butler blinked in surprise. Never for one moment had he anticipated that the woman would call it a day and break off negotiations. Perhaps she didn't have as much liquid cash available as he'd thought. Oh well, what did it matter? They still stood to make a killing from the British Museum. He rose to his feet.

'As you wish,' he said indifferently: 'But might I ask why?'

'Well let me put it this way. What would be the point of me bidding against the British Museum, when you and your partner are no longer in possession of the marbles?'

He frowned: 'What are you talking about? Of course we've got the marbles.

'Are you quite sure about that?'

'Of course I'm sure.'

'Then where are they?'

'I don't know where they are. And I don't want to. All I do know is that they're here. Somewhere in England, in the care of Captain de Souza.'

'That is not what I've been told.'

'By whom?'

'By the one man whose word I trust. John Armitage.'

Jefferson steadied himself against the back of the chair. Either she was up to something and lying like there was no tomorrow, or that swine of a Portuguese sea captain had already done a deal with the British Museum and walked off with the money. And why *should* she be lying? What could she possibly gain by breaking off all negotiations? It just didn't make sense. But what did make sense was, as he'd suspected, da Souza had been planning to screw him all along and, even worse, had apparently succeeded in doing so. He was probably on the other side of the globe by now. Dear God, was it really all over? After all he'd been through? With no job, no money and no place to live? With absolutely sweet bugger-all, in fact? His shoulders sagged. He could almost hear his world collapsing around him

Athena Papadopoulos noted her butler's air of utter desolation with grim satisfaction, then felt a sudden surge of anger. Had it not been for Jefferson's duplicity, by now, the marbles could have been adorning the Parthenon itself. The man needed to be taught a lesson he'd never forget. She reached inside a nearby bureau drawer and extracted a small, beautifully inlaid, mother-of-pearl handgun, which had been given to her by her late father for her personal protection – as well as giving her lessons in how to use it.

'And now, Jefferson,' she said bleakly: 'It's time for you to pay the price for your dishonesty, your disloyalty and total lack of respect for the daughter of the late, great Andreas Papadopoulos and his beloved Parthenon marbles. In short, you are a nasty little piece of doggie-do, who belongs on the sole of someone's shoe, instead of defiling my house with your presence and fouling the very carpet you're standing on.' She raised the gun: 'And I think maybe I shoot you, like the dirty little doggie you are.'

'God almighty!' shouted a horrified Jefferson: 'You're barmy!' He backed towards the door, his hands raised in supplication: 'Please, no. Don't shoot. Please?'

Her first shot ploughed into the Persian carpet, inches from his feet. The second shattered the valuable Chinese vase on the table next to him and the third neatly decapitated the equally valuable onyx bust of Adonis on the mantle-shelf, close to his head. While she would later severely chide herself for the sudden burst of uncontrollable anger that had resulted in the destruction of two priceless artefacts, at the time, it had seemed worth it, just to see the look of abject terror on the obnoxious little man's face.

The butler managed to wrench open the library door and run, howling with fear, into the hallway. With the expertise of an Annie Oakley, Athena Papadopoulos blew the smoke curling from the muzzle of the handgun and replaced it in the drawer. Settling old scores with her ex-employee had been the only bit of genuine enjoyment she'd experienced in weeks,

John J. Armitage was climbing out of the black taxi-cab when the mansion front door was suddenly flung wide open and a hysterical Jefferson ran down the steps to the street, looking wildly over his shoulder for any sign on pursuit. To Armitage, he shouted:

'She's mad! Your fancy woman's fucking crazy! I'm off – and if you had any sense, you'd be off, too!'

He continued along the pavement at a walking run, heading towards Victoria Station, presumably intending to put himself well beyond the reach of his obviously homicidal, trigger-happy, ex-employer. Armitage shook his head in perplexity and walked up the steps and into the house.

'Perhaps it just wasn't meant to be,' said Athena Papadopoulos, wearily.

'What d'you mean?' asked Armitage, pouring himself a coffee.

'You know very well what I mean. The Parthenon marbles. Two times we have them, two times we lose them. Maybe the Gods *want* them to stay in your British Museum.'

'Why should they want that?' grunted Armitage: 'And let's keep the deity of Mount Olympus out of it, shall we?'

'Maybe the Gods are all English,' she said stubbornly: 'After all, you English are everywhere.'

'Look,' said Armitage: 'This is not the end of the road. It's only a matter of time before they're put up for sale again. In the meantime, here's a sweetener.' He handed her a cheque: 'With the compliments and grovelling apologies of Captain Jaime Carlos António José da Souza for the quite unacceptable way he tried to take you for a ride.'

She studied the signature carefully: 'Who's G.H. Messiter?'

'The third member of our little team. The one you've yet to meet. We put de Souza's money through his bank account. Gavin is the only one who doesn't have an overdraft.'

She handed the cheque back to him: 'You keep it. For your out-of-pocket expenses.'

'You've already covered those. More than covered them.'

'Then buy yourself another pantechnicon.'

'The one they took was insured.'

'It could be a very long time before the insurance company pays up, so get a second one. We'll need it, for our business.' She saw his sudden frown: 'For *your* business,' she corrected herself swiftly: 'I owe you a great deal, John J. Armitage. For all you've done. For all you've tried to do.'

'You owe me nothing. The deal was payment on delivery.'

She sighed: 'Not that again. But very well. Have it your way.'

She took back the cheque, tore it into small pieces and tossed the pieces up into the air. As they fluttered, confetti-like, down to the floor, she shrugged and said:

'That takes care of that. Now, let's talk about more important things. Are you staying the night or not?'

'Not. Sorry, but I've got a business to run. But I promise you,' he added softly: 'As soon as things are running smoothly and I can afford to do so, I'll take you away to some exotic, faraway place in the sun, where it'll be just the two of us, without an army of servants hiding behind every palm tree.'

'Blackpool,' she said suddenly.

'What?'

'When I was very small, one of my many nannies came from your English Blackpool and she told me what a wonderful place it was, with a big tower, candy-floss, donkey rides, circuses and merry-go-rounds. To a five-year-old child, living in a big house in Athens, it seemed like heaven.'

Said Armitage carefully: 'Yes, well, I think I should warn you that the reality may not be quite as exotic as she described it.'

'Maybe. Maybe not. But I want to find out for myself. I want to feel like a little girl again and paddle in the sea and make sand-castles and do everything that she did and what my father did not allow me to do.' She looked at him anxiously: 'Or do you think I'm just being very silly?'

To Armitage, her child-like eagerness was quite touching. No matter how affluent her upbringing, or possibly because of it, he reflected, she couldn't have had much of a childhood.

He smiled and said gently: 'I think it's a wonderful idea. And if that is what you wish, it would give me great pleasure to take you there.'

'Thank you, John J. Armitage.' She leaned over and kissed him: 'You are a very nice man. Even if sometimes, you can be a pain in the bottoms.'

'I'll settle for that,' said Armitage. 'But in the meantime...' he nodded towards the pieces of paper, scattered across the floor: 'As trying to reason with you on more mundane matters is like trying to communicate with a breeze block, I will use the money to buy another truck. Because you're right. We do need one. And quickly.'

It was her turn to frown: 'A breeze block? What is this breeze block? And of course I'm right. I'm always right.'

Armitage smiled, despite himself: 'Goodnight, Athena.' He rose to his feet: 'But remember, the moment you're contacted about the marbles – call me immediately. Because whoever's holding them, unless they've already done a deal with the British Museum, we're still in with a chance. And hopefully, it'll be third time lucky.'

Who am I kidding? He asked himself, guiltily. He didn't know why, but he had a gut feeling that the marbles were probably gone for good. Just where and for whatever reason, he couldn't even speculate. If, he reasoned, they were still up for grabs, she would surely have been contacted within hours of them being hijacked. For her sake, however, he'd tried to be positive, simply to keep her hopes alive. That was the very least he could do for her and no more than she deserved. But don't hold your breath, Athena Papadopoulos, he told himself, gloomily. This really could be the end of the road.

☙

Quicksands, according to some geologists, are notoriously volatile and above all, extremely unpredictable. A sudden climatic change, a shift in the speed and direction of the tidal flow, or even a minor upheaval of the sea-bed and the shifting sands often take on a life of their own.

It was almost three months later to the day since Armitage had watched his hijacked pantechnicon disappear into the darkness, when he received a telephone call from the Suffolk police to ask him if *Armitage Transport International* was missing a large truck, on which was emblazoned its name, address and telephone number. Fortunately, to distance himself from having any connection with the pantechnicon's cargo, should the hijackers be apprehended in transit, Armitage had immediately informed

210

the police and his insurance company that his empty truck had been stolen from his unattended Essex depot, a couple of days earlier.

As events proved, he had been wise to do so. The two small boys, in shorts, bare feet and with shrimp nets in hand, who had been carefully skirting the beach area where the newly-erected signpost warned walkers of the quicksands which lay ahead, were suddenly stopped in their tracks. They watched, open-mouthed as, with a loud gurgle, first the radio aerial, then the twin vertical exhausts of a large truck, slowly rose into view, a couple of hundred yards out into the bay. The boys' eyes widened as the roof of the driving cab majestically followed and, with a final gurgle, the sands completely disgorged the huge container itself, like a regurgitating hyena, spitting out the indigestible bones of its prey. The boys looked at each other in wonderment, then turned and ran excitedly back towards the sand hills, to share their discovery with their friends, their parents and anyone else they happened to meet on the way.

'Yes, they're the genuine article all right,' said Gavin Messiter, as he, Beynon and Armitage inspected each and every exhibit in the British Museum's Duveen gallery.

'A pity they didn't catch the dozy bastards who went off with them,' grunted Beynon: 'They could have been lost forever.'

'That's one consolation, I suppose,' said Armitage: 'At least from Athena Papadopoulos's point of view. Better back in the British Museum than buried several feet down, somewhere off the Suffolk coast.'

'Even so,' said Beynon: 'She must still be feeling rather pissed off with us for losing them twice in a row.'

Armitage nodded 'Especially as she must now know there's no chance of us ever been able to lift them for a second time.' He indicated the security guards all around the gallery: 'They've doubled the security since the last time we were here.'

'So they're back,' said the voice behind them.

Armitage recognised the perfume immediately: 'Oh, hallo Athena. We thought you might drop in.' He indicated Messiter: 'This is Gavin Messiter. You've already met Ken Beynon.'

'I wanted to see the marbles for myself,' said the elegantly attired Athena Papadopoulos, as her uniformed chauffeur waited patiently in the background: 'So what do you intend to do about them?'

'Do about them?' repeated Armitage.

'Well, is not the situation – what do you English call it – simply a case of back to square one? My offer still stands, gentlemen.'

'If you mean what I think you mean, Miss Papadopoulos,' said Beynon: 'You've got to be joking.'

'I never make jokes, Mr. Beynon. Especially about the Parthenon marbles. And is there not another English expression that says that where there's a will, there's a way?'

'On the other hand,' said Armitage: 'There's also one that goes once bitten, twice shy.' He nodded towards the security men: 'The Museum would never make the same mistake again, Athena. It'd be easier to empty Fort Knox.'

He turned to Messiter, who was staring fixedly at the exhibits, though his thoughts were obviously elsewhere.

'Right Gavin?'

'Um?'

'I said –'

'I heard what you said,' said Messiter: 'And as everyone seems to be swapping Olde English saws and sayings, how about never say never?'

'Meaning what?' asked Armitage.

'Meaning I've just had an idea.'

Beynon groaned: 'Oh Christ, no. Not another one.'

Athena Papadopoulos beamed, slipped her hand through Messiter's arm and said: 'Why don't we all have lunch and talk about it?'

'Why not?' said Armitage resignedly, muttering under his breath: 'You bastard, Gavin.'

As they left the gallery and made their way towards the front entrance, followed by the chauffeur, none of them noticed the young man coming out of the souvenir shop, accompanied by the pretty young woman who usually served behind the counter. Lucas froze in his tracks and said, not for the first time:

'It's them! The truck driver and his mate! And look who's with them! The Papadopoulos woman! I told you they were all in it together!'

Julie Baker sighed. Oh Lord. Not those rotten marbles again. They had more important things to think about.

'So?' she said plaintively: 'What does it matter? The marbles are back where they belong; you've been promoted to be Mr. Bracegirdle's deputy and our wedding's just three weeks away. So why don't you just forget about the marbles for once and think more about the lovely time we're going to have on our honeymoon in Benidorm?'

Lucas hesitated. His natural instinct was to cry 'stop thief' and have them all arrested. Another hesitation. Arrested for what? Stealing the Elgin marbles? But they were all back in the Duveen gallery. Besides, what if it all came out that it was he and Anderson of the Yard who had nearly been the cause of the marbles being lost for all time? And with Anderson having taken early retirement, who'd carry the can for the whole sodding fiasco?

Barry Muggins, that's who.

He watched the group walk through the doors and out of sight, then took his affianced by the arm:

'You're right, darling. Let's go to lunch.'

As Athena Papadopoulos's limousine purred in the direction of *Le Caprice* restaurant, just off London's Piccadilly, in the sound-proofed compartment behind the uniformed chauffeur, Gavin Messiter outlined his thoughts on the possible future of the Parthenon marbles. The others listened in silence until his discourse finally came to an end.

Said Athena Papadopoulos eagerly: 'Well, John J. Armitage? What do you think?'

Armitage ignored the question, his brow corrugated in thought. The limousine turned into Arlington Street and came to a halt outside the restaurant. *Le Caprice's* doormen competed with each other to be the first to open the passenger doors, but the Rolls-Bentley's occupants made no attempt to descend to the pavement. They just sat there, deep in thought. Athena Papadopoulos tugged impatiently at Armitage's arm.

'Well?' she demanded again: 'Tell me. What do you *think?*'

'I think,' said John J. Armitage, slowly and reluctantly: 'That Gavin's idea might work.'

'Oh Christ,' said Ken Beynon for the second time that morning, glaring at the totally unrepentant Messiter. While he knew the elderly delinquent had been grateful for Armitage's offer of employment which, in the absence of a decent pension, had provided him with a financial lifeline, he also knew that Messiter had been eagerly looking forward to his retirement.

And who could blame him? After all, a million quid was a million quid and would enable him to live a life to which he would obviously like to become accustomed. To grow old disgracefully, while knocking back *premier grand cru* bubbly and munching the roe of the virgin sturgeon, as the old boy had once described it. So what the hell?

'In all honesty,' he muttered and totally against his better judgement: 'I also have to say that I think that Gavin's idea might work.'

Athena Papadopoulos smiled with delight:

'That's settled, then.' Her eyes lit up like a child who still believed in Santa Claus: 'Now. When do we start?'

END

Printed in the United Kingdom
by Lightning Source UK Ltd.
122022UK00001B/175-186/A